NANA BOO

Willow River Press is an imprint of Between the Lines Publishing. The Willow River Press name and logo are trademarks of Between the Lines Publishing.

Copyright © 2024 by Jackie Meekums-Hales

Cover Artwork and Design: Cherie Fox

Between the Lines Publishing
1769 Lexington Ave N, Ste 286
Roseville MN 55113
btwnthelines.com

First Published: Septber 2024

ISBN: Paperback 978-1-965059-00-5

ISBN: Ebook 978-1-965059-01-2

Library of Congress: 2024942094

NANA BOO

Jackie Meekums-Hales

For all those strong, caring, capable women I have the privilege
to call family and friends.

All characters and events in this novel are fictional, though you
may find something of your courage and love within these pages.

"The tragedy of growing old, is not that one is old, but that one
is young."

– Oscar Wilde

Chapter 1: Nancy

Crash! Slam! Breaking glass tinkled on the air like Christmas bells, pitched at different tones and volumes.

"Well, Tommy Tucker, what on earth...?" Tommy tipped his head on one side, listening intently through the bars of his cage and moving slowly along his perch. His reply was a quick "Gissakiss, Tommy", which usually meant he had a few more minutes' attention from the face on the other side of the bars. Today, it failed.

She'd never really wanted a budgie, anyway. She had enough to do, holding down her job and dealing with the family. Pestered by her children, she'd caved in, at last, to demands for a pet. She settled first for fish, then for a bird, both resulting in more cleaning, more work for her, and ultimately ignored by teenagers more interested in music and going out. The fish died a long time ago, but when the budgie died, she'd kind of grown used to having one, and James had come home with a replacement before the cage could be tidied out of the lounge. Her protests were too little, too late; there was no cool-off period for buying a pet, and he was here to stay. Unlike Tommy Tucker 1, this Tommy Tucker didn't sing very well for his supper, and his lack of conversation was a bitter disappointment. James had certainly tried to get the bird to talk to him, but since the only thing he ever said was "Gissakiss", he was in disgrace when visitors' startled faces indicated their lack of appreciation for his efforts. He hadn't even bothered with that since James was not there to laugh at it.

The yellowing leaves of the willow tree waved through the window, as if dancing to their own song of autumn in the September winds. Hopping across the newly dug flower bed, a robin seemed to turn its head towards her, listening for her through the open window.

"Cheerily, cheer up, cheer up," he sang, creasing her face with a reluctant smile. It seemed so much more friendly than Tommy, and she needed friendly today.

"Cheer up! Wouldn't that be good, now?" she thought. It was hard to believe it was only a year ago she'd stood in the garden, full of excitement at the prospect of taking off to somewhere around the world. She'd always been a great believer in the capacity of human beings to adapt to new situations and the indomitable human spirit, but her philosophy had been sorely challenged this year. She'd prided herself on inheriting her mother's strength in adversity, and she was digging deep, determined to find a way through the stubborn fog that swirled around her thoughts since James had gone.

Nancy Brewer slowly and carefully rearranged the flowers she'd placed in the vase on the window ledge. Sometimes, she wished she still had her net curtains. In what seemed like another lifetime, her frill-edged, cross-over, tied and sparkling white nets were her pride and joy, so much more fashionable than her neighbours', and oh-so-useful when she desperately needed to see across the road without being detected. *Not that I made a habit of that kind of thing,* she reassured herself, *but something's going on over there at number ten.* She could hear the rumpus over the polite tones of the Radio 4 presenter. There seemed to be a pile of CDs scattered across the gravel. She didn't think the younger generation had them anymore, but someone obviously did. More came flying out of an upper window - clothes, magazines. Tossed with the strength of a javelin athlete, they fluttered or zoomed to the ground. *He's surely not going to throw that - aargh!*

He did! A laptop joined the debris on view to the world. She felt her breath being drawn in and her lips forming "Oooooh!" as she forced her eyes to turn back into the room. The whole street would be full of wagging tongues and disapproval of the likes of Fred and Janet at number fourteen, who'd appointed themselves the guardians of these highly prized and highly priced houses. Fred shamed anyone who let their grass grow, by his dedication to the manicuring of the verge as well as his own lawn. He often bestowed his advice on Sean and Marta, the young couple in the semi adjoining his. What would he make of these shenanigans?

Doors slammed, a car screeched out of the drive, and suddenly everything went quiet. She could just make out the postman, who'd been hovering outside number ten, pushing his cart towards the front door as though some creature might suddenly jump out of the beautifully pruned hedge and attack him. She watched, as he rang the bell, parcel in hand, but got no answer. She craned her neck a little too long and almost knocked the vase over, as she saw him turn and head round the end of the street towards her own gate. As it creaked, she told herself, "I absolutely must get that fixed". It would not do for her house to be the one to let down the whole neighbourhood with things getting shabby, but it had its uses as an alarm, signalling the need to be ready to open the front door. She never used the front door herself, and she was always shocked, when she opened it and saw the cobwebs, carefully woven between the security light and the inside of the porch. He was tenacious, this wretched spider, she'd give him that. No matter how many times she cleared those cobwebs, sure enough there they were again, whenever she ventured their way. *Mental note to self: get rid of them again later.*

The bell played its cuckoo song, another of James's acquisitions. She took just enough time to retrieve the key from its hook, and to check her long, greying curls in the cloakroom mirror, to convince young Simon that he'd taken her by surprise.

3

"Good morning, Mrs Brewer," he chirped, as cheerful as the doorbell. "A lot of post for you this morning! Could you take a parcel in for number 10? They don't seem to be in."

She could have told him he was wrong. She was sure of it. Whoever was still there was just ignoring him, and she knew he'd seen what she saw, but instead she smiled sweetly at him. She hated taking parcels in for other people when the postman found she was the only one not at work these days. It was such a nuisance when they didn't collect them quickly, or when they did collect them, just as she was eating or trying to listen to a good programme. Sometimes, she felt like other people's convenience store. He saw none of this in her smiling face, as she told him of course she would, and he deposited the box in her hall. If she hadn't known him since he was a toddler, she might have been brisk and sent him packing, but when he looked at her with pleading chocolate-brown eyes, it was like being back in the classroom, when he so often needed that extra little bit of help. She guessed he really didn't want to have to walk past that pile of debris on the front lawn over the road again, and she couldn't blame him.

The package sat on the corner of the telephone table, as she went back to the window. She was sure someone was in. *Only one person's left, and they can't have been arguing with themselves*, but she could see no-one now. The wilting flowers were threatening to rebel against another rearrangement, so she decided it must be time for coffee and cake. There was nothing more to be learnt right now.

She gathered up her own post and settled down in the comfy old armchair in the conservatory, ready to be transported to faraway places by the persuasive pictures in the brochures she'd ordered. With her cup balanced on the arm of the chair while she organised her cushion at her back, she began to flick through the pages full of sunshine, sea and history, her imagination wandering ahead of her into places she'd never been, like the Parthenon or the Adriatic. The problem with teaching was that she and James always had to have their holidays when everyone else did, and that had made them so expensive. Her daughter often complained that they didn't have the holidays abroad that some people had, but then they'd always been struggling to pay the mortgage, run the cars, and keep up with the needs of their own parents and demanding jobs. Time or money, often both, had been in short supply. *Well now, I've got plenty of time on my hands, and I can't see any point in saving my money till I'm too old to enjoy it, so I might as well spend it. No use leaving it for my children to fritter away.* Ben earned more than she'd ever earned, and Poppy was perfectly capable of looking after herself and her children.

She and James had such plans for retirement, just the two of them, plotting to use their pension lump sums to travel like eighteen-year-olds on a gap year. They hadn't planned for one of them to be left wondering where, or whether, to go. They hadn't planned for him to abandon her like this. He was supposed to come too, not opt out on a cricket pitch, in front of his friends and family. She felt the anger surge inside her, as it often did — anger that he hadn't realised he needed to see a doctor, or he'd chosen not to believe that he did. Anger that he'd dared to go somewhere without her. Anger that here she was, having to cope alone. Anger that he'd spent his last minutes batting a ball instead of holding her and saying goodbye. When they'd carried him off the pitch, she'd thought he would be fine in a few days. He'd been fine that morning. It was nearly half-term, and they were going to the Lakes for a break. It was all planned. She was not going to be told he would never come home. It couldn't be true. He was only in his sixties, not old. She saw again, in her mind's eye, the ambulance, the hospital, the curtains they pulled round the bed after frantic attempts to bring him back. He would not come back. He just would not.

Sometimes, it seemed so unreal, as if he'd suddenly appear at the back door, saying sorry for being so late, kiss her on the cheek and sit down to eat his meal. Sometimes, she just felt overwhelmed by missing him. People said she was doing well. Friends had rallied and included her in events. Her children had their own grief, missing their father. She kept her feelings locked away in front of others, literally putting on a brave face, but it was those times in the night when she still cried, faced with nothing but the dark and the loneliness. She knew he would tell her to do what they had always done, pick herself up. They'd talked about one of them being on their own eventually, some time in the future, and they'd agreed they'd want the other one to carry on living, not give up and mope around for too long. In some ways, she wished she was still at work, where there was company, but in other ways, she was glad that there was one less place where she'd have to pretend, have to answer, "I'm fine, thanks," to the kindly questions about how she was doing. *What d'you tell people, anyway? They wouldn't want to know the truth.*

She wished she still had the confidence of youth to take off on her own to explore new places, but she was determined to fulfil some of their dreams, and she certainly wasn't going to let herself sit in this house, wasting precious time and waiting to be past it. She'd gingerly told her daughter about what she was thinking of doing. The response was predictable.

"What on earth do you think you're doing, Mum? You can't just take yourself off somewhere. What if you're taken ill? You're not young anymore, you know. Don't you think you should be deciding where you're going to live now that you're on your own? Why don't you concentrate on getting the house on the market and moving down near me? You could move into one of those retirement complexes, where you'd have company and all the facilities."

Retirement complex! Facilities! Huh! Nancy wasn't ready to trade her walking boots for carpet slippers yet! She knew Poppy meant well, but she still had her own life to live, thank you very much. She mustered her most indulgent smile, her reading glasses perched half-way down her nose.

"Poppy, dear, I know you worry about me, but you don't need to, you know. I'm not in my dotage yet, and I can still look after myself. Perhaps, next time I come for a visit, we could have a look around, to see what there is near you."

But perhaps not, she added to herself, without uttering the words. She loved her daughter dearly, but the easiest way to ruin their relationship would be to live too near. Poppy would take on the burden Nancy was not ready to be, and they'd each be acting in the other's best interests, pulling in opposite directions.

She felt as if she should cross her fingers, like a child creating a convincing lie. When did it happen — that switch from being the mother that worried about the daughter to the daughter that worried about the mother? She'd of course done the same with her own mother, but her mother had been plagued by arthritis, her father the victim of years of smoking, and she'd been the capable one, doing the caring balancing act so many of her generation had done.

Flicking through the brochures, her eyes were drawn to the prospect of rail journeys across half of Europe, escorted so that she wouldn't have to deal with everything herself. How she would love to ride that Glacier Express! She'd go into the travel agent next week, and get it all planned out, before she told her family. Once she'd paid the deposit, they wouldn't be able to dissuade her. *Sometimes,* she thought, *they would do well to remember I've been the one in charge of a whole class, or in charge of half the school, and brought them up. I haven't suddenly become incapable because James is no longer around.* She certainly didn't think of herself as old. In her head, she was still a teenager, who'd want to get up and dance, a daughter and a mother who would do the looking after. She now understood why, to her own mother, the "old ladies" had become older as she herself had aged, so that when she was seventy, they only qualified as old ladies in their eighties. Thinking back to her own childhood, someone in their sixties would have seemed old, worn down by housework and children and dressed in pinafores and granny shoes, but there was no way she was going to look like that! Her jeans were the same as her daughter's, and her shirt was stylish, if not the latest fashion. She didn't have much use for her smart shoes now, but even her comfortable shoes weren't like Granny Marchant's had been, and she certainly wasn't going to let anyone give her the standard "older lady" haircut.

"I'd love to style your hair," Gino had said, as he ran his fingers through it before her last trim. "Have you ever thought of having it cut short?"

Nancy winced at the thought of letting a pair of scissors chop off more than the few inches she conceded as necessary. A polite, "No thank you," had acquired that clip on her voice she'd used for naughty children.

When the phone rang, it almost made her knock her coffee across the room, her Bakewell tart with it. Her daughter had phoned a couple of days ago, and she wasn't in the habit of doing that too often, as she was usually exhausted at the end of a long day. Her son would message her on her mobile, unless it was a weekend, or he was cooking an evening meal, or he was out for a walk. He rarely used the landline during the working day unless there was an emergency. She grabbed at the handset, hoping it didn't do that irritating thing of stopping before she found out who was trying to sell her what, or who had a wrong number, so that she could tell them the error of their ways. If they thought she was fair game, being a lady of a certain age, they could think again! She held the receiver at arm's length and put it on speaker phone, while she deposited her cup on the table.

"Hello," was all she said to it. "Never give them your number," she'd taught her children. "Don't confirm that they've got who they think they've got."

"Nana Boo," said a familiar, but still startlingly deep, voice. "How are you?"

She took a deep breath, her fingers reaching for the locket at her neck, as she unconsciously moved it back and forth on its chain. The voice so dear to her, yet so rarely heard, since he grew into the man she hardly recognised as the child she doted on when he arrived. He was her first, beautiful grandchild. The memory of his tiny hands wrapped in her own and his

8

curly, blond head resting on her chest, as he snuggled into her lap, took her back to the toddler who struggled with her name. For some reason she would never understand, her son-in-law had insisted that the children called their grandparents by their surnames. They had "Nanny Brewer" and "Grandma Castleford", so she became "Nana Boo", re-christened by him, and adopted as this new identity by Poppy's other two children, as they followed him. She'd never told her son-in-law, but she was secretly delighted not to have to be a "grandma". She was far too young, and the thought of having to behave like some staid and frumpy pensioner horrified her. She still refused to be staid and frumpy, even if she had to finally admit to being a pensioner, but "Woe betide anyone who implies that I'm less than the person I've always been".

Upstairs, in the bedroom where the children had all slept when they stayed, were still the Rupert annuals and Roald Dahl books he'd loved, when they had laughed together, and she'd taken him to the bridge to play Pooh sticks. She remembered the child who cheated at board games, who couldn't bear to lose, and she let him win, just to see the satisfaction on his face. She felt the sadness, buried most of the time now, in the pit of her stomach, like a winding punch, at so much missed in his teenage years away at school, the bond between them stretching like a piece of weakening elastic, finally breaking as his adult life had moved beyond her, physically and mentally. She'd been left with a shipwreck of abandoned love, as his life floated on friendships, girls, social life, and work, leaving no time for her. Like his sisters, he sat in a photo frame on the side table, his latest image sporting his school leavers' ball suit.

Yet here he was, suddenly breaking into the silence of her humdrum life, and her heart skipped.

"Nana Boo? Are you there?" insisted the voice.

"Yes. Yes, I'm here, Jake. I'm here. I'm OK, thanks. And you? Where are you?"

9

What kind of trouble makes you ring your Nana when you don't usually bother? She gulped back the unspoken question she longed to ask, like a lozenge too big to swallow.

"I'm in my car, at the motorway service station. I've got a bit of study leave, before I go back to uni, and I was wondering if you'd like a lodger for a couple of days."

Nancy felt the blood rush to her cheeks, as she wanted to shout "Hooray!" to the world, but she mentally checked that everything would be ready when he arrived.

"Of course you can stay," she said as calmly as she could muster, her hand shaking with excitement. This was new — her grandson choosing to come on his own.

"OK then. I'll see you in about an hour. Bye for now, Nana."

She sat staring at the phone for a few seconds, until she wondered whether she'd nodded off and it would all turn out to be a wistful dream. She smoothed her hot hands down her old jeans and sprang out of the chair as if she'd been scorched.

"Well, Tommy Tucker, what do you think of that then?" she launched at the bird cage, as she whisked up her empty cup and headed past him. *Cake. He must have cake.* She hated cooking, but for him she would do it, just to see the smile on his face as he tucked into his favourite butterfly cakes. She'd learnt how to make them at school, in lessons that held no interest for her, other than the taste of sweet products. At least they were easy and quick, so she didn't need the skill she'd never craved in the kitchen. She would never understand the craze for cookery programmes on the television, with all those chefs indulging in producing pretty plates of very little food, which disappeared almost as soon as they'd created it. It seemed to be the province of men now, anyway, she reasoned, which freed her from the yoke her grandmother and mother had carried. Luckily, James had quite liked cooking, as she'd only done it out of necessity. She preferred creating something to use in the classroom, which might have a slightly longer survival rate.

The cakes were in the oven when she saw him arrive, waving through the kitchen window. He headed for the back door, as they always had when he was small. His smile seemed to warm the whole room, even before he came inside, and she felt herself smiling from her eyes to her heart.

He dumped his holdall in the utility room, as if he'd been there yesterday, and they met each other in a hug that said more than either of them could have put into words.

"Oooh! Cakes, Nana? You're spoiling me!"

"Take your bag up to the guest room, and I'll get them out of the oven. Coffee?"

"Thanks, Nana. Which room am I in?"

"You get the big one, since you're on your own. It's all ready."

"Whew! Mum's old room! She'd be miffed, if she knew."

"She's not here, is she?" They grinned at each other.

Jake swung the holdall up over his shoulder and made his way up the familiar staircase. As he tossed it on the bed, he looked out of the window, over the fields beyond the garden. He remembered when he could hardly see over the windowsill, when he'd watched the stars in the night sky, mesmerised with how they twinkled where Nana lived. They didn't twinkle outside his bedroom in the middle of town, where the light destroyed the magic. He would stand and stare upwards, trying to recognise the shapes he'd seen on the wallchart at school. He'd learnt how the sailors had navigated by the stars and wondered if they got lost on cloudy nights. He imagined what was out there, and fantasised about whether ET might come flying through the darkness.

He opened the window and took a deep breath, as if ridding himself of the town air. He picked up the old teddy, still sitting on the chair in the corner of the room and gave it a squeeze. Nana never changed, and here he could feel as safe as he'd always felt. He sensed his stomach muscles relax for the first time in weeks. A tiny purple light flashed on his phone, telling him there was a message, but he ignored it. His smile waned, like the sun disappearing behind a cloud, and he threw the phone onto the pillow before striding across to the door and hurtling down the stairs, back to the comfort of the kitchen.

Nancy was tidying away the brochures she'd been looking at, as he glided into the room.

"What's that, Nana? You planning a trip?"

I was till you arrived, she thought. She said, "Well, Granddad and I had planned all this travelling, and I was thinking maybe I'd do some of it for the two of us." Annoyingly, she could feel the catch in her voice, not something she wanted Jake to hear. She kept her head down, as she shuffled the papers into a tidy pile. "I thought I might go on a train journey."

"Oh wow! You should try what we did last year, Nan, inter-railing! Have you ever looked at that?"

"No. That's just for young people, isn't it?"

"Not necessarily. Here, have a look on your phone. If you got a global pass, you could just keep going, through 33 countries!"

Nancy loved the way he saw no barriers for her. Unlike her daughter, he didn't see the hazards, just the adventure, and the adventure was what she wanted before it was too late.

"Here. Have a look at these while I get a meal ready," she said, as she passed him the pile of brochures.

He strolled off into the lounge, and she heard him say, "Watcha, Tommy! How're you doin' old bird?"

"Watcha Tommy! Watcha Tommy!"

What? That contrary bird! It had hardly said a word since James died, and suddenly, there it was, talking to Jake as if it always had! *Well, if that isn't the final straw – a misogynistic budgerigar in the house!* She'd spent all these years fighting for women's rights, only to find two beady little eyes and a pile of green feathers hid the enemy within. He might be the only thing she'd to talk to sometimes, but his appeal was rapidly descending to that of an earth worm. He'd definitely been James's bird, and she was sure he was sulking on finding she was the one he had to live with now.

She heard the television go on, filling the house with chatter. She found daytime television beyond her tolerance level most of the time, preferring the radio in the background to keeping herself busy, but Jake played the channels, just as his grandfather had done, and settled on some film that her mother would say had "come out of the ark".

As she peeled the potatoes, she heard him talking again, this time, she assumed, on his phone. She tried not to listen, but with no sound other than the peeler in the kitchen, she found herself tuning in, just as he said, "Look, don't tell Mum yet, OK? I need some time to think."

Hmmm. There was obviously something on his mind. Perhaps he would tell her in his own time, but meanwhile, where did Poppy think he was, if she didn't know he was here?

Chapter 2: Nancy and Jake

It was a bright morning, the sky promising one of those days when Nancy just itched to be outside. Autumn sunshine was bursting through the clouds and turning a spotlight on crimson and yellow leaves, as if it had been let out of jail. She decided, as she sipped her second cup of coffee, that Jake needed to be prompted to get out of bed and get dressed. It would do him good to get some fresh air. She rummaged in the cupboard in the hall, and after shifting a few boxes of things that might never see the light of day again, she found what she was looking for.

Jake woke with a start. What was that? Somewhere in his memory, something stirred, as he opened his eyes to the best spare bedroom.

"Clang, clang, clang! Clang, clang, clang!"

For a second or two, he'd thought it was the end of playtime, but then it came back to him. Nana! *That blasted bell she used to use to get us all to come down for dinner!* What was she up to?

"I'm awake, Nana!" he shouted down the stairs. "I'm awake! You can stop that thing now. Please, please stop!"

Nancy was grinning to herself. It had always worked, that brass bell. Someone was bound to buy you a bell, if you were a teacher, and this one had come in handy, when teenagers didn't get up or children didn't hear you calling them above their playing shouts and screams.

14

"Come on, then, Jake. Get yourself dressed. We're going out!"

She knew he would groan, but she couldn't hear it downstairs, so she put the bell on the hall table and went to wash her coffee cup. She heard the shower, and she guessed he would be at least another ten minutes, even if he was quick. She had time to sort out her bag, decide which coat to wear, and to clear the passenger side seat in the car; it was a handy side-table when she drove alone.

As Jake appeared, she thrust a breakfast bar in his hand.

"Here. Eat this on the way. We're going to pay a visit to the RHS garden at Harlow Carr. I haven't been there since your granddad died, and it's always lovely in the autumn. Grab your coat. I'll treat you to lunch at Betty's Tea Room."

He almost dared to say that he was a grown man, that he was twenty now, and he didn't need to be organised like a child. However, since the famous Betty's had opened one of its tea rooms at Harlow Carr, the mention of lunch there was too tempting. Like a lizard's tongue stretching out and catching nothing, he whisked it quickly to the back of his mouth, an artificial cough into his hand disguising the halting sound.

There had been a time when his parents thought he might study botany, as he'd been enthralled by flowers, but that was before he discovered girls and testosterone deepened both his voice and his disinclination to work. It had been a battle to get him to study for his exams. It was only because he was very bright that he'd achieved a good set of results in most subjects in Year 11, although biology wasn't one of them. A re-think for his last two years at school had set him on a pathway that had led to his future in the world of artificial intelligence, which his father disparagingly thought an appropriate description of his own talents. Uncle Ben was the only one he could talk to about what he was doing, as he understood computers in a way that his father never would, though the man used them all the time in his accountancy business. Sadly, Uncle Ben was not someone he knew very well. He wasn't sure why, but his mother seemed luke-warm about her brother, and they were not as close as he felt to his own sisters. Uncle Ben had a far more exciting life, it seemed to Jake. He'd worked for an international company, and he'd been all over the world. Poppy, Jake's mother and Ben's sister, called him a snob, but Jake had no idea why, other than the fact that he had a swanky address on the outskirts of Leeds. Jake had loved visiting him, taking a walk round Roundhay Park. The only problem had been children having to be on their best behaviour for the whole visit, not daring to touch anything in the house or run around unless they were outside. He did seem to be quite proud of where he'd settled, but then he had a huge, detached house, compared to their semi, and it was full of the latest gismos, like curtains that shut themselves at the touch of a button. Jake thought maybe his mum was a bit jealous of his tales of where he'd been, who he'd met and how thrilled he was with what he'd bought.

Once out of the street, they were soon driving past the fields of sheep and cattle that seemed to have been there forever. Nancy still felt a twinge of satisfaction, when she saw the cattle, but Jake wouldn't remember the year they disappeared when foot and mouth disease ravaged the countryside at the beginning of the century. Over six million cows and sheep were slaughtered that year, before it was defeated. She would never forget being near Skipton during a half-term holiday, driving down the dale towards the town, hearing the gun shots; notices fixed at farm gates, saying "No entry". She'd shuddered at what that signalled for the farmer. She still found it miraculous that farming had somehow recovered from the blow, as it did from so many others, never knowing which years would be good or bad.

In the distance, the "golf balls" of Menwith Hill air force base were shadowy structures on the horizon, as they made their way towards Harrogate. The avenue of trees lining the open grassland of The Stray stood like a guard of honour as they passed, their leaves presenting to the world their last flourish of red and gold, waving like flags before they fell. They drove alongside the open space, where dog-walkers and runners, strollers, and striders, made the most of what had been preserved for their generation. It was, of course, at its best when the crocuses bloomed, carpeting the grass with the promise of spring in shades of purple, white and gold, but it was a blessing for the town in all seasons.

They parked easily, since it was a weekday, and they passed quickly through the reception area, thanks to Nancy's membership card. On the map of the site, Jake noticed all the changes that had taken place since he'd last visited. Once through the gate, they turned to their right, where they were greeted by a splash of colour from a wildflower bed, magnificent in its disorganised display that seemed to be nature shouting out "We win!" in competition with the controlled, managed beds on the opposite side of the path. Nancy and Jake stood for a minute or two, trying to recall the names of the blooms that were so familiar. He remembered having a little Ladybird book when he was at primary school, and he'd struggled to read the words, his eyes reluctant to be pulled away from the vibrantly coloured pictures to the less attractive print. Nana might remember, he thought. The reds, blues, whites, and yellows wafted back and forth in a gentle breeze, almost hypnotic as his eyes fixed on them. Out of the depths of his memory, he recognised some scarlet poppies among the dandelions, daisies, and St John's Wort. They were a wonderfully chaotic, kaleidoscopic celebration of colour. Intended to attract the bees, they also drew in the less useful human visitors, who were mesmerised by the scale of what would normally be labelled weeds, but here were trumpeting their worth. He became aware that he was smiling, something that had been a rare event in the last few weeks.

"Oh look!" Nancy cried, on cue. "Do you remember these, Jake?" The smile on his face was matched by her own. To the left, dahlias cried "notice me", with their brilliant hues of scarlet, purple and gold, like royalty waiting for people to pay them homage. As they approached the alpine house, they stopped to admire the sculptures that had been added. One of the joys of visiting the garden again was making new discoveries among the plantings. As they followed the paths, they came upon the deer sculptures and an enormous bee. Then there were the little bridges that Jake had loved running across. He just had to sit on one of the swing seats, while Nancy laughed at his boyish pleasure. As they reached the sculpture of a rabbit, Jake moved to line up a photograph on his phone, while Nancy stood still, keeping out of the way. Just as he was about to take the shot, he swung round, his back to what she thought he was going to photograph. Asking Nancy to smile for him, positioning himself to take a careful snap, he diverted her surprise into co-operation with his playful intent. As he finished the shot, his arm spun her round by the shoulders.

"Come on, Nana. Let's head to the woodland. Do they still have those birdsong boxes round there?" He whisked her on, through the middle beds, where usually he would stop to admire the colour and survival of the carefully tended blooms. She had no time to object, as he ran ahead – just as he had as a boy – and waited for her behind a tree, laughing as she walked as fast as she could, never quite catching up with him. He moved on to the vegetable beds and down the slope towards the queue waiting to buy teas.

"Slow down, Jake!" she laughed. "My legs are a bit older than yours!"

He grinned at her, as if he were still five years old, without a care in the world.

Once past the tea queue, they walked slowly on, into the wood, and there, just as he remembered them, Jake found the bird song boxes. He pressed each one in turn, delighting in the recognition of what he'd learnt. At the bird hide, they sat down, so that Nancy could catch her breath, and they peered through the window at the scene in front of them. Some tiny birds were pecking away at the feeders hanging from the branches, their colourful breasts standing out against the drabness of the bark.

"They won't be here much longer, will they?" Jake ventured. "They seem to be feeding up for winter."

"They won't all migrate, Jake, but yes, they do seem to be eating to build up stores. It always amazes me that we can see such a variety of different species in this tiny area."

"It must be great to be able to just take off, into the air, when you've had enough of where you are," muttered Jake, his eyes fixed longingly on the robin that had just had its fill and fluttered away. Sometimes, he would love to be able to remove himself as easily as that. He imagined flapping his wings in boring lectures or tricky situations, and suddenly, whoosh, there you were, out of there!

A lone magpie came into view. "Oh, I hope there's another one of those somewhere near," said Nancy.

"Oh yes!" Jake started singing quietly:

"One for sorrow, two for joy,

Three for a girl and four for a boy.

Five for silver, six for gold,

Seven for a secret never to be told.

Seven for a secret never to be told…"

His voice faded as his vacant eyes fixed on the glass, until a noisy crow frightened the smaller birds away and snapped him out of his trance.

"Well, that's all right then, Jake. That nursery rhyme could count magpies or crows, so I guess we have two!"

"So, he has a secret never to be told," she said to herself.

They wandered back, past the children's playground, and Nancy almost expected him to make a beeline for the swings, but he slipped his arm through hers, as if she needed to be steadied, and she felt herself being steered towards the exit.

"Time for tea, then, Nana? You must need to sit down by now."

No, I don't, thought Nancy, but she wouldn't discourage him from being thoughtful, as he'd obviously had enough of walking around.

"OK. Betty's it is, then. We'll have to queue, but it's not usually too bad here. The exit will take us through the shop."

They walked past the plants for sale, into the shop. Nancy thought Jake might want to browse a little, but no. He ignored the plants, the seeds, the colourful displays. He headed straight for the exit at the other end. Maybe he was very hungry, she thought, as he'd only had the breakfast bar this morning.

It was probably some time since he'd had the treat of going to Betty's. She smiled to herself at his seeming excitement at the prospect.

As always, the queue, no matter what the time of day, stretched back from the entrance to the restaurant to the door of the shop, but no-one seemed to mind. The goods stacked at the side wall and in the centre gave them ample opportunity to take in the possibility of what they could treat themselves with on the way out. Meanwhile, the girls behind the counter offered the kind of service that encouraged their customers to continue to flock back. Like the waitresses, they wore unique uniforms from a bygone age, lending the atmosphere a touch of nostalgia that never seemed to lose its appeal.

Menus were thrust into their hands as the manager, with his customary efficiency, asked how many were together, and offered them the chance to choose what they wanted while they queued. Nancy and Jake pored over the pages of offerings. Nancy knew she would choose tea, despite the fact that she usually drank coffee at home. This was Betty's, and Betty's tea was not to be passed up, as long as you remembered to use the tea strainer that came with the pot! It was not yet lunch time, so lunch somehow didn't seem right.

"All day breakfast, eh, Nana?" grinned Jake, just as Nancy was thinking that was what she would have. It had always seemed decadent to her, to have breakfast in Betty's, but today was as good an excuse as any, with a grandson in tow.

"All day breakfast it is, Jake," she returned, with a smile that lit up her face.

They were lucky to be sent to a table by the window, at the far end of the restaurant, where Jake allowed her to look out over the autumn colours, while he had his back to them. Nancy relaxed into the chair, surrendering herself to the sense of privilege, and relishing the polite, refined service, famous across Yorkshire.

"Tell me, what have you been doing with yourself over the summer, Jake? Your mum said you'd been off to Spain with a friend. Did you have a good time?" Safe ground, she thought. Maybe she could somehow get him to reveal why he'd decided on this visit, out of the blue.

"It was great!" he answered, with enthusiasm that sounded genuine. That was not the problem, then.

She listened, as he told her about the sights they had seen in Barcelona, bringing back memories of when she and James had been awed by the City of Gaudi many years ago.

Their meal arrived, and as she poured out their drinks, she asked, "You were with Connor, weren't you, your old school friend?"

He nodded, now intent on savouring his sausage. As he finished his mouthful, he volunteered, "I feel as if I've known Connor all my life, so it's easy to be with him. He's studying medicine now, you know, Nana."

"Is he now? Not a mathematician like you then? I seem to remember you two getting up to all sorts of things when you were at school. Was Barcelona ready for you?"

She'd liked Connor when she'd met him. Poppy had told her about what a tough start he'd had in life, with his mother dying of cancer when he was tiny, and a father in the army, being brought up by grandparents who adored him but were not a match for an energetic, mischievous teenager. Boarding school had been his refuge, and he'd spent a lot of time with pastoral staff. He'd seemed a bit of an attention seeker in lessons, courting popularity, but Jake had seen the other side of him, the vulnerable side that he covered up by playing the clown. Despite his apparent inattention, Connor had sailed through exams with an ease that astonished Jake, and he'd always been destined to become the doctor his mother would have been, had she lived. It had been an unexpected friendship between the two of them, but having a best friend had calmed Connor down and given Jake confidence. They'd become inseparable until they left school and went on to study at different universities.

They tucked into their breakfast, enjoying both the meal and the chatter about Jake's school days. In hindsight, he acknowledged how lucky he'd been to go to such a good school, but of course, when he was there, he only saw the restrictions of boarding, rather than the advantages, and he knew he and Connor had not always worked as hard as they might have done, until they realised just how much they wanted those A level results, to get into university. He admitted they'd been surprised at how hard it was to leave school, at the end, and shocked that they suddenly had to face the big, wide world without the safety net that had always been there to catch them.

"What struck me this summer, Nana, was how much more serious Connor was, how sensible and responsible, compared to when we were teenagers. Hitting our twenties seems to be making us grow up, I guess, and sometimes Connor even sounded like my mother!"

Out of the corner of her eye, Nancy saw a very elegant, well-dressed woman peering through the glass from the outside, as though she were looking for someone, brushing her auburn hair away from her worried eyes, as the wind caught it. She was obviously with a friend, who was bent over, tying the laces of her walking shoes, talking as she did so. As the friend stood up, the woman turned her head back towards the entrance steps, and they moved on.

"Something fascinating out there, Nana?" Jake wondered aloud.

"Oh, just some woman looking in through the window. She's gone now."

Jake swigged the last of his tea and swallowed the last of his meal. "I'll be back in a mo, Nana," he said, as he placed his napkin on his empty plate and headed for the toilets in the corner of the room.

Nancy took the opportunity to pay the bill, ensuring that when Jake finally came back to the table, she was ready to leave.

She decided to take a different route home, avoiding the town, so she headed out through Beckwithshaw and Killinghall. She much preferred driving through the lanes and countryside to driving through the traffic. Besides, it gave her more time in the car with Jake. She would avoid the main roads, going the long way round, so she could enjoy being able to speed up now and then. It was better than sitting in a queue at lights, and she could relish being flanked by stone walls and grass, instead of buildings hemming her in.

Jake chatted on the way home, about the flowers, about the sculptures, about the memories, but Nancy was waiting for him to do what he'd done when he was a teenager, when he would take the opportunity of sitting beside her in the car, not having to face her, to tell her what was on his mind. His mind seemed to have told his tongue not to breathe a word, and like the robin out in the cold of the morning, he chirped his cheerful song as if he could do nothing more. It had been a thoroughly pleasant morning, such precious time with her grandson, and she was determined to store it up in her memories, to keep her going when his life moved on again.

Nancy opened the front door, ready to find the cafetière, so that she avoided Jake's abhorrence of her instant decaf made in a cup, but as she deposited her keys on the hall table, she noticed the little red light on the phone flashing. She pressed the "play" button, expecting it to be a message she would need to hear. She was not sure whether to laugh or not, when she heard:

"Rock-a-bye baby on the treetop,
When the wind blows the cradle will rock
When the bow breaks, the cradle will fall.
Down will come cradle, baby and all."

Nancy and Jake looked at each other, looked at the phone, and looked back into each other's eyes.

"What on earth is that all about?" Nancy's rhetorical question elicited a shake of the head and lifting of the shoulders from Jake, who was as bewildered as she was.

"Must be some kind of sick joke, Nana. But why a nursery rhyme? Scammers are usually trying to sell you something, aren't they? Maybe you'll get another call, offering you some kind of security device!"

"Perfectly feasible," thought Nancy, as she deleted the message, then wished she hadn't. She wanted to remember what the voice was like.

"Best ignored," she said, as she hung up her coat and headed for the kitchen.

"Absolutely," Jake agreed. He silently puzzled at the vague familiarity of the voice. It had been well disguised, but there was just a tiny tell-tale sound in the way "baby" and some other words had been said that struck a chord deep down in his memory. Where had he heard that before? What was that accent? He shuddered, despite trying to convince himself that it was just a silly prank.

He stuck his head into the lounge, as he passed, and tested the new-found voice of Tommy Tucker. "Watcha Tommy!"

"Watcha Tommy. Gissakiss! Rockabye!" screeched the bird.

"Rockabye? How did he learn that?" Nancy was flabbergasted. The lounge door had been open, so the bird must have heard the nursery rhyme being recorded and then replayed, and he obviously responded to a male voice far more easily than Nancy's. She was even more convinced that he was prejudiced, and she fervently hoped he would forget the last bit.

Nancy tried to forget about the phone call, as she settled down for the evening. Jake disappeared upstairs for a while. He had some reading to do before he started the new term at Cambridge, and she was left to doze in front of one of the few programmes she actually enjoyed. She tried to focus on what was happening on the screen, but nagging away at her brain was the message on the answerphone. She found herself quite glad she was not on her own, as it might have seemed more sinister, and she thought it might be one of Jake's friends, doing something they thought was a joke. She remembered teaching Angela Carter's *The Bloody Chamber* to her A level literature group one year - an anthology of tales that demonstrated just how much gothic potential there was in stories supposed to amuse children. She remembered when she'd been a child, how they'd skipped to "My Father Was a Captain on the Lusitania", singing away, never realising what tragedy was behind the rhyme. The innocence of childhood learnt the words, heard the rhythm and rhyme, and cared little about the meaning behind them. Some distant memory lurked in her mind, and she reached for her laptop, to look up the origins of "Rock-a-bye Baby". As children, they'd just assumed it was about a baby in a cot, a lullaby, but now she wondered. If Red Riding Hood's grandmother could be eaten by a wolf, there was no telling what lurked behind nursery rhymes.

There it was. It was possibly a death wish for the son of James the Second, expressing the hope that there would not be a Catholic king. The metaphor of the wind blowing, breaking the bough and the baby falling could easily be lost in the assumption that singing about a baby was cute. The sinister meaning attributed to it made her wish, even more, that she'd kept the recording. Who would send such a message? Was it a harmless prank, or was something else going on here? She was quite glad Jake had heard it, too, as she wasn't sure who would believe her if she told anyone.

She could imagine the sideways look indicating suspicion that it was a figment of an old lady's imagination. She could already hear the whispers:

"Well, you know, she's getting on a bit. Maybe she imagined the whole thing and thinks it's real. It's way too weird to be true! She might be on the verge of developing Alzheimer's at her age. Maybe we should encourage her to be tested. She might not be safe to live alone…"

She was not losing her mind, and she was not imagining things. They could whisper all they liked; she had a witness.

Chapter 3: Poppy

"Oh hi, Anita! Sorry I missed your call earlier. Rushing around as usual. My phone was in my bag while I was shopping. Didn't see the missed call until just now. Tim's always saying, 'Poppy, you must slow down. You're trying to do too much!' Well, that's easy for him to say, isn't it? How am I meant to do it?"

Poppy's forced laugh hung in the emptiness of the hall. Her friend, picking up the tension and not knowing what to say, other than that she didn't know, hoped she sounded sympathetic.

"He doesn't have a solution. I know he doesn't. But he's right - I am doing too much. I'm so tired all the time. How am I supposed to keep up with my job, the kids, Mum? I don't know. It's easy for Ben, when he's got a wife doing everything for him, and Harley's just a baby. Try having three older kids, all over the place! Being like a single parent most of the time is no joke. Tim seems to be quite happy to ignore most of what's going on as he gets absorbed in his latest brief — especially since he got the London flat. I don't think he's living on this planet."

"Has he been behaving himself lately?" enquired Anita, not really wanting to hear news of Tim. Not after the chaos he'd caused in his drunken declaration of love for one of the bridesmaids at her sister's wedding. She'd been so embarrassed, and he'd deserved the way he felt the

27

following day. They'd known each other most of their lives, having grown up on the same street, gone to the same schools, shadowed each other at Cambridge and included each other like family for so many years. The Tim she'd known had always had a strong sense of justice, and it was no surprise to her that his integrity had gained him a position of trust in his finance company, but lately he seemed to have abandoned his principles, as if he were having a mid-life crisis that was making him reckless. When Poppy had come to her in tears after the wedding, it took her by surprise that she felt more loyalty to his wife than to him.

"Thank goodness Cassie's the sensible one. I don't have to worry too much about her — she's always been a good kid. I do miss her, though. It was great, having her home for the summer, even if she was out a lot of the time. I'm not too sure about that Miles she's keen on at the moment, but with a bit of luck it won't last, now that she's away."

"Oh! I do hope she isn't heading for heartache, then, Poppy. Poor girl!"

"He seems a bit wishy-washy to me, to be honest, but he obviously adores her. At least he seems to have been brought up with some manners, so he isn't a yob! As I'm not keen on men right now, maybe I'm being unfair."

"What about Daisy?"

"God knows what I'm going to do with Daisy! One day she's all grown up, the next like a sulking child. I never know which she's going to be when she gets up in the morning, or which she's going to be when she gets home from school. Exhausting! I do hope she knuckles down and gets her head round what she needs to do to get good exam results this year. At least the other two made it to university; she might not if she doesn't buck her ideas up. All she seems interested in, this year, is her sixteenth birthday party. It's worse than planning a wedding!" Another forced laugh.

"I'm not sure we can ever get it right, when they're teenagers, can we? I remember Lydia's eighteenth - like planning a ball for about a hundred people!"

"It's going to cost me a bomb. No concept of making ends meet, that one. I've somehow got to persuade her to leave a few people out, and she won't be happy!"

Poppy glanced at her watch. It was just as well she didn't have to be at the school gate. With a bit of luck, Daisy would be home late today, as she'd said was going to her friend's house after school.

"Right! I'd better get the rest of this shopping put away, before one of them rings and wants to chat about their latest disaster. I've got to sort that PowerPoint for Monday, too. At least Mum seems to be OK, though goodness knows what she's up to, planning to take herself off on trips all over the world! I don't think she thinks of herself as in her sixties! I know she's missing Dad, but we don't talk about it much. It would just be too upsetting for both of us. I wish he would just walk through the door, with that indulgent smile of his, and take charge. He was always the voice of reason, wasn't he? I think she may be losing it a bit, the way she talks to that budgie as if he really understands anything. They say loneliness can affect mental health. Maybe I should persuade her to go to the doctor, before it's too late."

Having spilled her thoughts over the phone and ending the call with a hurried "Goodbye", Poppy grabbed her bag and made her way to the car, just as the landline was ringing in the background. She couldn't stop. Whoever it was would ring again, if they genuinely wanted to speak to her, and if it were one of the kids, they'd call her mobile. She heaved herself behind the steering wheel and sat for a few minutes, taking deep breaths to calm herself down. Why had she made the excuse that she had to put the shopping away? It could wait. Anita was her best friend. Surely, she would have understood what Poppy was about to do. But she'd been Tim's friend first, and Poppy didn't entirely trust that she would not be in touch with him herself.

Breathe. Stay calm. You've got to drive this thing in a straight line. It just won't go away, the memory of that day, will it? It was so humiliating! When I challenged him with "What the hell do you think you're playing at? What's going on between you and that woman?" all he could come back with was: "What are you on about, Poppy?" as if nothing had happened. He must think I was born yesterday. It's pretty obvious that he's been up to something behind my back. And as for her, the slut! The least she could have done was to send him packing, rather than encouraging his stupidity in front of so many people! Anita said she'd been embarrassed, but she didn't seem embarrassed to me. I think she thought it was funny. He's known most of them since they were children, but I don't remember her, and that wasn't child's play. I've been living with him for twenty-one years, and I know when he's lying. He's no good at it, anyway. Goodness knows how much he'd had to drink, but it was obviously more than he should have had. We don't drink a lot, usually, just a glass of wine with dinner, when he's here for it, and maybe a bottle or two at the week-end. At least, that's what I drink. What he drinks when he's away on business is anybody's guess, but when he's staying in a hotel on expenses, I've no doubt it's a fair bit more! You'd think he'd be able to hold it, wouldn't you? There was something ...something in their eyes ... that spoke volumes. Well, he's on a plane from Dubai now, and I can't live like this. I have to know the truth. Maybe this investigator Jonty recommended will be able to find out. Right, here we are. We'll see what secrets you've been keeping, Timothy Castleford, while I'm busy holding everything together.

"Mercury and Mars" was up a steep flight of stairs, covered in old linoleum and edged with metal, obviously having seen years of wear and tear. The mustard-coloured walls did nothing to ease her mind. At the top of the flight, a bell tinkled as a heavy fire door opened onto a surprisingly light foyer, a vaulted ceiling making it seem larger than it was. Tasteful welcome notices hung on the walls, sporting reassuring compliments and reviews. Among them were the friendly, smiling faces of the partners, Jason Mercury and Hector Mars — if you could believe they were their real names and not some attempt to sound as if they had god-like powers.

From an office to the left, a tall, balding man in a pristine suit and tie emerged and proffered a hand to shake. He was nothing like fictional detectives Philip Marlowe or Cormoron Strike, and he was certainly nothing like a god.

"Good afternoon, Madam. I'm Jason Mercury. Can we help you?"

The next half an hour was spent explaining what sounded feeble now that she voiced it. She didn't trust her husband of twenty-one years. She thought he was having an affair. She was no longer sure when, or whether, he was away on business. She wanted to know. Did she mean she was gathering evidence for a divorce? Well not exactly, no, not yet. She hadn't decided. It might be nothing, mightn't it?

She left, having asked Mr Mercury to "undertake discreet enquiries" on her behalf, as he'd phrased it. She hoped he would at least live up to his name and deliver a speedy result. Ironic, she thought, that Mercury had been the god of financial gain, but also of tricksters and thieves! She had her own bank account, and he need never know she'd done this, if she was wrong. She hoped it would come to nothing, but at least she could stop picking at an open sore, never letting it heal.

She looked at her watch again. Good. She would be in before Daisy. Inappropriate as it was, she found herself smiling at the thought that here she was, doing exactly what she was disapproving of - a secret meeting she would not divulge to anyone in the family. She was learning how to play a double game.

"Where were you?" greeted her, as soon as she emerged from the garage, finding herself face-to-face with an irritated Daisy. "I phoned, to tell you we were leaving Laura's early, but you didn't pick up. I've been sitting in the garden for ages, and I'm frozen!"

Ah! The sound of the phone ringing as she left the house crept back into her memory. She'd assumed someone would phone her mobile, if it was urgent, but of course she'd turned her mobile off while she was with the investigator. It was still off.

"Oh dear! Look at that! Must be a dead battery. Come on Daisy, let's get you in and warmed up. Did you have a good day?" *Sometimes, lies come so easily, don't they?*

Daisy was already through the front door ahead of her, throwing her rucksack at the stairs, as if they had done something wrong, and heading straight for the fridge.

"You never have anything decent in here, do you?" she flung at Poppy, as she slammed the fridge door shut and dived into a drawer to find some chocolate. With that, she stomped out of the kitchen and up the stairs, phone in hand, already starting to message someone. It never ceased to amaze Poppy, how teenagers could use their fingers and thumbs so quickly and nimbly, tapping out the letters and numbers almost as fast as they could speak. She'd thought it was quite something when she'd learnt to touch type, to make it faster to use a keyboard. However, her thumbs couldn't seek out the tiny pads on her phone, and she knew Daisy laughed at her tendency to use one finger to type a message. They were actually quite clever, these kids, she thought, but she wouldn't dare say that too often to her own daughter. There would be something wrong with saying it, no doubt.

As she reached for the coffee machine, a sign of true decadence, only excusable in her own mind because it was a present, she could hear Daisy laughing upstairs. Why didn't she laugh downstairs anymore? When she was about five, her mum had been her bestest friend. What happened? She was probably her leastest friend now! Mum would be the last person she would confide in.

Mum would be the last person she would confide in. Well, look at you. When did you last confide in your own mother, then? What would she make of private investigators? With a sigh, she began to put away the waiting remnants of the shopping.

Chapter 4: Cassie

"Write it down," they said at school. "Get it out of your system." To be honest, I was never sure how much help that would be, if I was upset, but maybe it'll clear my head, so that I can get on with what I've got to do.

Cassie grabbed her pristine pad of A4 paper Poppy had insisted she might need, her mother not quite understanding that Cassie didn't intend to write too much down by hand. She would record some of her lectures and talk into her laptop, so that it typed the notes for her. Never mind – it might have its uses. She picked up her pen and started, enhancing the first "W", as if it were part of an old, illuminated text, while she allowed her brain to find a gear. Once she started, she found the ink flowing over the page, her hand struggling to keep up with her thoughts, not being used to this kind of exercise much these days:

What on earth am I going to tell Mum when she phones? I can't tell her the truth. She'll hit the roof. She seems to be a bundle of nerves lately, and I don't think she's handling me leaving home very well.

She thinks I didn't notice, when she dropped me off at my digs, but I saw the tears in her eyes. I felt the extra-long hug, before she finally went. You'd think she would be fine with me going off to Leeds, wouldn't you, when she's already got Jake at Cambridge? I won't be that far from home. It's what your kids do, grow up, leave home. And anyway, I'll be back at Christmas, so it's only a few weeks I'll be away. She left me with what she thought were words of wisdom, the same old stuff that parents always trot out, hoping we'll enjoy ourselves, but secretly hoping we work hard and make the most of what they see as our chance to make good. She said she trusts me. Of all her children, I'm the one she sees as the sensible one. No pressure, then!

It felt very strange, as I shut the door to my room and realised this was it. This was where I was going to be living, at least for now. Compared with my room at home, it's just so dismal! No pretty curtains and comfy cushions here! It was only the excitement of being here that made it all right to have so little space and a bed that had definitely seen better days. Mum had made sure I had a mattress protector, just in case... I could see, in her eyes, the condemnation of its stark otherness. The room looked clean to me, but she insisted on cleaning the toilet herself, and she left me plenty of bleach. Compared to my room at boarding school, the university one does look deprived - a bit like a room in a sorry, dilapidated hotel. I wanted her to stop fussing, but I didn't have the heart to tell her so. I wanted her to go, and yet I didn't want her to go, if you know what I mean.

I need to go and follow the noise down the corridor, find someone to talk to, someone who knows what it feels like but won't make me cry. The last thing I want to do is cry. It's so exciting, suddenly being able to be me, without having to be theirs at the same time. Scary though now that I've got to make my own decisions and sort things for myself. Can't blame them if it goes wrong now, can I? Well, at least I won't have to go shopping for a few days. Mum's left boxes of food here, as if I'll starve if she hasn't filled my cupboard. I hate to tell you, mother dear, but eating in is probably not what I'm going to be doing for a while!

It's a shame Dad couldn't come too. He always seems to be so busy these days. I'm not even sure I'll miss him, to be honest. Not that different from not seeing him when I was at school, except for the fact that I won't have a half term holiday to catch up with him. He did at least leave me a note, and an envelope with some money in it. That should come in handy, anyway.

I've put my "Good Luck" cards on the window ledge. Nana's is, of course, the biggest one! "Let me know how you get on," it says. She knows she won't hear for a while. She knows a lot, does Nana, far more than Mum gives her credit for. I used to say I would listen to Nana's "wise words" when I was younger, because she didn't get angry with me, just talked to me, and somehow, she always seemed to find the right thing to say. When we Face-timed her before I came away, she had such a wicked glint in her eye, when she told me not to do anything she wouldn't do in Freshers' Week. Not sure I can stick to that one, Nana!

Freshers' Week has been something else! Awesome! Like one big party for days, till we were all exhausted and wanted to sleep for a week, but no-one was going to be the first one to give in. I think we must have tried out nearly every club in Leeds. They're so much better than anything we've got at home!

The other girls on my floor are a great crowd, honestly. None of us had ever met before we came here, but that didn't stop us partying in our shared kitchen, as if we'd known each other for years. They all seemed just like people I knew at home, until the shots flowed. I don't even want to remember what we did by day three. It was just a haze. I thought I had freshers' flu, I felt that ill, so I ended up in bed all day on Friday. I nearly phoned Mum, but I'm glad I didn't — I couldn't have taken her disapproval and fuss. By Saturday, I just wanted to stay in bed. Tomorrow, I've got to get my head straight and be ready to listen to lectures.

The only other time I've ever felt that bad was that time we celebrated Sadie's eighteenth birthday last year, on that trip to Blackpool for the weekend! I'd never been there, but I'd heard about it, and it looked fantastic on the screen. We'd all heard about Blackpool Tower ballroom, of course, because of Strictly being such a popular TV show, though no-one admitted to watching it. When Sadie said she'd got us some "late rooms", I thought we'd just have a bit of fresh air and that might be a good thing, clear my head and make me feel like facing the next week. How wrong can you be?

Cassie sat back in her chair, flexing her cramped hand. The painful memory flooding back, making her flush with remembered embarrassment as she continued writing:

OMG. How did I let myself get talked into that? I thought Blackpool was sand and lights, you know, and kids having fun. I thought, staying at a nice hotel, opposite the beach, we'd be civilised, eat some cordon bleu for a treat, enjoy the sunshine, walk up the pier.

It was going well when we first arrived. Sun was shining to order, even if it was an autumn day. Just what we needed. We got there a bit late. Sadie's car is just ancient, and it hasn't got Satnav, so we took a wrong turn when we came off the motorway. Nearly ended up in Lytham instead. The radio was blaring, and Julie and Becky were singing along to Adele's "Hello". I was trying to watch the road signs, but Sadie said she knew where we were going. She'd been there before, in her boyfriend's car. It was a good job I had Google maps on my phone, so we eventually got there. We were all starving hungry by then, so we piled out of the car at the hotel. Julie said, "Let's go and get some fish and chips".

So much for going for a nice meal! Sadie was already on her way across the road, towards the row of shops, where the smell of fish and chips made it pretty easy to find. I hoped I didn't get fish and chips down my new top. I certainly looked smarter than the others, with Becky in her over-sized jumper, Julie in ripped jeans and Sadie in a pair of crop trousers I know she wore last summer, though that was hardly going to matter now. I hoped we weren't going to walk far, when I hadn't put my walking shoes on, either. I was already wishing I hadn't gone with them.

I looked across the road, where the music was blaring out of the amusements that were full of teenagers and old men. I did hope we would be able to walk through that quickly and get out to the end of the pier. I hadn't been on a pier for years.

"D'you want vinegar?" asked the young man serving us, with a leering smile on his face.

"Yes please," I said. "And salt."

He plonked the containers down in front of me, and I plonked them back down when I'd used them, not impressed. It was just getting worse by the minute. I should have listened to Mum. I thought she was just being a snob.

We took our lives in our hands crossing the road. The cars were whizzing up and down, and as we crossed the tram tracks, I could see the bus stop we'd need later. We headed down some steps, and we were on the sand, with the sea lapping on it like a gentle invitation to jump in.

"Just look at the tower!" Becky said. I looked. I didn't think it looked that impressive, to be honest. Not quite the Eiffel Tower, was it? I expected it to be sparkling, like the inside you see on the television. The dancers always seem so thrilled to be there!

"Have you ever done any ballroom dancing?" Sadie asked me.

Well of course I haven't. Mum sent me to ballet lessons. "Not my thing, really, Sadie," I said. "Have you?" I couldn't imagine Sadie in one of those dresses, not with her figure, though I wouldn't dream of saying that to her.

"Well," she said, "my cousin Saffron competes at national level. She taught me a thing or two, and we all used to go to watch her in her competitions, when we were younger."

"Wow!" said Becky. "You'd better take a photo of the tower, to send her. Tell you what, I'll take one of you, with the tower in the background, if you like."

So, there we were, fish and chips, no shoes, and Becky taking a photo for Sadie to give to her cousin. "What on earth do we look like?" I thought to myself.

We headed back to the hotel to unpack. I wasn't used to sharing a room, but at least I was sharing with Sadie, who was less giddy than the other two. I was a bit disappointed in the hotel, to be honest. It was far worse than my room in hall is, and I dread to think what Mum would have made of it!

We met up outside and headed for the pier. At last, I was going to get to go to the end! I told myself not to look down through the gaps in the wooden slats, or I'd start to feel dizzy. I thought there would be something at the end of the pier - a theatre or something, but there wasn't. We walked up it anyway, and we stood at the end, looking out at the sea. Julie pretended to be on Titanic, and we all gave a rendition of "My heart will go on." I don't think the elderly couple sitting on a nearby bench were very impressed.

As we walked back down, the sun was setting, so we stood and watched as the lights began to come on. I felt quite excited, like a little girl. I was so busy watching, I didn't see what was happening until I heard Becky shout, "Julie, don't be so daft! Get down!" Julie had decided she wanted a better view, and she'd climbed on a seat and had one foot on the rail at the side of the pier. Any minute now, she could disappear over the side!

A woman passing by with her small son hurried him on, saying, "There's a silly girl, there, Bobby. Don't you ever do that, will you? It's very dangerous."

Bobby obviously wanted to stand and watch, hoping she would fall, but just in time, Sadie grabbed her by the elbow and pulled her down —

sadly not before her sunglasses landed with a plop in the sea and floated off towards Ireland, like two eyes staring at her in disbelief, just as hers stared back at them.

The sun went down, the dark closed in, and we made our way to the bus stop to board the tram. Everyone was looking forward to this. The queue just kept growing, but we managed to get on the first tram — just. We clambered forward, along the carriage, finding seats where we could. Oh, whatever Mum thought of Blackpool, the lights were awesome! We travelled up the road, beyond the beach, and they shone and shone, some of them making tableaux and some of them like animation, all of them full of red and blue and white and green, lighting up the night. I actually found myself smiling, excited, feeling about ten years old, as I stretched myself forward, to see the next display. The tram went all the way back along the sea-front road, before it turned us out at the stop where we'd boarded. We were all feeling very cheerful as we got off, so we agreed it was time to find somewhere to have a drink. Let the celebration begin!

Well, I never expected to find myself in that pub with all those loud and very drunk men. Big mistake! And the women in that hen party, carrying that disgusting blown-up thing, with their "kiss me quick" hats and raucous laughter. That man leaning on the other side of the bar, covered in tattoos, and things stuck through his eyebrows, must have thought I was one of them. He kept eyeing me up, grinning at me. I mean, every time I looked at him, all that metal and ink just made me shudder. I was glad when we got out of there, away from the rabble, before he could get anywhere near me. My ankle still hurts from falling up that step on the way out. I think I must have got something in my eyes as we came out — it was very hard to find our way back to the hotel. No-one was talking much when we got up the next morning.

It was a very quiet drive home. As far as Mum knows, we had a lovely weekend, and the lights were just spectacular. End of story. Mum thinks I'm the sensible one, and maybe I am, most of the time, but it's a good job she doesn't know everything. She'd have a fit! She'd probably tell me she was right that I shouldn't hang out with that lot, because they're a bad influence! Ah, in some ways I'm not going to miss those girls this year!

And now, this... my brother is being a pain, as usual, and I'm supposed to just keep quiet, tell Mum nothing, pretend I don't know.

Thanks a bunch, Jake!

She slammed the pen down on her desk, just as someone called through the door.

"Cassie. We're off to get a burger. You coming?"

Chapter 5: Daisy

"She drove me to it. I know I shouted "I hate you!". I know I shouldn't have done that. But I do hate her sometimes." Daisy tossed her frustration at the empty air of her bedroom. Her unchecked thoughts tumbled round her head:

Why is it always me that can't have what everyone else in my class has? Suzie's parents are getting her a stretched limo, so that her friends can arrive in style. And what do I get? Tell them to come by bus or taxi or get a lift! Thanks a million, Mum. I'll be the laughingstock of my year! Most of my friends are hiring somewhere to have their party, and Melissa's parents are putting up a marquee. Laura's dad is going to use one of the barns on their farm, and he's hiring a band. They're all going to have fantastic parties, and mine's just going to be such a load of rubbish! I wish I had different parents! I can't wait till I can get out of here and do what I like, like Cassie. It was all right for her – she had no trouble getting her grades, Miss Goodie Two-shoes. Sailed through, didn't she?

I wish I were dead! Maybe then someone would miss me, and they'd be sorry for nagging on and on about getting down to work and not spending money, and not wearing so much eye make-up, and not having tattoos. I just want to be like all the others, but I'll never be like them.

Throwing herself on her pillows, Daisy sensed the blackness smother her, feeling that nothing was ever going to be right again. Nobody loved her, and she was just going to be SO embarrassed in front of her friends that she almost wished she didn't have to have a party at all. She wouldn't even have a boy to hang onto now that Aaron had decided he didn't want to go out with her anymore — not that Mum knew she even had a boyfriend in the first place. *No good telling her because she would not understand, anyway.* Everything was going wrong. Her Instagram and WhatsApp fuelled her misery, as, one after another, posts boasted about what was going to happen. She even dared to look at Facebook, which she hardly ever used these days, hoping that one of her 175 "friends" would be saying they would not be having a super-duper celebration, but not one of them did. She picked up her laptop and opened the diary she'd secretly been writing for the past year. One day, she just might let her mother see what agony she went through, but for now, the diary was just her best friend. She could tell it everything, which was more than she could say for talking to her parents. Ever since she'd read Anne Frank's "Diary of a Young Girl" at school, she'd found her confidante at the end of her fingertips, just as Anne had.

Dear Diary,

Well, it's another boring day, and I have the worst mother a girl could have right now. I wish you could see what I see, when she gives me that look that says I'm making a fuss about nothing, being a nuisance, asking too much. She has no idea. I don't think she was ever really my age. She can't have been my age and be like she is. She seems to be ratty all the time just lately, and totally unreasonable, if you ask me. What am I going to do? I can't face all my friends like some kind of Cinderella, can I? She says I'm a spoilt brat. Huh! Spoilt? I don't think so! She's the one behaving as if she can't have what she wants, all the time! She's in a rush, got a headache, too busy, too tired, especially if I try to get her to see that I desperately need my sixteenth to be special, if I'm not going to lose all of my friends. I'll only be sixteen once, and she's talking as if I can celebrate any time. It's always 'We didn't do that in my day'.

Nahnahnah... Well maybe she didn't, but everyone does now. It doesn't even seem to do any good if I cry. She tells me to wipe my nose, as if I'm about four years old. And Dad's no help. He's never here, anyway, and when he is, there's some job he's just got to do, rather than spend time with Mum and me. It's pretty obvious they're not getting on. Maybe I'm going to be a child from a broken home, on top of everything else. They think you don't notice, don't they, that there's a permanent frost in the air, when they sit down for dinner, when he's got home late? The only time they're nice to everyone is when we visit Nana, and we can't do that very often now that we live so far away. I wish I could have stayed at boarding school, like Cassie and Jake did, but no, that's out of the window as well now that we've lost Granddad. Money. It's always money with parents, isn't it? Maybe if I ran away, I'd be a bit more precious. I could live in doorways and play my ukulele to collect donations from people who'd be sorry for me. They wouldn't care, would they, those two? They might just be glad I'd gone, that third child they never meant to have. They've told me, and anyone who'd listen, I was an accident. They laugh! My life started as a tragedy, and I'm going to end up fading away with misery. Then they might be sorry!

Ping! From behind the fluffy pink case came the signal that a message had just landed. It broke the spell of the downward spiral of gloom, as Amelia's voice announced:

"Hey, Dais! Me and Hannah are heading into town. Some of the others are gonna meet us at the precinct. D'you fancy coming?"

"OK, yeah. Give me five minutes to change, and I'll meet you at the bus stop."

"Right. Bring some money, 'cos we're gonna grab a burger. See you in about ten, then, yeah?"

Amelia, alias Millie, was one of the few people Daisy felt close to at school. They had hit it off on Daisy's first day, when Millie had been

43

assigned as her buddy, to show her the ropes. That didn't go down well with Hannah, Millie's best friend. Daisy knew that Hannah tolerated, rather than liked her. The jealousy of everything she said and did was sitting there, just under the surface. Millie was the friendly sort, who knew everyone and oozed a kind of gentle confidence in smoothly gliding from one group to another, somehow never making enemies. Under her wing, being the newcomer had been a little easier than it might otherwise have been. But Daisy knew that stepping over the line from just one of the crowd, to close friendship, would meet with Hannah's wrath, and she didn't dare chance it. Nor did she dare miss an opportunity to join in, or she'd have been that stuck-up girl from a boarding school, Miss Posh.

Daisy grabbed her bag, dropping her phone into it and checking that she had enough left of her allowance to buy a burger. She didn't want to ask her mother for an advance that would just mean more moaning about how much she spent. She tried combing her hair, but it seemed to make no difference to how awful it looked, sitting on her shoulders as fed up with life as she was. Hidden in the bottom of the wardrobe was the dye she intended to use on her birthday, turning herself into the blond she wished she'd been born, instead of mousy brown. She just had to get her eyebrows sorted before the party. Turning sixteen had to mean looking at a woman in this mirror, and she was going to find a way to make that happen, whether her parents approved or not!

She ran down the stairs, calling out to Poppy that she was going out, and she would not be back for tea, slamming the front door behind her, before her mother could get to the bottom of the stairs to ask where she was going, and who with, and what was she having for tea.

Poppy stood there, looking at the door, rooted to the spot for a minute or two, her face a contortion made of anger and dismay. She could hardly shout down the street after her daughter, and anyway Daisy would be halfway to the bus stop by now.

"Did she take a coat?" Poppy wondered, looking at gathering grey clouds through the window. "That girl will be the death of me!" She wandered up the stairs, as if in a daze, finding some consolation in the fact that Daisy's phone was gone. She could at least call for help if she needed it. Maybe it was a good sign, going out, because she must be meeting friends. Maybe they were turning a corner, and Daisy would snap out of the doldrums. She'd often wondered what her own mother meant by that, but when she'd looked it up, it seemed to fit the current situation perfectly — part of the Atlantic Ocean "with calms, sudden storms, and light unpredictable winds". Calm would be good. Calm would be very good.

Chapter 6: Jake

Messenger
Tim Castleford to Jake Castleford
Where are you? Call me.

email
from Edthefred99@hotmail.com
to jaketherake@gmail.com
Are you OK, mate? You looked as if you were mad as hell after you'd been to see your dad. Did you get to your nan's? I hope you've had time to cool off. When are you planning to get back? Are you going to be registering for the term on Monday?
Using email cos I'm attaching what we've had from the landlord. rent needed asap. I've paid your share for now, but that's my food and drink you're borrowing.

from jaketherake@gmail.com
to Edthefred99@hotmail.com
I'm fine. I got here OK. I think she was a bit surprised when I rang, but I knew she wouldn't turn me away. She's always been there for me. Can't remember a time when she didn't welcome me as if I were a Christmas present she'd always wanted and couldn't wait to hold. She'd

take me, no questions asked. I told her I had a few days study leave, and she swallowed it. Didn't turn a hair when I turned up in Dad's car.

We went to some gardens yesterday. You wouldn't know them, but they're pretty famous up here. She knows I used to love flowers and plants, so that was fine, but then I had a shock. There she was, that woman, right in front of me, coming down the path with another woman. What the heck? Last thing I expected, as you can imagine. I don't think she saw me, to be honest. I managed to turn my back to her, just in time, and Nana was hidden by some giant sculpture I was about to take a photo of. I could hear them chatting, but it got further away, so they must have gone down towards one of the bridges. I thought I was going to burst with panic, like some over-blown balloon! Whew! I don't need shocks like that every day.

Anyway, the last couple of days have been quiet. We've been up to Masham and Ripon, visiting some of the places we used to go when I was a kid.

She hasn't asked any questions, but I can tell she's dying to know why I've turned up out of the blue. I'm stalling so far, but she's nobody's fool. Cassie knows I'm here, but I can do without Mum charging in like the cavalry, as if some battle's got to be fought. I'm still trying to decide whether or not to say anything. It's going to cause a bundle of trouble if I do, and I'm going to feel guilty as hell if I don't.

Don't worry. I'll be back to register. Got to, to make sure I get my loan, or I'm sunk. I'll probably drive back on Sunday, if I can hold out that long, without giving anything away. Get some beer in! I'm gonna need one! I'll message you. I'll get the rent money to you as soon as I get back. The old man's given me some extra, to keep me quiet!

Messenger
Jake Castleford to Cassie Castleford
Hi, Sis.

Hope you have surfaced from Freshers' Week!

Arrived at Nana Boo's house yesterday. Don't tell Mum where I am, for goodness' sake. Decided I needed some time out. Things were getting too stressful. Will let you know when I'm back in Cambridge, though right now, I don't feel like facing another year of blood, sweat and tears. M&D will be expecting me to get a first, and I don't think that's gonna happen. Talk soon.

Cassie Castleford to Jake Castleford

What are you playing at, Jake? Don't tell Mum? She's like a bloodhound! She'll find out soon enough, won't she, if she phones Nana? What's going on with you lately? You're being even more of a pain than usual! What have you done now? No, don't answer that. I don't want to know. You can't drop out now, you idiot! Get your sorry backside back there! Who cares if you don't get top marks for your degree? You could at least get something, and stop messing around with that liability, Ed. It's his fault you've gambled away half your allowance. I bet Mum and Dad don't even know that, do they? They think you're the shining light I've got to live up to. Huh! You might be older than me, but it was me who had to rescue you at school, not the other way round. It's a good job I love you, brother!
And, yes. Survived Freshers' Week — just. Will tell you all about it when you are back in Cambridge. Call me — Today!
Your poor sister.

She'd given him another talking to when he'd managed to sneak in a quick call. He had to use all his powers of persuasion, to convince her that he was not going to gamble any more. He'd learnt his lesson. It was only thanks to the money Dad had given him that he could pay his rent. He told her to stop worrying; he was sorting it all out.

Jake sat back against the wall, pillows piled up behind him and laptop on his knees. He felt as if he could throw it across the room. Why didn't everyone just leave him alone? His head hurt; his thoughts churning round and round, as if his brain had been put into a tumble dryer. Who was he supposed to please? He had no idea what was right here. He yawned, tiredness sweeping over him as if he'd just run a marathon, instead of pottering around Nana's garden, helping her with the tidying of autumn leaves, piling them into bags, to wait for bonfire night. He could imagine her standing there, on her own, doing what they had done every year when he was small. Would she still roast chestnuts, as she had for her grandchildren, or would she not bother? What did you do if you were on your own? He'd never stopped to think, before, about what it was like not to have a family to surround you, or a family you wished you could avoid. Nana was OK, wasn't she? She seemed it, quite content with what she did every day. He wished he could be content, but every time he got close to it, it seemed something got in the way, and life got difficult again. He hadn't meant to lose all that money. He hadn't wanted to get mixed up in what his father was up to. He didn't want the stress of his exams. Why was everything so complicated all the time? He hadn't slept well last night, and he was so tired. Despite this, he was delighted to wake up, this morning, to get out of the dream that had him trapped in guilt and disaster.

He rarely remembered his dreams. You just don't, do you? But this morning was different. He'd been awake till about three a.m., finally falling asleep only to come to when someone was suddenly at the window. It took a few moments for his brain to work out what was going on, until he recognised the swish, swish noise against the glass and heard the ladder move. Of course! The window cleaner! Why did he have to turn up early in the morning, when a man had only just gone to sleep? He groaned, cursing and thanking him at the same time.

In his dream, he'd appeared inside a picture he'd seen in Nana's newspaper earlier that day. There was a deserted stadium, eerily devoid of human presence. Something about it had made him shudder. Somehow, it was all his fault that the stadium was empty. He saw himself as a criminal who had wrecked lives. There he was, creeping like a lifetime thief into the arena where so many had lived and died. *Light at the end of the tunnel,* they say. He couldn't see a way out. He wasn't sure where the light would lead him, even if he could reach it . He wanted the chocolate-coloured comfort of darkness to wrap him in its soft blanket of ignorance. He didn't want to acknowledge his past actions. How could he face them now? Champions all, cheering, lifting them, year on year, until the axe fell and the money ran out. The hands of childhood mascots were imprinted on the rails, peacock pride parading for the crowd. All gone. He wrapped himself in his own arms —the only ones left — and savoured the smell of the banner dust, before he reached up to take them down, closed the doors and walked away. The crowd's roar was singing in his ears. He could hear a chant, as he shut the outer gate, "Get Jake! Get Jake! Get Jake!"

He woke soaked in sweat, startled until he saw the familiar walls. The window cleaner had saved him. He dragged himself up, showered and dressed, and put on a determined smile as he reached the bottom of the stairs, where Nana's smile spread warmth through the chill of fear.

Chapter 7: Nancy and Jake

If he thought he'd fooled Nancy, he was very much mistaken. As he appeared, with his wet hair and smile that seemed to be the effort of someone trying not to look as if they hated the food they had just tasted, she thought to herself, *He looks as if he's been awake half the night. Somehow, I need to get him to talk. I think he wants to, but something's stopping him. All I can do is keep giving him the opportunity to spill the beans, I suppose. He's said he's staying till the weekend, so there's time yet.*

"Shall we pop out again today, Jake? The forecast's good. I need to go into Knaresborough, to collect my glasses. Would you like to come with me? We could have a walk along the river, get some fresh air, before you do some more studying. If you fancy it, we could have a bit of lunch at one of the cafés down by the boats."

"Of course, Nana, if that's what you'd like to do." He hoped he sounded more enthusiastic than he felt. His fourteen-year-old self would have protested that he didn't want to be dragged out, but he was too old to be that awkward now, and he knew Nana was enjoying being able to take him to places that would fill up her cup of nostalgia, as she remembered his childhood.

She took him by surprise, as she suddenly suggested that he drove.

"Are you sure, Nana? You trust my driving? That's more than my parents do!" Indeed, his mother had refused to take him out for any practice when he was learning, and she was less than pleased when his father gave him the car, instead of trading it in. She couldn't see why he didn't wait until his new one arrived, instead of insisting that, as he used the train for work, he could do without one for a few weeks or use his old Jeep that seemed to spend most of its life in the garage.

"Well, Jake, I'm assuming you will be aware of your cargo, if I'm on board, and you will take it far more steadily than you would if you were on your own. You will drive more carefully than you did on the way up here, I'm guessing!" She turned her back, so that he couldn't see her grin, leaving him unsure how to take that comment.

Why does she always seem to know what younger people would get up to? It's as though she's got some kind of second sight. Surely, she's always been a steady driver herself; she was always a bit too careful, as far I remember, when she had grandchildren to ferry around to some playground somewhere. He remembered one time, when she'd stopped the car, refusing to go any further unless he and Cassie stopped squabbling on the back seat. He felt rather like that child, being chastised, as he took the driving seat. You didn't contradict Nana. *I'd better get it right.*

He parked with exemplary precision when they arrived at the car park near the castle. He'd driven slowly all the way, ensuring that he was always a little under the speed limit and changing gear as if he were taking his driving test. Alongside Nancy, he felt like a learner again, waiting for disapproval of anything he got wrong. He was expecting her to do what his father did — tell him what to do and how to do it, as if he knew nothing and needed constant instruction, even if he was now qualified to drive on his own. Instead, she sat calmly, saying nothing, and that, in itself, was a little unnerving.

Nancy bit back her inclination to say, "Well done!", knowing that judgement was not what you wanted, when you were twenty. It had been a comfortable ride, because Tim didn't buy cheap cars, and she'd rather enjoyed the leather seats. No-one had given her a car at Jake's age – she hoped he realised how lucky he was. At the opticians, she collected her glasses. It took only minutes, as she'd used her old frames. She didn't see the need to pay out for new ones, when she was still fortunate enough to need them only for reading. There was a quick procedure of trying them on, to make sure they worked as they were intended to work, and as she peered at her own reflection in the mirror, she saw Jake checking his phone, twitching on his feet like a child impatient to get to a party, his distraction registering as she carefully folded the glasses back into their case, smiled at the receptionist and paid the bill.

They walked past the ruins and through the beautifully tended castle grounds, standing, as so many had stood, to look at the majestic viaduct reflected in the river below. Camera at the ready, Jake joined those crowding round the ravens being shown to tourists near the top of the steps that ran down to the river. It was the view so often sent to other people on postcards. Even at this time of the year, the town drew the visitors to its history and spectacular viewpoint. Down below, the swollen river was flowing swiftly, after the rain of the previous weeks. Undaunted, visitors of all ages ran, walked or strolled along the riverside, towards the black-and-white chequered house, past where the boats were all tied up for the winter and the ducks could claim the water as their own. There was still a thrill of excitement when a train appeared on cue, rattling its way over the viaduct, suspended above the water below.

As they descended the steps, Nancy empathised with a young mother trying to climb upwards, toddler and buggy to hold on to. The girl took the steep slope, rather than the steps, a little easier on the last stretch, but still a challenge. At least she had sensible sneakers on, unlike some of the silly shoes the tourists wore to clamber up and down.

Whew! I could do that once, thought Nancy. *Nowadays, it's enough to try to get myself up these steps without having to rest on the way!* She knew she was fitter than a lot of people her age, but nevertheless, she was no longer able to take them like a mountain goat, even going down, and Jake was soon a long way ahead, laughing as he leant on the railings to wait for her.

"Don't you laugh at me, young man!" she called, her smile filtering into her voice. "You wait! One day, if you're lucky, you'll be my age!" She was pleased to see he was relaxing.

It meant nothing, of course, to Jake, who thought, as a twenty-year-old will think, that her age was such a long way off, and he would be just as agile as he was now, if he got that far. His grandfather had often said you could be run over by a bus, so you never knew what was round the corner, and his grandchildren had known that the likelihood of them being run over by a bus was so remote as to be ridiculous. They had the feeling of near-immortality that only the young can have, and contemplating old age was for grandparents, not them.

They passed the overhanging rocks, now covered in wire. Apparently, there had been too many crumbling pieces tumbling to the ground, and the wire protected passers-by from injury.

"Remember how you used to love going under the overhang, when you were short enough to do that, pretending to be a caveman?" Nancy asked.

He remembered. He remembered all the times she'd taken him and Cassie out, when they had come to visit, while their parents had spent time relaxing or helping their grandfather with jobs that needed to be done. It seemed much longer ago to him than it did to her - a different life-time called childhood, when he could run and hide and pretend to escape, leaving any upset behind in an instant of distraction. *I used to tell you all my secrets then,* he thought, *even when I didn't tell Mum, like where I hid my best tractor, to stop Cassie finding it and breaking it, and where I buried my pennies in the garden, so we could pretend to be pirates and find them from the treasure map.* Sadly, he remembered that hadn't worked, as the precious map fell into the paddling pool, and he forgot where he'd buried them, so he'd lost his pennies for good, until one day when Daisy was digging in the garden and found what her brother had planted. Triumphant, she'd clutched them in her hand, holding them up in the air, and the screams as he'd run towards her and snatched them from her grasp could be heard several streets away.

Although the cafe right on the edge of the water was closed, they managed to find one open, so that they could eat lunch and look out towards the opposite bank, where Mother Shipton's Cave was hidden behind the trees and rocks. That had been another favourite place to visit, during half terms when Poppy and Tim were busy, or Nana just wanted some precious time with her grandchildren to herself.

Sometimes, she'd just had one of them at a time, but Jake remembered how she gathered up the three of them when they all visited, rather like their teacher did, organising them without the stress their own mother seemed to have at the thought of getting them all out through the door. She would shepherd them along, taking no nonsense but seeming more than pleased to be able to spend the day rekindling the thrill of watching her own children discover the magic of some of the places she could take them.

Pointing across the river, he smiled, as he recalled, "There were teddies and hats and shoes all turning to stone, as the water dripped over them over there at Mother Shipton's, weren't there? They fascinated me!" He became quite animated as he reminded Nancy of how he'd thought it might be good fun to put Cassie in the water, to see what happened. Luckily, she was too heavy for him to lift, and when she caught sight of his plan, she suggested that perhaps he should volunteer his Action Man instead.

"D'you remember how we loved to walk along the riverside to the tiny chapel in the rock on the other side of the main road?" he asked.

"Oh yes!" answered Nancy. *That's where history and fantasy could feed a child's imagination,* she thought. They would climb the steps and irreverently play "King of the Castle", while Nancy tried to instil into them a sense of decorum. By the time Daisy was old enough to do the same things, Jake was feeling far too grown up, in the top class of primary school.

Then he was off to boarding school, and more inclined to want to be with his own friends than with two younger sisters, who were a drag on a boy trying to impress his fellow boarders. As he entered his teenage years, he wanted to be off doing adventurous things, and visiting Nana hadn't been so much fun anymore. She'd wanted to know about his school reports, his sports successes, how he'd grown, but somehow, he'd lost that feeling that he could tell her his secrets, and he knew she'd clung to the Jake she'd known as a child, rather than the Jake his parents had dealt with as a teenager. Right now, it felt as if he was reclaiming that space he'd vacated for a few years, as he confessed to her:

"You know, Nana, I wish I'd kept up my rugby when I left school. I used to be pretty quick, but I don't think I'm as fit as I used to be! Too much enjoying myself. Too much beer and too much rubbish food since I escaped from Mum's beady eyes and healthy eating!" He laughed, glancing down at his tuna mayonnaise sandwich.

"I think you're probably right there, Jake!" She looked him straight in the eyes, and he felt their questioning, even if nothing passed her lips. You couldn't fool Nana, ever, it seemed. In that instant, he knew she was waiting for him to tell her what it was that was behind the laugh that didn't reach his eyes. She could still read him like a book, even if she couldn't decipher the writing! He broke away from her stare, bending to do up shoelaces that were not undone, to cover the flush he could feel mounting from his throat to his cheeks.

"*Damn!*" he thought. "*How much longer can I keep this up?*"

When he straightened, she'd finished her soup and was tidying her napkin, ready to leave. He swigged down the last of his too-strong coffee and took her cue to stand up and make their way to the till.

They walked along the path to the steps up to the gardens, and Nana decided they would climb back up to the car park this way. She thought he might like to see the plants. He didn't argue. He watched her pace herself, her breath becoming shallower as she climbed, shock hitting him, as he realised how much he'd taken for granted that she could still do everything she used to do. She stopped at the paddling pool, retrieving her inhaler from her tiny rucksack, and indicated that she needed to sit down. She let him take her arm, something no-one had done regularly since James had died. As he watched her, his concern drew his eyebrows closer, his lips apart, and she saw his face grow older in an instant. Not the child she'd known, nor the teenager who tried the patience of them all, but suddenly a man, who was no more inclined to fit into a mould that others would have him fit than she was.

She recovered her breath, and they reached the exit to the garden before tackling more steps, to emerge in the castle grounds again. Nancy was able to take the flat perimeter path at a brisk walk, and they headed for the car, just as the rain clouds gathered overhead.

While Jake locked the car, Nancy opened the front door and deposited her coat on the hall stand. The red light flashed on her answering machine, beckoning her towards it. Strange! Again, a missed call, but no-one had tried her mobile, when they couldn't get her on the landline. Another scam?

As she pressed the play button, Jake shut the front door behind her, and both of them stood like statues, as a heavily disguised voice sounded as though someone were talking through a scarf:

"Georgie Porgie, pudding and pie

kissed a girl and made her cry

when her boy came out to play

Georgie Porgie ran away."

"Same crank as before, do you reckon?" Nancy asked Jake.

"No idea, Nana. Someone's got a weird sense of humour if it's a prank!"

Jake felt a surge of unease rise from his feet to his head, but he couldn't quite work out why. He knew nothing about nursery rhymes, other than that he'd had a pop-up book full of them when he was little, and he used to sing them with his mum. One of his favourites had been "Ride a Cock-horse to Banbury Cross", though he'd no idea what a cock-horse was, or who the fine lady might be, as he bounced up and down on his mother's knee. If this was someone's idea of a practical joke, it wasn't funny.

Nancy's finger hovered over the "delete" button, but this time she stopped herself. She didn't like the fact that she'd had two of these messages, and she wished she'd kept the first one, to compare it with this one. She knew it must be some kind of prank, but who would do that, and why? She was glad Jake was here, she found, so that she was not on her own. How strange, feeling that he was some kind of protection, when not so long ago her instinct would have been to protect him. She felt more vulnerable than she'd felt at any time since the funeral. Was she becoming the frail old lady her daughter believed she should be, at her age? Surely not!

She found she felt a bit shaken by the call, but she didn't want to worry Jake. He seemed to have enough on his mind. She decided she needed something quick and easy for dinner, and rummaging through the freezer did nothing to inspire her taste buds.

"Jake, how do you fancy pizza tonight?"

"Pizza, Nana? Are you feeling all right? Am I not going to have to eat my meat and three veg, to build up my muscles?"

"Cheeky monkey! I think your muscles have been built up quite enough if you ask me! And don't sound so surprised. Granddad and I didn't always practise what we preached, you know, when you children were not around, when we didn't have to be the perfect example in front of our younger generations." She playfully hit him across the shoulders with the tea towel, as he made an exaggerated duck.

"OK. I'm just going to pop to the supermarket. What kind of pizza do you like these days?"

"Oooh! A large one, Nana!" Jake grinned. "With plenty of meat on it. I'll leave the vegan trend to Cassie!"

"Right. You'll be OK on your own for a while, won't you? If the phone rings, don't answer it!"

58

She grabbed her car keys and was gone before Jake could answer her.

Jake realised he'd never thought about how his grandparents had had to be on their best behaviour for him; it had always seemed to be the other way round. Suddenly, Nana was treating him as another adult, and it took a bit of getting used to.

The phone rang five minutes after she'd gone. He did as he was told and ignored it, although it rang three more times. Her mobile rang, too, as she'd left it on the worktop. He couldn't answer that, as her screen was locked, so he took himself into the lounge and turned on the television.

"So, Tommy Tucker, what should we watch?" he muttered.

"Watcha Tommy, Watcha Tommy," was the only answer, as Tommy tilted his head expectantly.

Jake sighed. No Netflix here, of course. He would have to take pot luck with what he could find by running down the channels, unless .... ah! At least he could try catch-up TV, as long as the internet was working.

Chapter 8: Poppy

"No answer. Where the heck is she then? She usually answers her mobile, even if she doesn't answer the landline. She'd take it with her if she went out. Is she ill? Has she had a fall? Has someone stolen her phone? And why isn't Jake answering, either? As if I haven't got enough to cope with already! Now my mother and my son seem to be conspiring to give me even more to worry about. They've both gone AWOL!"

It had been a bad day at work for Poppy. More and more kept landing in her lap as a senior teacher, whatever it involved, and starting to plan the Christmas concert and carol service had just wound all of the children up to a pitch of thinking term was nearly over, when it had hardly begun. It was always the same at this time of the year. Christmas adverts would soon be on the television, social media bombarded with sales pitches, and families planning what they were going to do. Some of what she called her "naughty but nice" students were being more naughty than nice this term, and her group of "bad boys", who were usually very likeable when you got to know them outside the classroom, were getting themselves into hot water with their antics inside the classroom. She had parents complaining over the phone, because they wanted to take their children out of school before the end of term and didn't see why a trip to America couldn't be called education, and parents crying down the phone because their daughter was about to be suspended for the second time, on a last warning, and they were at their wits' end. There was a child whose friend had died in a car accident and another who felt she was being bullied by one of the clique leaders in her year. Every day, there was something new, and all of the welfare and discipline issues were her responsibility. Poppy felt there was just not enough of her to go round. She felt as if her head would split in two, and Daisy's dramatics certainly weren't helping.

Oh Cassie, if only you were still around to help with that one – you were so good at being a big sister!

In Poppy's opinion, Cassie should have been the oldest of the three children, in fact, because she often seemed to be more reliable than Jake. She shook her head. *Heaven knows, Jake's Jake, and on a good day, he can be wonderful, but then I know he'll do something stupid and not know how to get himself out of the mess he got himself into.*

The coffee machine in the corner of the kitchen was blinking, and after what seemed like a long time, it settled its green lights, and Poppy was able to make herself a strong, black coffee. As she collapsed into an armchair, she tried to calm herself down. She found herself talking aloud, and part of her brain was reminding her that this could be the first sign of madness.

"OK, so think. Rational explanations. Jake might have dropped his phone into a pint of beer. It wouldn't be the first time, would it? Or it might be broken, the screen smashed as he thrashed around in a mosh pit somewhere, with his friends."

He'd gone back to Cambridge early this year, supposedly to put in some study time, but she was under no illusion that he would conscientiously study once he was with his friends. She'd been very surprised, to say the least, when Tim had suggested that he have the old car to get him around a bit more. They hadn't discussed it, but then they didn't discuss much of late. It had been a relief that she didn't have to pile all of his things into her car and make the trek to his student house, as it was quite enough to deal with getting Cassie to Leeds and leave her there.

Why was it so hard to let them go, even when you knew it was high time they flew the nest? You want them to go to university. You want them to do well. Yet when you stand there, saying goodbye and leaving them, you want to wrap them in your arms and bring them home again.

She thought she might cope better with the second one, but no. It was just as hard, if not harder, the house so much quieter, the chatter and the coming and going gone. She found she even looked forward to the washing piling through the door in a great holdall, when Jake brought his home, so that she could play at being mother for a while. However exhausting it was, she found she missed the chaos of their presence.

It was only as her own children left that she'd begun to understand how her mother must have felt when she and Ben were no longer around. Her parents had seemed happy enough, and they certainly enjoyed meeting up with their friends and doing their own thing. Her father had always liked a game of golf, and her mother had been as busy as she was herself, when she'd been teaching.

Did you feel like this, Mum? Maybe you felt this combination of relief and desolation, the strangeness of having spent so many years building your life round your children's needs, and latterly their social calendar, only to find that you then missed it when it was not taking over!

"And Mum," she said aloud. "What's going on? Now I'm worried. I really don't like you being on your own, where I can't see that you're all right. You tell me you are, but then half the time we tell each other what we think we should, rather than being honest about what we think, don't we?"

She knew she didn't tell her mother everything, like how she feared Tim was having an affair, or how she'd had a cancer scare two years ago. It was easy to avoid telling all over the phone. It would be harder in person because she knew Nancy could read her, somehow. She had that instinct, that sixth sense that seemed to pick up when something was amiss. Sometimes, it was a good job they were miles apart, but sometimes it would be so much easier if she were down the road, where Poppy could pop in and not have to take a whole weekend to visit. Now that she had Cambridge and Leeds and Daisy's social life, fitting in one more demand on her down time was near impossible.

Her thoughts raced. *I'll try ringing again tomorrow, or maybe I just won't bother and make the trip after work instead. Friday night traffic will be a nightmare, but I'm just going to worry myself silly, churning it all over and over, unless I go and check things out for myself.*

She twisted a piece of her hair round and round, until it hurt, as if her body just had to feel what her mind was suffering.

Chapter 9: Poppy

"Cassie, do you know where your brother is? He's not answering his phone."

"Oh, hi Mum. I'm doing fine. How are you?"

"Cassie, I'm sorry. Please don't get clever with me. I'm worried about Jake. I know he knows I'm trying to get hold of him, because he cut off the call, instead of it going to answerphone yesterday. What has he done now? Please, if you know where he is, tell me. Is he back in Cambridge at all?"

"Don't panic, Mum. He's all right. He's gone to Nana Boo's."

"What? Why has he gone there? He's supposed to be getting through his reading list before term starts. I thought he had a tutorial to go to."

"Well, I don't know about the tutorial, but I know he's safe and sound at Nana's."

"Right. And what about Nana? She's not answering, either!"

"No idea on that one, Mum, I'm afraid."

"Right. I'm just going to have to go and find out myself, aren't I? I don't know which one I'm more worried about, or which one I'm more annoyed with!"

"But Mum, Jake's twenty. He's a big boy now, and Nana's old enough to sort herself out, isn't she?"

"That's the trouble, Cass. She's old enough not to sort herself out, and Jake will be useless, if there's a problem. They both need looking after sometimes!"

"Well, I bet they're both fine, Mum, but if you're that worried, can't you get Dad to drive you up there?"

"No. He's still in London. He's staying there this weekend."

"Oh!" Cassie couldn't think what else to say, in view of what Jake had told her. Sometimes, she thought it was her mum that needed to be looked after. She was still smarting at the fact that it didn't seem to matter how she was. She could feel her own irritation with her brother and her father taking over, as she mustered her self-control, to suggest that Poppy try phoning again the next day.

"I won't sleep, so I might as well just get myself there. If I find out tomorrow that there's a crisis, it's a bit late to start out. Look, I'm sorry I didn't ask how you were, but we did message yesterday, didn't we? Is everything still going well? Have you made new friends? Oh, Cassie, I do miss you, you know! Look, when I come, I'll take you out for a meal, probably the weekend after next, OK?"

"Actually, Mum, I'm going to be busy that weekend, so would you mind leaving it a couple of weeks? I think there's a party next Saturday, and a few of us are going to a gig the weekend after. There's such a lot going on here, and if I don't join in, I'm going to look as if I don't want to know."

"Ah, got it. Don't rain on my parade, Mum!" Poppy laughed, realising that Cassie needed to be able to establish herself before parents came crashing in.

"Something like that, Mum. Oh, and while you're on the phone, could you bring my boots with you, when you come to see me, and if you've got any food that needs using up, it would apparently be gratefully received here!"

Poppy remembered how Jake had pounced on the food boxes they had taken, every time they visited him. She knew what Cassie would want would primarily be biscuits and rice and pasta, plus anything they could snack on. But definitely chocolate ... and wine. When she'd been a student herself, they would drink anything cheap, but these days it seemed it had to be something they considered "decent", to keep up the street cred with their peers.

With promises that they'd talk after the weekend and food would be delivered, they parted, neither of them entirely pleased with how the call had gone. Poppy was beating herself, mentally, for not having asked about Cassie first, knowing she'd got it wrong. Cassie was still annoyed, yet also concerned that her mother seemed so torn between the generations she worried about. She knew she'd lied, and it didn't sit easily with her.

Poppy gathered some basics together, threw an overnight bag into the back of her car, and set off with grim determination to sort out whatever catastrophe awaited her. Protests from Daisy rained on her ears, as she was wrecking plans for a trip to the cinema tomorrow, and she felt as if she could just go to the bottom of the garden and scream. It seemed everyone pleased themselves, and no-one saw how she had to bend like a tree in the wind, whichever way their demands blew her.

"Why can't I just stay here on my own? You don't care about me, do you? It's always Cassie and Jake. Never me. I'm not going, and that's that. You can't make me. I'm nearly sixteen, and I promised I'd meet up with Laura. You told me we should keep promises, didn't you? You did. You know you did."

The tirade went on, while Poppy gathered what they needed. Daisy threw herself on the sofa and turned on the television, determined not to be dragged away from her own plans because her mother would not choose to stay put.

"Life's so unfair! Just because I'm the youngest, I'm always last on your list of priorities, aren't I? It's always 'We've got to take Cassie or Jake here' or 'We've got to get Cassie or Jake from there', always playing frigging taxi for them for as long as I can remember. What about me? Being the youngest sucks," she threw at Poppy, the pout she'd perfected spreading across her face and her big, brown eyes glaring at nothing in particular.

"Get some things in your rucksack, or you'll have to manage without, Daisy. I have no choice. Something is wrong, and I need to find out what. Now come on, please. Help me out here. You're not breaking your promise, are you? You can blame me, or Nana, or Jake. Take your pick. Look, I'm sorry, love, but there'll be other weekends. I know you're nearly sixteen, but I can't leave you on your own, and your dad isn't going to be here. What if anything went wrong for you? What about being on your own all night? No. I can't do it. You have to come with me. I'll make it up to you somehow."

"Huh!" muttered Daisy. "That'll be the day. You're always going to do that!"

"Please, Daisy! Will you just get your things? I just can't cope with you showing off right now. It's not the right time. I am truly, truly sorry, but I need you to do this for me. Look, you'll probably get to see Nana Boo, and you love seeing her, don't you? She'll be delighted to see you ... when we find her. You can tell her what a terrible mother you have, and she'll probably agree with you! But think about it. If something's happened to her, and you cared about going out more than you cared about her, how would you feel tomorrow? Would you honestly prefer to go into town rather than make sure she's OK? I don't think that's the Daisy I know and love."

Wow! The L word! thought Daisy, still determinedly rooted to the sofa. How often did her mother tell her she loved her these days? When she'd been a little girl, it had been every day, when she had her cuddles, but in recent months it had been noticeably absent. They'd been like strangers, Poppy never seeming to understand her point of view.

With almost imperceptive movement, her rigidity eased, as if it flowed out of her into the floor. She unfolded her arms and, saying nothing, ambled reluctantly to the stairs. As slowly as she could, she climbed them and disappeared into her bedroom.

Poppy almost held her breath. No point in shouting at her. Just wait. Seconds turned into minutes that felt like hours.

Daisy walked down the stairs as if performing on a catwalk, her rucksack poised on one shoulder, her head high. Silently, she exited the front door, leaving Poppy to follow her to the car.

On the motorway, the headlights coming towards her did nothing to alleviate the headache that was pounding, as Poppy fought to keep her eyes focused on the darkness ahead. She hated driving at night these days, and she was beginning to understand why her father had avoided it, if he could. Luckily, the mist that had come down the previous night had cleared during the day, and the rain held off, so she made good time. She thought about pulling in at the service station, to try to warn them she was coming, but decided against it, in case they tried to tell her not to come. If she just turned up, they would have no choice.

She'd just seen the sign saying she had about sixteen miles to go, when the steering wheel acquired a sudden life of its own, juddering in her hands and refusing to hold the car in a straight line. It took a few seconds for her to register what was happening.

"No!" she said aloud, hitting the wheel with her hand, so hard it would have hurt, had she been able to pay it any attention. She glanced over her shoulder and into her mirrors and took her foot off the accelerator. "Brake gently," she told herself, because braking hard could send her into a spin. As she eased off the carriageway, onto the hard shoulder, she just wanted to put her head down onto her arms and cry. This couldn't possibly be happening, could it? She hadn't got a flat, in the dark, somewhere on the motorway, with no-one knowing where she was. She couldn't change a tyre in daylight, let alone in the dark, and she knew that meant waiting until the breakdown service could find her.

Gingerly, she clambered out of the car and headed for the grass bank beyond the barrier, urging a sleepy Daisy to follow her.

"Keep it together," she told herself. "Just keep it together. You've got the number in your phone. You've just passed an exit. Get your head straight."

She tried to sound calm as she told the woman on the other end of the phone that she'd blown a tyre and gave her some idea of where she was. She realised she was near a bridge, and the woman told her to go under the bridge, away from the car, so that she had shelter. Someone would be with her as soon as they could, but it might be a while.

Poppy paced up and down, like a caged tiger, but eventually talked herself into accepting that there was nothing to do but wait. Luckily, she had a blanket on the back seat of the car, so she risked opening the door to grab it, wrapped Daisy in it, and leaving her sitting on the grass under the bridge, she climbed to the top of the bank, not caring whether there was any mud there or not. At least while she waited, she could sob her tears of frustration into her arms, and no-one could either hear her or see her, unless their headlights caught her for a few fleeting seconds. Daisy had her music on her phone, and she was still in no mood for talking. For the first time that week, Poppy found herself still, with no control over what was happening, and it was almost a luxury to be able to let herself go, to let the stress wash over her and bury her in its cloak, as black as the night.

By the time her knight in black and gold armour arrived, forty-five minutes later, she'd cried out the worry, the anger and the sadness that had held her rigid, and she could feel nothing. She watched him swiftly and cheerfully change her wheel, signed his piece of paper, and was back in the driving seat, a numbed version of herself.

It was quarter to eleven, when a ring at the doorbell startled both Nancy and Jake. Nancy was in the process of locking up and turning everything off, having made her hot chocolate and thinking she would drink it in bed tonight. Jake had already gone to his room, on the pretext of going to bed. He was lying on the bed, his eyes shut, listening to music through his headphones, so that Nancy wouldn't hear it. He'd escaped into his own fantasy world, and the doorbell was a rude disturbance, as it seared through the guitar solo with its birdsong.

Nancy approached the door with caution, wary of who would dare to be at her door at this time of night. After the messages on the answerphone, was this someone coming to attack her, thinking she lived alone? You heard about all sorts of things on the news ... and now that she was a woman in her sixties, she might be considered an easy target.

The bell rang again.

"Who is it?" she called through the glass at the side of the door.

"Mum! Let me in! It's Poppy and Daisy!"

"Poppy? What on earth are you doing here? What's wrong?"

"Just let me in, will you?"

Nancy fumbled for the key, and it seemed like an age to Poppy, before the door opened and she almost fell through it.

"Good grief, Poppy! Where have you been?"

"Sitting at the side of the road, waiting for a tyre to be changed. If you'd answered your phone, I might not have been there. Where have YOU been, and why didn't you answer your landline or your mobile? I've been worried sick. And what is my son doing here?"

The words tumbled out faster than Nancy could process them, and Poppy made for the kitchen, where she sat herself down at the table and looked at Nancy as if she demanded answers. Nancy hugged Daisy, with little in the way of a response, as the music flowed on in Daisy's ears, blocking out the reality of a world she didn't want to be in. A feeble, wan smile was as much as she could give — even for Nana Boo, who was very obviously OK — so written all over her face was why, oh why did she have to be here at all?

"You didn't need to come rushing to find me, you know, Poppy. I'm fine. I just forgot to take my mobile with me, when I went to the shop."

"But you don't do that normally, do you Mum? And your answerphone was turned off, too. Are you getting forgetful?"

"No, Poppy. No more than usual." Nancy attempted to laugh. Everyone of her age was becoming forgetful to some extent, and colleagues younger than her had joked about it starting to happen to them, but she knew where Poppy was going with this. Getting old. Not fit to be on your own. What would she say, if she knew about the phone calls as well? She'd have Nancy carted off to some place where she had "care" she didn't yet need. This was a tricky situation, because without the explanation, she had no reason why she'd turned off the answerphone.

"I didn't need the answerphone, because I was in, and then I went out, and I was only going to be a few minutes. My psychic powers let me down, I'm afraid, and I didn't realise you would choose right then to phone!" The tone of her voice was, she hoped, enough to put Poppy off the scent. She could see her daughter bridle as she said it, and she would rather have her anger than the alternative. "Look, I'm so sorry, Poppy. I wouldn't have made you worry for the world."

Poppy heard, in that instant, how her own apology to Daisy had fallen on deaf ears. Mothers and daughters, criss-crossing generations with love that somehow turned into expressions of anger and regret. She wanted to reach out, hold her mother tight, allow herself to demonstrate the relief she felt at finding she was not in some hospital ward, dreadfully ill, but the caring blocked the instinct, and instead, all she could do was give vent to the pent-up feelings of frustration at imagining the worst, just as she would with her children.

"Well, I do worry, don't I, when I know you're on your own? What if you'd had a fall, and you'd been lying there?"

"Yes, well I'm not, am I? And I do appreciate your coming, and Daisy..." Nancy could imagine what it had taken to get a reluctant teenager to join them, as her voice tailed off.

"Now you're here, we'd better sort some beds. You can't drive back tonight. It's too late, and the fog's coming down. I'd be doing the worrying then, with you on the motorway. Let's talk in the morning. I was just going to bed when you arrived."

"Well, we're all tired. That's for sure. Yes, I think we need to have a long talk tomorrow, so I presume I can go up to my old room? Or can I? Is there anything you need to tell me tonight, Mum, like where my son is?"

"Jake? Well yes, he's here. I assumed you knew!"

"Not a word from him. I've been trying to phone him, as well, and he's been blocking my calls. He didn't tell me. You didn't tell me. It's like a conspiracy! If it were not for Cassie, I wouldn't have a clue. He's supposed to be back in Cambridge, and instead he's here. Why? What's going on?"

"I've no idea, Poppy. He hasn't told me anything. We've had a lovely few days, and he has done some reading, I think, but he said he had some study leave and thought he'd come for a visit. I'm afraid he's in your old room, because I didn't know I was going to have more visitors! You two will have to make do with Ben's room and the box room, I'm afraid. There are plenty of bedclothes up there."

"Right. He's here. You're here. At least I might be able to get some sleep. I'll sort Daisy out and see you in the morning."

Dismissed, like one of her pupils, Nancy poured herself a drink of water to put by her bedside and left Poppy to it. She didn't envy her daughter, telling Daisy she was sleeping in the box room, but tonight it was not her place to interfere, as doing so might just make matters worse.

"I see Nancy's got more visitors turned up, at this time of night!" Fred tutted, as he pulled the bedroom curtains to. "Whatever happened to this neighbourhood being quiet and peaceful?"

He turned to Janet, who was already in bed, book in hand. She didn't often manage to finish a novel, but she'd seen this particular Catherine Cookson dramatized on the television, and she loved the story. She was glad she hadn't been born a woman in those days, with all that poverty and hard work to deal with. She liked her respectable life, with her washing machine and vacuum cleaner helping her to keep everything clean.

"I don't know what it's coming to, Janet. Cars coming and going, strangers walking the neighbourhood, and people asking questions, even if they don't know you. There seem to be some nosy parkers around here now, don't there, pulling the tone down? After all that rumpus the other day, I'm sure I don't know what some of the neighbours must think. I bet we have 'For Sale' boards springing up all over the place, and they're just so tacky! I would've thought Nancy would have more consideration and would tell her visitors to turn up at a respectable hour, wouldn't you?"

"Yes dear. But then look at that expensive car sitting on the drive, and that looked like her grandson driving it, when he arrived! Thoroughly spoilt, some of these young people nowadays! I dare say he's been racing down the motorway or got himself into some sort of trouble. That's his mother's car, isn't it, that's just arrived? I recognise it from her last visit. Downright dangerous to let him loose behind a wheel if you ask me. Mind you, that woman from number ten didn't drive too carefully the other day, either. With all that stuff on the front lawn, she just drove across the verge when she left. She's left great big tyre tracks in it. It's disgraceful!" She peered over her reading glasses and shook her head in disapproval.

"I'll be out there tomorrow, Janet, sorting it out. I can't see him doing it, so it'll be down to me to keep the street looking respectable, won't it? Goodness knows what was going on there, but surely it can't get any worse, can it? Shouting and carrying on! I bet it put off that young woman looking for a house to buy. She must have been horrified. Didn't stay long, did she? Good job she bumped into us and met someone who wasn't making a junk yard of the place. I told her, didn't I, that we're not all like that, that it's a nice, quiet place to live, with nice neighbours? I don't know whether I convinced her. She seemed very interested in what had been going on and who lived there. Might be a bit of a nosy parker, anyway. Perhaps it's just as well if she doesn't move in nearby."

"Oh well. Nothing we can do about it now. Let's get the light out and get some sleep. Hopefully, tomorrow will be calm and peaceful."

Chapter 10: Tim

Messenger

Daisy Castleford to Tim Castleford:

Dad, for goodness' sake come and rescue me. I've been carted off to Nana Boo's in the middle of the night, and I've just got to be home tomorrow. Mum's car broke down, and Jake was missing, and I've got to break a promise to my friend!

WhatsApp

Poppy Castleford to Ben Brewer:

Ben, I need your help. I think Mum's showing early signs of going senile, and Jake is holed up with her for some reason. I need a summit meeting. Can you get to Mum's for dinner?

Ben Brewer to Poppy Castleford:

Calm down, sis. I'll have a chat with Sarah and see what I can do. Can't promise anything, because it might depend what kind of night we have with Harley. He's teething, and we're not getting much sleep.

Tim looked at his daughter's message, feeling a stab of guilt for deciding to stay in London for the weekend. He was still hoping that

Felicity would change her mind and join him. He was sure she didn't mean it, when she said she didn't want to see him anymore. He'd tried to contact her, but he knew he didn't dare phone her mobile, in case she faced questions about who was phoning. He'd messaged her, but she wasn't answering, and he was becoming despairing of managing to reach her. He hadn't expected to fall in love again at his age, but it had hit him with such a force, like a tsunami, that he didn't know what to do with these feelings that seemed to take over his thinking. He'd been married to Poppy for such a long time, and he still loved her, but they were not in love, like they had been years ago. It was different. They cared about each other, and he didn't want to leave her, yet he found himself pulled towards this beautiful, auburn-haired, soft woman he'd met at a conference a few months ago. He hadn't been able to take his eyes off her in the meeting, watching her every move and tearing his eyes away when she noticed what he was doing. Her voice, calm and quiet, had somehow commanded respect and attention, in a room full of experts in their field. Her charisma held them, as she put forward her ideas for the corporation. He'd never seen her at the meetings before, but she was standing in for the Managing Director of her branch, who had fallen ill just days before. When he offered, during the coffee break, to show her some of the sights of the capital before she went home, he'd felt the warmth from her, like the glow of a winter fire. It became inevitable that they would meet again. It couldn't be anything else.

And so it began, the lies and the juggling of lives. It was not what he'd set out to do, and he knew it didn't sit comfortably with her, either, but it was as if they were compelled to seek each other out, drawn together as if some unbroken thread bound them to each other. The meetings became more frequent, weekend work more pressing, despite the guilt eating them up. When she told him she thought her partner suspected, he told her it would be all right. They would be careful. He had no proof. She appeared, one Friday night, with bruises around her wrists, and still he told her all would be well. He didn't ask her to leave her partner. He didn't ask himself to leave his wife. There was no endgame in sight. Then she told him she couldn't handle it anymore. It had to stop. She wasn't sure that she would stay with her partner, but she knew he wasn't going to take the final step, to leave his family that he obviously loved. It was a hopeless journey they were on, like a runaway train, and she'd decided to get off. They were in danger of being outed if they were seen together, and their little secret world would be shattered. She'd left in tears, as he begged her to think again, telling her he would be in the flat all weekend, if she changed her mind.

What was he to do? If he left, he would never know whether she tried to come back again. He would have to accept the end. If he didn't leave, his youngest child would feel abandoned to whatever her mother was in the throes of dealing with, because he was not there. She would blame him. Her cryptic message left him wondering and worrying, as it was intended to do, and he knew he couldn't turn his back on her, ignore his missing son, not care that his wife had gone to the rescue of her mother, after dark, and that meant there must be something seriously wrong.

He felt as if he'd been punched in the chest, his breath coming in short, sharp gasps. The panic told him he had to go, had to stay, sent his mind whizzing round in circles, avoiding decision. He leant on the worktop, forcing himself to breathe slowly and deeply, forcing himself to calm his body, in order to calm his mind. He knew. He had to go. He had to let go of whatever it was that had netted him like a guileless fish in open water. Felicity was right. He could never turn his back on his family. He'd almost lost the game, when Jake had confronted him, and it was only diverting his attention by giving him the old car that avoided a full-blown session of inquisition. He'd quickly managed to brush aside the accusation, so far, but Jake was bright. Jake was onto something, and it was too dangerous to think he could have carried on.

Next morning, as he turned the lights out and pulled the door to behind him, he whispered "Goodbye. I'm sorry," as if she could hear him.

Chapter 11: Ben

Henry seemed to want to bark as much as Harley wanted to cry last night, thought Ben. *Oh, for a good night's sleep! All that keeps going through my head is 'Macbeth shall sleep no more', as if I've somehow done something very wrong, and now I'm paying the price. They don't tell you about this bit of being a dad, do they, when they tell you how wonderful it is to have a baby? I thought they were supposed to feed, sleep and smile at you, but I'm beginning to wonder what wicked fairy put a spell on Harley, to make sure we were too exhausted to enjoy anything anymore. We could do with a break. I was glad to get away from home a few years ago, but right now, I'm wishing Mum was round the corner, if only to take the pram for a walk, to let us sleep! Poor Sarah's shattered, I can see that, and there's certainly no danger of conceiving another child, when we finally fall into bed! How come Poppy's had three children, and all of them were good as gold? I know he's really cute, and we really wanted to be parents, but we're pushing forty, and we haven't got the energy packs we had in our twenties. 'It'll be worth it,' our well-meaning friends say, and the health visitor thinks he's a very bright baby, but bright or not, it feels as if we're only half human during the day, and even less than that when he wakes up in the small hours of the morning and thinks it's time to play! We're told to make the most of it, because time passes so quickly, but time seems to be passing at snail speed here. What were we thinking, starting a family at our age? We'd never have thought we'd wish our mums could pop in, but Sarah was having one of her weepy days yesterday, and all she wanted was her mum. She's hardly going to come back from Cyprus to play nanny, is she? Oh, it must be so good to be sitting in the sunshine, carefree and rested!*

Ben's thoughts wandered round and round the fact that he was feeling like a zombie. He'd been so thrilled when Sarah had gone into labour two days early, on a Friday night, and he'd been there for the magic of the birth of his son. At last, they were a family, after almost giving up hope. They'd had two rounds of fertility treatment — costing them a huge chunk of their savings — and they were becoming resigned to being childless while their friends were all immersed in doing things with their kids, family holidays, and reliving some of the things they had enjoyed themselves when they were children. It seemed like a wonderful excuse to go back to Legoland, visit Disney World, go kite-flying, swimming, fishing and bike riding, climbing all over castles or building them out of sand, playing football or watching the match with a fan at your side. The romantic images they encouraged him to see didn't include the smell of nappies needing to be changed at 2 am, the trying to fit in a meal for yourselves between feeds, the crying you couldn't stop, and this dragging yourself around as if your eyelids and feet were made of lead. He couldn't imagine playing games when you were tortured with no sleep. He thought he was doing well in the first few weeks, being a modern man and taking an equal share in caring for their son, but as they both began to feel defeated; he and Sarah had found themselves bickering over who did what, something they had never done before. Walking the dog had never been an issue, but now each of them thought the other should fit in a sprint to the park, and Henry must be wondering why they ran so much these days.

And now, here was this demand from Poppy, the straw that broke the camel's back. He had nothing more to give, and what she expected him to do about their mother, at this moment in time, was beyond his comprehension. Surely, she realised they just needed to focus on getting through the next few months with Harley. How was he to broach yet another need with Sarah? He knew his sister, and if she was determined to organise him like she organised her classes, it was futile to come up with reasons why he couldn't comply, unless they were watertight excuses. He loved her dearly, and they'd always been close as children, but she was always a teacher, even when she wasn't in the classroom, and she had a way of making him feel as if he should jump, if she snapped her fingers, especially when she got that edge on her voice that said, "Don't try to say no". Their mother had the same tone, honed to perfection after years of dealing with teenagers. He was more like his father - easy-going and not inclined to rush at things, his relaxed management style having endeared him to his team, if not to his family. What Poppy thought was urgent, he thought could wait a while, and he knew he'd infuriated her at times.

He tried to make his body move with casual ease, as he approached Sarah, who was sitting in a nursing chair by the French windows, Harley feeding and starting to fall asleep. He thought he'd better get on with it, before she put the baby down, because if Harley slept, they needed to just grab the opportunity to try to nap, one on each end of the over-sized corner sofa.

"Sarah, I've had a message from Poppy. It's a bit strange, but basically it amounts to the fact that she's had to go to Mum's, because Mum wasn't answering her phones. She thinks it's time we had a chat about how Mum's doing since Dad died. She wants us to pop over there tomorrow. How would you feel about that? It would be a chance to show Mum how Harley's doing, and maybe, if there are plenty of people there, someone would give you a bit of a break. What do you think?"

He was aware that he gabbled his way through what he was trying to say, putting a positive spin on what could be a very negative request. He stood with his hands in his pockets, waiting for Sarah to gather her thoughts, hoping she'd grasped the last point and would sanction it.

She groaned. He felt his throat muscles tighten and a headache start to hover over his eyes. She was not going to like this.

"Your family seems to be incapable of sorting out its messes without dragging you into them, doesn't it?" she eventually sighed, keeping her head down. "Look, if you're going to go, we all go. I'm not being left here to cope with the baby and the dog on my own, right?"

This was better than he could have hoped for.

"Right. OK. I'll drive, and we don't have to be there till dinner time, so there's no rush. We can leave when it's convenient to us, between feeds. How about that?"

"Do I have any real choice, Ben?" She lifted her chin, and her blue eyes sagged in front of him, her usually beautiful blond hair pulled back into a ponytail, the only way she could keep it out of her way while she held the baby.

"Thank you," he said, as he bent to kiss her forehead, this wonderful woman who had made his life so much more than he'd imagined it could be before he met her.

He had found himself in Italy after heartbreak had left him diminished and totally lacking in self-confidence, she had shone into his darkness quite unexpectedly. Mistaking his olive skin for local origins, she struggled to ask him where to catch the boat in broken Italian. As he spoke only a few words of his late grandmother's native tongue, he frowned and told her he was sorry, he didn't speak Italian.

"Scusa. Non parlo italiano. Sono inglese."

She'd chuckled behind her hand, the sparkle in her eyes reaching something deep within him.

"Oh, that is such a relief!" she'd said in perfect Yorkshire English. "Can you help me, please?"

They had both laughed, and before he knew what he was doing, he'd turned back from his own path between the bays and escorted her to the boat that ferried visitors along the Amalfi coast. By the time they reached the jetty, he knew he had to see her again. If there was to be "The One", she was it. He'd come alone, in search of solace, anchoring himself in the

81

familiarity of this tiny place, while putting a distance between him and the life he needed to rebuild. She'd come with a friend who had gone to a family reunion in Sorrento, and she'd made herself scarce, to avoid being in a room full of chatter she wouldn't understand, in a culture she didn't know, feeling like an intruder. Better to play the tourist. She'd wandered further than she'd intended, when she got off the ferry, and she'd been worried that she'd miss the last one back if she didn't find the terminus quickly. As she climbed aboard, he scribbled his mobile number on the back of a receipt and passed it to her, saying, "Ring me! Please, please ring me!" His imploring face was what she told him she remembered, as she sat on the boat and watched the coastline pass her by. When she reached the hotel, before she went inside, she took out her own phone and texted him.

"Hi! Ben, this is me, Sarah, so that you have my number in your phone."

The next day, she'd filled his thoughts, as he took the Sentiero dei Limoni from Minori to Maiori. He climbed over four hundred steps, hardly noticing them. As he looked out between the lemon trees, he found his eyes searching for her suddenly appearing on the jetty. He looked at the beautiful blue and aquamarine of the Mediterranean below, but all he saw was her smile. He thought he would contact her when he got home, but his fingers obeyed his heart, not his head, and before the day was out, as he sat eating his meal in the fading sun, he'd already sent her a message, telling her he longed to see her as soon as he got back. He didn't care where, but could he take her out for a meal somewhere that she would enjoy? He could barely remember the walk back to the hotel, after descending into Maiori, but his feet seemed lighter than they had been for months, and he wanted to spread his arms and say "bon giorno" to the world. When the waiters smiled at him indulgently, he realised that, try as he might, he couldn't stop grinning.

They married in the tiny parish church near his home, and Sarah's parents had come over from Cyprus, staying with her aunt in Wetherby.

They'd resisted the suggestion that they honeymoon in her parents' villa, their plan already made. They'd go back to where they met, and this time they would explore the area together, more intent on sight-seeing than seeing only each other.

The day after Poppy's summons, Ben climbed out of bed in the middle of the morning, having done the 2 a.m. slot to let Sarah sleep. He quietly packed the car, still mind-blown by the amount of "stuff" it took to go out for a day with a baby. How could one little person need so much gear? He double-checked against the list now burnt in his memory, having started out as a post-it among other post-its, stuck to the fridge. Mentally, he was saying "Check" each time he was satisfied, and it was only as he was about to shut the boot that he realised he didn't have the buggy. He loaded it as quietly as he could, then crept back into the kitchen to put the coffee machine on. There was no way he could make that quiet, but at least he'd managed to give Sarah a few extra precious minutes before she woke up. He took her a cup of strong, white coffee, made just the way she liked it, placing it by the bed as he whispered, "Good morning". She smiled at him, touched by his thoughtfulness, and raised herself on one elbow.

"Thanks," she whispered back, neither of them daring to make much noise, in case Harley broke the spell with his waking cry. She swung her legs over the side of the bed and sipped the coffee.

"I'll disappear, to let you come round," he said. "If Harley wakes, ping me on the intercom, and I'll come and get him, so that you can get showered and dressed in peace." He kissed his fingers and motioned them towards her, shaping his lips into the words "I love you".

Chapter 12: Nancy

I wish I hadn't forgotten my wretched mobile when I went out! All this fuss, and now I've wasted Poppy's time and upset Daisy, and everyone's going to be fractious with each other! Here I am, trying to tell Poppy that I don't need looking after and then giving her even more reason to think I do!

Well, at least I managed to get some sleep last night ... eventually. I'm not sure what to do about these prank calls, but I'll sort that out when Poppy's gone home. She'll just make a drama out of it, and I don't want to worry her any more than I've already worried her. Right, let's go and get some breakfast. This is one of those mornings when I'm glad I've got my own bathroom. Daisy's been in the other one for about half an hour! Just like her mother was at her age.

Nancy got to the bottom of the stairs as Poppy came out of the guest bedroom. As she stepped into the hall, she saw a piece of paper on the doormat in front of her. She bent down to pick it up and had just begun to read it when Poppy appeared at her shoulder.

"What's that, Mum?"

"Oh, nothing important. Looks as if the milkman's left me a note, in case I need any extra before he goes away."

Nancy shoved the piece of paper into the pocket at the back of her jeans, where she knew it would not fall out. She'd just had time to see the typed message:

84

"THREE BLIND MICE".

"Well, that's the third message," she thought, "so maybe it means it's finished. They've had their fun." She was beginning to feel unnerved by this now, and she hoped it would just stop. Who on earth could want to send her these messages? Could it be ex-pupils, with some kind of revenge on their minds, because she'd disciplined them in the past? She couldn't think who it might be, and as far as she knew only Simon knew where she lived. He wouldn't do something like this. He was a nice boy, a nice man, and she'd had a good relationship with him all the way through school. She thought back to a time, many years ago, when she'd lived in a small house not far from the big comprehensive where she had her first job. She'd had some tricky characters there, and one of them had moved into a rented house on the opposite side of the road. More than once her valve caps had disappeared, as her car was parked on the road, and one morning she'd found the windscreen covered in sticky-backed plastic, like they used so often on that Blue Peter show the children loved. It had come off easily enough, but it had made a mess of the windscreen, and it had taken a lot of effort to get it clean. Surely, in this area, after such a long time, she couldn't be a target again. If it were to be ex-pupils, they wouldn't be children anymore. What could they hope to gain by trying to frighten her?

Over breakfast with Poppy, the two of them having decided not to bother to wait for Jake or Daisy, she kept the conversation away from anything that might suggest she was afraid. She empathised with Poppy's workload, sympathised with her for having a flat tyre on the way there, apologised again and again for causing her to dash across the Pennines like the cavalry, when there was nothing wrong. She promised she would not go out without her phone again and tried to calm Poppy's angst about Jake having taken time out to come to visit her. Being truthful with herself, she knew she still hadn't got to the bottom of what was eating away at him, but there was no point in telling Poppy that right now. She managed to make her daughter laugh, telling her about how Jake had bounded his way round

Harlow Carr and loved playing with the bird song machines. His boyish charm was just so endearing!

Jake ambled into the kitchen, running his hands through his hair, and wrapped in the old dressing-gown that lived in the wardrobe until one of them came to visit. He'd given up waiting for Daisy to come out of the bathroom, and he was thirsty. Seeing his mother and Nana smiling, he felt a surge of relief, but he also guessed that Poppy still didn't know what was going on here. Poppy told him to sit down. She went to find the orange juice she'd brought with her and found room for in the fridge. She had her back to the table, and Nancy was able to hold up the note, so that Jake could see it. She shrugged her shoulders and pulled a face, as he stared ahead. He shook his head and mouthed at her, "You must tell someone, Nana!"

"Later," she mouthed back, as she started to clear away the dishes from her own and Poppy's meal.

"Toast or cereal?" she said aloud.

"A piece of toast will be fine, thanks, Nana. As you know, I don't usually eat much first thing in the morning. I don't usually *see* much of first thing in the morning!" He flashed his grin at her.

Daisy appeared eventually, looking as if she were about to go somewhere special, her hair carefully straightened and eyebrows carefully shaped. She strolled across the kitchen, helping herself to a piece of fruit from the bowl in the middle of the table. Nancy glanced at her, but decided it wasn't worth saying anything, under the circumstances. Better to pretend she hadn't noticed, as her granddaughter poured herself a glass of water and headed for the lounge.

"Is that all she has for breakfast now?" she asked Poppy, concerned that she was of an age when some girls ate too little, too often.

"Sometimes," was the answer, "but other days, she tucks into muesli and coffee and toast, or bacon butties at the weekend, so at least I know she's not starving! Honestly, Mum, I don't think I can get anything right with her, in her current frame of mind! If I didn't teach teenagers, I'd think we were totally abnormal, but when I'm talking to other parents, I know we're not. She can still be our lovely little Daisy, at times, but she's so busy trying to impress her peer group that we're those nasty people who stop her doing it as well as she might. How she's doing so well at school, I don't know, but she must be working hard somewhere, somehow, and I'll settle for that. I have to pick my battles, or we'd end up at loggerheads all the time."

Nancy was relieved to see her daughter relax, despite the fact that she could tell something was amiss. They decided to take a walk down to the stream after lunch, leaving Jake to study and Daisy to watch a DVD. It seemed to amuse Daisy that Nancy probably wouldn't pay monthly for anything that provided extra programmes or films and still had DVDs. Despite that, she quite enjoyed rummaging through them to find a favourite film. Not able to do what she'd wanted to do, she was obviously bored enough to resort to doing nothing until she could escape and join her friends.

Jake put his plate in the dishwasher and made a discreet exit, leaving his mother and grandmother to share their tales of battling with teenage drama. He had to message Cassie. Maybe she would be able to suggest something he could do. He wondered whether he should just tell Poppy about the messages, but he couldn't bear the thought of making Nana furious with him, feeling betrayed by him. He had to get her to talk about it herself.

Chapter 14: Cassie

Messenger

Jake Castleford to Cassie Castleford

Mum's only gone and turned up here, with Daisy! I need a rescue party! Now what?

Nana's had these strange messages, some weirdo reading nursery rhymes. Rock-a-bye Baby and Georgie Porgie, and then this morning a note through the door saying 'Three Blind Mice'. It's freaking me out, but she doesn't seem to care. She's not telling Mum, it seems. She's told me not to breathe a word, because it will only alarm Mum, and she's sure it's a prank that will stop if she ignores it.

Cassie Castleford to Jake Castleford

We did something about nursery rhymes in history. I can't remember the details now, but they weren't as cute as they might sound, Jake. That's not good. Be careful.

Cassie tried to concentrate on the forms she was trying to fill in and the bundle of information she'd been given during the week. So much to organise now that she was having to settle into life on campus. She was very glad her rent was being paid by direct debit, so she didn't have to try to sort that out, but there were all these other things to think about, since she was no longer living with her parents. Poppy had arranged insurance for her things, but she needed to get her head round all these words on bits of paper she had to keep safe. The box file she'd been reluctant to acknowledge now made sense. She was going to need it.

She pushed the pile of papers to the back of the desk and put her head down on her arms. She absolutely must stay sober this week. Everyone had been a little subdued in the last few days, as they had to get themselves to lectures, buy books, sort out tutorials. It was all getting real now. She was here for three long years and somehow, she had to come out at the end of it with a degree. She didn't quite feel ready for all this responsibility. For the first time in her life, she found she missed being at home, even missed Daisy's whining. She missed her mum fussing round her, paying all the bills and doing all her washing for her! Her room seemed tiny, and the bare brick and plaster made it feel like someone else's. She had her posters in the corner, ready to go up, but they had warnings not to use anything that might damage the paintwork, or they would be charged for putting it right. They had warnings about keeping their possessions safe, and the possibility of break-ins. She was not on the ground floor, where girls were considered more vulnerable, but that didn't entirely make sense these days, did it? Anyone could be vulnerable, anywhere. She checked the lock on the window, knowing she would never be able to leave it open on a hot night. The blind was cold comfort, compared with her stylish curtains at home. She shuddered at the thought of sharing a bathroom and was grateful that this hall did, at least, have en suites. She knew some of the people she'd spoken to didn't have that luxury. At least she now had some things on the shelves, relieving their bareness. She'd bought some fairy lights and strung them along the edges, and she'd brought with her a fluffy cushion to put on the bed. She had some hard copy books, but others she'd been able to download, saving her carrying so many around.

Not able to concentrate, she googled "nursery rhymes" and started to look at their origins. There it was — proof that her vague memory of what she'd been told in history was true. The only one she'd been able to remember was "Ring-a-ring-a-roses", with its probable connection to the black death, but her teacher had said it was not the only one that had started out as something less than pleasant. As she tracked down the meanings of the two Jake had mentioned, she felt as if her body was frozen to the spot.

"Rock-a bye Baby" would normally be thought of as a lullaby, and one explanation was that it was about women letting the wind rock their babies to sleep by hanging the cradles from the branches of trees, but it had a more sinister meaning — the hope that a baby actually would fall down when the wind blew — because it was about wishing harm to the son of King James II, a Catholic heir to the throne that some wanted dead. No-one would sing a lullaby down the phone, would they? But what if they meant to harm Nana Boo or Jake? She shuddered. Nana really should tell someone. This might not be a joke, and if it was, it was a very sick one! Then there was "three blind mice", not about mice at all, but about three Protestant bishops burnt at the stake for their beliefs. What was she to do now? It always felt as if Jake landed things on her and expected her to sort them out.

Here we go again, brother of mine! Somehow, I've got to get Nana to tell someone, get help to stop the prank, if that's what it is. I know you're right, of course. If we tell Mum, she'll go ballistic, and then Nana will be mad at us, and we'll just get the flak from both sides, and it won't solve anything. We're going to need to tread carefully.

She realised, as soon as she thought it, that suddenly it had become "we". She couldn't just ignore this, could she? So, cancel plans to go to a club tomorrow - it looked as if she was going to be getting the train instead. If she and Jake could get Nana on one side, or one of them could, while the other distracted Poppy, maybe they could talk some sense into her. That was going to take some machinations.

Chapter 14: Nancy and Poppy

Nancy and Poppy crossed the field at the end of the road, heading towards the church, where so many of their shared memories were anchored. There was an autumn mist hovering just above the fields, like a giant muslin sheet, suspended in mid-air. It hung over the beck, which was running fast, and dew drops sat on the reeds like discarded jewels. They stopped on the footbridge, looking down into the water where the children had played Poohsticks, running from one side to the other, shrieking with excitement. The horses grazed calmly in the field next to the church, one of them sporting his winter blanket, and everything was as still as if it belonged in a fairy tale, with a spell cast over it. They popped into the church, where Poppy signed the visitors' book, as she'd done every time she'd ventured inside since the day she got married there.

As she wrote her own signature, she felt the sadness of not having Tim by her side. It had been such a wonderful day, the day they had stood together by the choir stalls, vowing till death parted them. Where had they lost that magic? It seemed to have happened so gradually that she couldn't pinpoint when she first noticed that he was working more, away more, making more excuses not to join the family outings. She knew, now, that there was someone else, but not who she was. The investigator had been so terribly kind, when he'd delivered the news, over the phone, that he'd found no more evidence yet. Tim had been on his own at the London flat. No-one else had gone in or out all week. "OK," she'd said, "just keep going a bit longer, will you? He's not coming home this weekend, and I want to know why. I can't believe he has to work all day tomorrow. Just one more week, please."

She could tell the investigator thought she was wasting her money, and he was not the sort to take it from her, if he couldn't give her anything in return, but she just had a gut feeling she couldn't explain.

"It's such a special place, this, isn't it?" she asked Nancy, looking around at the stained-glass window, the ancient stone pillars, and the familiar pews.

"Yes, it is." Nancy touched her daughter's arm, squeezing it gently, as if she understood exactly what was going through Poppy's mind.

They walked back down the gravel path and headed back to the house, Poppy feeling the stirring of courage, as she reached the end of the road.

"So, have you given it any more thought, Mum, coming to live near us?" She tried to sound casual, not as if she'd been planning to broach the subject all along.

"Poppy, I'm not moving anywhere yet. You know that. I need to be where my memories are for now."

Stubborn and awkward, thought Poppy, not daring to say it. She held back the "Here I am, worrying myself silly about you, and you're busy digging your heels in."

"Right," was all her tongue would manage.

"What about you, Poppy? Are you all right? You seem to be carrying a lot of stress, my love."

"Stress? Well, you've done the job. You know what it's like! I'm working all the hours God sends, and I'm trying to sort out three children, who all seem to still need so much organising!" She saw her chance to deflect the attention. "It was awful leaving Cassie at her hall, I have to say, but I thought I could rely on Jake to get himself to Cambridge and stay there. Have you found out why he came yet, Mum?"

"No. I think I was getting close, before you came," offered Nancy, "but he wasn't talking about himself at all, which is, I know, most unusual! Maybe he just needed to unwind a bit, Poppy. It's a lot of pressure, being somewhere like Cambridge, knowing you're expected to come out one of the highest flyers, not some average Joe Bloggs. Maybe sometimes he just wants to be Joe Bloggs."

"Hmmm..."

So, he's not talking, and you're not talking, and I'm not telling you about the pranks, thought Nancy. *A fine bunch we are, aren't we?* If she'd been less preoccupied with events, she might have seen the similarity in their characters, so much the same, while also so very different.

As they turned the corner and approached the drive, Nancy spotted a blue car seeming to turn into it. Did it turn into her drive? It looked a bit like Ben's car, but surely Ben wouldn't just turn up, unless something was wrong. Her steps quickened, and as they walked up to the back door, there it was! It was Ben's car! Sarah was just lifting little Harley out of his car seat, while Ben was unfolding the buggy and toting the changing bag.

"Ben!" she called; amazement clear in the tone of her voice.

"Hi, Mum!" His hair fell across his eyes, as he had no hands left to sweep it to the side, and she was struck by how like his father he looked, his head at exactly the same inquisitive angle, and his tall frame looking too big for the buggy without stooping. His old, familiar leather jacket was slung on the back seat, and his jeans looked as if they could do with ironing. The bags under his eyes were new, she thought, courtesy of a teething baby. Sarah looked frailer than ever, as if her legs would give out under her.

"Shall I take him?" Poppy offered, while Nancy opened the door and told them to come in, out of the cold, bewilderment but delight careering round her body.

"What are you doing here? Can you stay for dinner?" She hurled questions at him faster than he could answer her, so he just got hold of her and gave her a huge hug, to stop her in her tracks.

"Can't a son come to see his mother, then, and bring his baby to have a cuddle from its gran?"

"Of course you can! I just wasn't expecting it, that's all. I thought you two would be too exhausted to come right now. I was thinking I might come down to stay in a few weeks and help you out."

"That would be great, Mum, honestly. It would be good if someone could just wheel him up and down in the pram for half an hour today! We are in need of adult company and two free arms!"

"You saw that your sister's here, didn't you? Daisy and Jake, too. It's quite a house full, all of a sudden!"

"It'll be like Christmas, early," he grinned. She'd bought it, it seemed. Just a surprise visit.

As Harley whimpered, Tommy Tucker squawked in the background, "Gissakiss! Watcha Tommy! Gissakiss! Rockabye!" as if competing for attention.

"Can't you shut that bird up, Mum? He'll make Harley cry!" pleaded Ben.

Poppy passed Harley to Nancy and went to round up her unsociable offspring, to say "hello" to their aunt and uncle. Jake shook hands with Ben, feeling that he was far too old now to do man hugs with an uncle, and he nodded at Sarah, hands in pockets, not sure what to do with them. He couldn't kiss a beautiful blond who wasn't related to him by blood. It seemed the wrong thing to do, even if she was a lot older than him. The baby, he gave the obligatory glance, totally sure that he wasn't going to offer to hold it. He sat himself down near Ben, so that they could talk about sport, much safer ground than babies.

Daisy produced her first smile that day. However much she despised pink and frilly skirts and any suggestion that she was somehow soft and cute, she melted when she saw Harley in Nancy's arms. She ignored the adults, going straight up to him and saying, "Isn't he gorgeous?"

"Hallo, Uncle Ben and Auntie Sarah," prompted Poppy, wishing Daisy would just remember the social niceties, without having to be reminded all the time.

"Oh sure. Hi!" Daisy turned to them and gave them a wave. Poppy squirmed. Daisy turned back to Nancy. "Can I hold him?" she asked.

"Sarah? Would that be OK?" asked Nancy for her.

"Sure. Why don't you put him in the buggy and push him round the garden, Daisy?" suggested Sarah. "He gets heavy."

Daisy became the unexpected treasure of the afternoon, besotted with Harley and willing to play with him as much as he would let her. He seemed more content than he'd been for days, and Sarah would have given Daisy the biggest auntie hug, if only Daisy had let her.

Nancy and Poppy insisted that Sarah sit herself down and take the opportunity of a rest, while they prepared a meal, concocted from what Nancy had in the freezer and what Poppy had brought with her. By the time they finished, they had a roast chicken, surrounded by sausages, with sliced gammon to complement it. Luckily, Nancy always had some frozen vegetables, and Poppy had managed to bring some carrots and potatoes, so they cobbled together enough to feed five adults and a teenager, as they collected chairs from all over the house. The house was full of the smell of roast dinner, and Nancy's heart was full of joy, with her children and grandchildren around the table.

They were just about to start eating when the doorbell rang. The smile was wiped from Nancy's face, as she wondered who was there, and there was an awkward silence, while Poppy went to answer the door.

"Tim!" Nancy declared, as he followed Poppy into the dining room. "What a lovely surprise! Today's full of surprises!" She looked from Tim to Poppy, from Poppy to Tim, not knowing what to make of this.

95

"Hello, Nancy. Lovely to see you. Daisy told me she and Poppy were coming, so I thought I'd make it a family affair, and let the work wait for a change." He deposited his briefcase on the floor. "I hope you don't mind."

"Of course not. Grab a chair from the kitchen, Tim. I'll find you a plate. I'm sure we've got more than enough for another one."

Poppy had said nothing. Nancy heard the others chatting to Tim, as she took her time finding him a plate and cutlery. Had they even greeted each other, she wondered?

Daisy had told him they were here, but she suspected that was not the whole truth. He would not have come, just because he knew the others were here. Perhaps she'd sent him a dramatic version of events, but perhaps she just needed her dad. Sad, Nancy thought, that Daisy was not happy.

Chapter 15: The Family Gathers

"Oh! You managed to get away from work then?" Ben asked, as he turned to Tim.

"Yes. Yes, I did. I decided whatever else needed to be done could wait till Monday," Tim answered.

How did you know we were here?" Poppy's question cut through the air with the speed of a well-aimed knife, and everyone fell silent.

Tim looked straight across the table, his eyes locking with the fierceness of his wife's. "Daisy sent me a message," he said, trying to sound as innocent as he should be.

"Daisy?" Poppy spun her head to her left, towards her youngest child, who was nonchalantly poking her roast potato round her plate. "You didn't tell me you had let your dad know. When was that?"

Like someone who knew that if she was not careful, she would be heading for a dive into very hot water, Daisy spoke slowly, carefully choosing her words. "I ... I just thought he might need to know that we weren't at home," she said. "You know, in case he tried to phone and got worried, because there was no answer, like you got worried about Nana and Jake."

Poppy felt as if she should accept this explanation, on the surface quite plausible and quite thoughtful. She was, in essence, right. The fact that she hadn't bothered to communicate what she'd done to her mother made it less convincing, but then she was not best pleased with Poppy for dragging her away. Maybe it was just that as they were leaving the house, she wanted her dad to know where they were going.

But then ... "I gather you've had a rotten journey, something about a puncture and having to wait for ages in the cold?" Tim asked, with concern that was genuine, if somewhat misplaced, in the context of having been missing himself. As soon as he saw the flash of realisation dart across Poppy's face, the muscles contracting as if she'd been slapped, he regretted what he'd given away.

"It seems you know about the puncture, then?"

Ben shifted awkwardly in his chair, and Sarah muttered an excuse about needing to see to Harley as she left the table. Jake was transfixed, watching the invisible duel between his parents. Nancy was doing the verbal equivalent of sitting on her hands, longing to interrupt and sort it out, but knowing that was absolutely not the thing to do. *Oh, if only James were here!*

Tim stopped abruptly, his fork dangling in mid-air, on its way to his open mouth. He rested the fork on the side of his plate.

"Yes. You poor things!"

"You've been having quite a conversation with you father, then Daisy?"

"I just thought he would want to know." Daisy refused to look at her mother. She was not about to explain that she only sent one message, and that it was a plea to be rescued.

"Well now I'm here, I thought maybe I could take Daisy home after dinner, if you want to spend some time with your mum," Tim offered, doing his best to protect his daughter from being completely found out. He might be planning to have a word or two with her in the car, but not in front of everyone at the table. "I thought there must be something wrong if you hadn't planned the trip. I presume you're OK, Nancy? No broken bones or anything?"

"I'm all in one piece, thank you, Tim, and yes, I'm OK. I'd switched off the answerphone and forgotten to take my mobile, when I went out, so unfortunately, I had my daughter imagining me lying at the bottom of the stairs or rushed off to hospital, or worse. Entirely my fault, I'm afraid." She felt like one of the teenagers she'd reprimanded in the past, giving the classic promise of "It won't happen again".

"Well, no harm done. That's the main thing, isn't it?" Tim ventured.

Daisy was busy checking her phone, seemingly unaffected by the tension building.

"And what are you doing here, Jake?" Tim said, in a calm, slow voice that sent shivers down Jake's spine. The others might not have noticed it, but he was very aware of the question behind the question – *What have you told anyone else?*

"I just thought it would be nice to see Nana, before I get stuck into another term of slogging away."

He was amazed, how easily the lies came, when you felt as if you were cornered. The last thing he'd expected was his father turning up.

"You seem to have quite a family reunion on your hands, Nancy, don't you? Most of my family, and Ben turned up as well! Fancy that! What a coincidence!"

Ben was frantically trying to gather his scrambled thoughts, to think of some reasonable excuse for being here, other than being summoned by his sister, and it was with huge relief that he suddenly heard the doorbell go again.

Eyes darted round the table, seeking some indication of anyone knowing who else might be appearing. Jake shot out of his chair, offering to go to find out who was there.

"Oh, Cass! Thank goodness it's you!"

99

"Well, you practically snared me into coming," she spat at him. "Leave me with the burden of knowledge, and duck out, as usual! What's going on? How many people have we got here now? That sounds like a party!"

"Hardly a party, as Dad turned up, thanks to Daisy, and Ben and Sarah turned up with their baby, not thanks to me or Daisy, so I have a suspicion that Mum wanted them here for moral support."

Cassie peeled off her coat and deposited it on the coat stand.

"Look, I've done some research on those nursery rhymes," she hissed at Jake, trying not to let her voice carry into the dining room. "I was right, Jake. It's creepy! Two of them sound like death wishes, and I'm not at all happy that she's keeping quiet about them. We're going to have to let the parents know, I think, so that they can make her see sense."

"Well, that should be fun, shouldn't it?"

Cassie let Jake lead the way into the dining room.

"Look who I've just found at the door," he said, as merrily as he could manage. He produced his best smile, avoiding direct contact with anyone at the table. Poppy looked aghast at her daughter, and Nancy looked as if her head would explode. Cassie could almost read on her face, *Who else is going to turn up? What on earth is going on here?*

Daisy broke the ice by leaping out of her seat and running into the arms of her older sister. Maybe she hadn't realised how much she'd missed her being there, as the buffer between her and their mother, but right now, she was obviously so pleased to have someone break the spell that hung over the room, and to avoid any more awkward questions.

"Cassie!"

"Hiya, kid sister," Cassie returned. "Hello everyone. Oh, Sarah, how lovely to see Harley! I didn't expect to find you here as well!"

"As well as who?" Poppy was starting to feel as if life had completely slipped out of her control. Anarchy seemed to be reigning in her family, and they had all descended on this house as if they had homing devices pulling them in.

"Well, well! Now I have the whole set!" exclaimed Nancy. "Both of my children and all of my grandchildren in one room, at the same time! It's a Christmas miracle come early! Now, to what do I owe the pleasure of your company, Cassie?"

Cassie looked at Jake. Jake looked at Cassie. There was no excuse she could dream up right now, faced with a room full of family, who all seemed to have avoided telling each other so much.

Jake appeared with the chair from the study and motioned for her to sit down. He pushed his own chair a little way away from the table, so he was sitting next to her. It felt safer that way.

"My brother being such a brave young soul, I guess I'll have to kick off then," she started.

Tim jumped out of his chair. "Cassie, I'm sure there's no need to upset anyone tonight," he began. "There's nothing anyone needs to worry about right now. Let's just enjoy all being together." He could feel his heart thudding under his ribs, and his head started to match the rhythm. Panic engulfed him. That toerag of a son of his! He'd spilled the beans, hadn't he? Now they were going to denounce him in front of everyone. Somehow, he'd to stop it happening. What could he do?

He didn't have to think up anything, as luck would have it. He felt the blood draining from his face, and his head was suddenly full of cotton wool. He could feel himself about to fall.

He hit the floor with a thud.

"My God, he's passed out!" observed Ben. Not that it had gone unnoticed. He lay in a crumpled heap between two chairs, as everyone suddenly moved at once. Daisy started crying, putting into practice the dramatic moves she'd learnt in the school play, as if the world were about to end. Harley decided to pick that moment to remind everyone that he was there, to let them know it was his dinner time, and Jake stood with his back pressed against the wall, already wondering what they would do if his father were dead.

101

"Right. Everyone get out of the way," said Nancy, shooing her daughter into the doorway. Poppy's very apparent confused emotions seemed to leave her no room for reason. She didn't care, yet cared, as she watched others hover over Tim.

Nancy knelt beside him. She'd been a first-aider at school, and she'd often dealt with teenage girls, sometimes teenage boys, who'd passed out for one reason or another. At least they didn't seem to do it deliberately these days, as she remembered some of her peers doing, to get out of assembly!

"He's just passed out," she declared. "He's got a pulse. He's OK. Perhaps he's been working too hard, too many hours."

"Huh!" muttered Poppy.

"Open the back door, someone. Let some air through."

Cassie did as her grandmother asked, the only other person in the room not behaving as if she were in shock.

Tim started to rally, as Nancy waved a napkin in front of his face. She spoke gently to him. "Tim? Tim, you're OK. You just fainted, that's all. Can you hear me?"

He gave a feeble nod. "Tim, can you stick your tongue out for me, please?"

Tim felt too strange to bother about whether or not he was being rude. He stuck his tongue out, and Nancy seemed satisfied.

"His face doesn't seem to have dropped. Tim, can you sit up now? Ben, Jake, come and help him."

Ben and Jake helped him into a sitting position, leaning him against the wall, rather than trying to lift him onto a chair. As he opened his eyes, Nancy said, "Tim, would you please just lift both of your arms into the air for me?"

Of course, Poppy thought. *She's checking to see if he's had a stroke. Why didn't I think of that? I was so busy being angry with him, I couldn't see past the fact that he dared to be here at all, and then he dared to disrupt everything by*

102

passing out, when I wanted to get the conversation round to what we're going to do about Mum. Selfish, to try to wreck my plans with his own agenda.

"That's all we need!" Jake whispered to Cassie, as she poured a glass of water in the kitchen.

"Oh right, so never mind that our father has just collapsed, Jake!"

"You know what I mean. We have to try to talk to Nana and get Mum and Uncle Ben on side, Cassie. She might be in danger."

"I know. I know. Look, let's try to sort out one thing at a time, can we? We'll try again, when this calms down."

Cassie carried the glass of water into the dining room, trying not to spill any, as her hands shook. Jake followed. Nancy took the glass and put it to Tim's lips, encouraging him to take a sip or two.

As he came round, she suggested he needed to rest, and maybe he should go into the lounge and lie down on the sofa, while they finished their meal. Unable to protest, he leant on the arm offered to him by Ben and settled himself down, asking Ben to leave the door ajar, so that he could still hear the chatter across the hall. Thinking this would help him to feel part of the family gathering, Ben readily complied, telling Tim to call out, if he needed anything.

"He's on the sofa now," Ben reported to the others.

"Right. Thanks, Ben. I'll pop in and check on him in a minute. Jake, would you nip upstairs and get a blanket, please, my love? Your dad might feel cold, as he comes round properly. Take it in to him, and if he's fallen asleep, just put it over him. OK?"

Glad to have an excuse to leave the room, Jake nodded and bounded up the stairs, two at a time. He got the blanket from the end of his bed and took it down to his father, who was, by now, starting to feel more himself.

"Blanket for you, Dad. Nana said you might feel a bit chilly." He tossed the blanket over his father's frame, startling the budgerigar.

"Georgie Porgie! Watcha Tommy! Rockabye!" Tommy Tucker jerked his head back and forth, frantically moving up and down his perch.

"Don't you dare split on me, Jake," Tim managed to say through gritted teeth. "You got the car. You promised you wouldn't say anything to upset your mother. There's no point. It's over. Don't go and cause more trouble than there needs to be."

"I don't know what you mean, Dad. I wasn't going to say anything about what you've been up to. I think she has a fair inkling anyway, if you ask me. You're not as clever as you think you are, you know, where Mum's concerned. She's not easily fooled by anyone. Anyway, it wasn't about you. It isn't always about you, believe it or not! So that's why you fainted, is it? Hah! I'm glad your guilty conscience is strong enough to make you dread the consequences of your actions! Well, sorry to disappoint you, but this time you have no reason to see me as a failure of a son. I have kept your secret, not for your sake, but for Mum's. I'm not going to be the one to shatter her life. No. This time, it's about Nana."

"What about Nana?"

"She's been getting some weird messages, and she hasn't told Mum. We think she needs to do something about them, so I asked Cassie to come and back me up. Now I'm going to go back in there and try to protect someone who deserves to be protected. You stay here, because it will make it a whole lot easier for me, if you're not around to make it harder!"

Jake spun on his heel and headed back to the dining room. His father's feeble attempt to shut him up had just given him a stronger resolution to do what he knew he needed to do. As he walked into the room, everyone was chattering away, apart from Daisy, who sat in melancholy silence, tears creeping down her face. It was easy for Jake to assume that she was in shock, upset by Tim's faint, but she was now acutely aware that she was definitely not going to get home in time to go out with her friends. She sent a very sad face to her group, with a brief message:

Dad taken ill. Can't leave him tonight.

It would elicit the required number of sympathy replies, which would make her feel very slightly better.

Jake beckoned Cassie to sit back at his side, and this time, he took the lead.

"Nana Boo, you know we love you very much, don't you?"

Wondering what dreadful news he was going to give her, with his solemn face and tone, and the prerequisite of mutual love, she answered, with a frown on her face, "Yes, Jake, I hope you do. I certainly love all of you very much."

"Then I hope you'll forgive me and understand why I'm doing this."

"*What IS he going to do?*" thought Nancy. It sounded as if he was going to do something that would upset her.

"Everyone, listen up. Nana has been getting some strange messages, and Cassie and I, well, we think she should tell you and do something about them, but she doesn't seem to want to do that. And I'm sorry, Nana, but I had to tell Cassie, because I knew she would feel the same as I do. We know you don't want to worry Mum, and you probably don't want to worry Ben, either, but if you're in any danger, you need help."

"What on earth are you on about?" said Poppy. "First your father passing out. Now your Nana in danger. What's going on here? Mum, why haven't you said anything?"

Nancy sighed. She should have known that she couldn't expect her grandson to keep it to himself. She knew she would now have to tell all, or it would just get worse.

"Mum?" Ben walked over to behind her chair and put a protective arm around her shoulders. She leant against his hand, feeling herself giving in to the inevitable.

"Okay, okay. Look, I'm all right. I'm sure it's just some silly prank, but someone seems to think that nursery rhymes are funny. The reason I turned off the answerphone, Poppy, was that two of the messages were left on there. Jake and I went to Harlow Carr, and when we got back, someone had left me a message. When we played it, it was baffling, because it was someone singing 'Rock-a-bye Baby'; the whole rhyme. I half expected it suddenly to turn into a pop song, or something, but no, it was just the rhyme. Then, when we'd been out again — and your son is a good driver, by the way — there was another message, this time 'Georgie Porgie, Pudding and Pie'. There doesn't seem to be any logic to it, so I had a look on the internet. I knew a lot of nursery rhymes had very unsavoury beginnings, but you think nothing of them when you're a child, do you? Anyway, the last message was this morning, and this time it was a note through the door, which is, I must admit, a little more alarming. I could have believed it was just a wrong number, or someone playing a prank on a random dialling stint, but a note through the door is a different kettle of fish, isn't it? I was going to wait until you'd all gone, so I could think clearly and calmly about what to do, but obviously my grandchildren are two steps ahead of me."

"Nana, I remembered doing something in history about 'Ring-a-ring-a roses', and how sinister some of these rhymes are, so when Jake told me he was worried, I looked them all up. You know, you need to take this seriously. Someone is not just playing a prank, but a nasty one, if it is that. Surely there's something we can do about it. Should we tell the police?"

"Why didn't you tell me, Mum?" Poppy's voice was almost cracking.

Ben's arm tightened round Nancy's shoulders. "Mum, what did you do with the messages?"

"I just deleted the first one — I thought it was a lot of nonsense, and someone had obviously got the wrong number. The second one is still on the answerphone. The third one is here." She pulled the piece of paper out of her pocket and put it on the table, in front of them all. They expected something like letters cut out and stuck on, but no. It was just a piece of printer paper, with the rhyme of "Three Blind Mice" typed on it.

Old films were going through Ben's head, where ransom notes or threats had been typed on typewriters that all had their idiosyncrasies and could be traced. But this would just have been typed on a computer and printing it out could have been done anywhere. The note had been folded into four, so that the message was not immediately visible. What was the point - to give Nancy a nasty shock, or to warn her that something was going to happen? Either way, the thought of his mother being vulnerable horrified him. She'd always been the capable one, the strength they all turned to. Unlike Poppy, he hadn't assumed, until now, that she would need to be taken care of. She was not old yet, was she?

"I have to say I agree with the others here, Mum. We need to do something about this, put a stop to it. If someone is trying to frighten you, I'd like to find them and punch their lights out!"

"Ben!" Sarah had never heard him speak like that before, and she was shocked at the thought of him involving himself in violence, especially as he might end up being the one that was hurt.

"I'm sorry, Nana, but you see why we had to tell, don't you?" Cassie hoped, desperately, that she would not be seen as a villain. "Jake and I were just so worried. We couldn't keep it from Mum, or we'd never have forgiven ourselves if anything had happened to you."

Nancy looked down the table at her two grandchildren who seemed so suddenly adult, full of protective purpose.

"I understand," she smiled at them. "My goodness, here you are, all sensible and grown up, and I'm so very proud of you both." She hadn't realised quite what tension she'd been holding, since the second message, but she felt herself filling with emotion at the thought of their caring so much about her. She'd always cared about them, but somehow taken for granted that the love flowed in that direction, and here it was, coming back, not from children, but from who they had grown into.

"Right, Mum. First thing in the morning, we need to decide on a plan of action," said Poppy, ever the organiser. "We need to get in touch with the police, and we need to think about how we can protect you. You see, now, why I keep saying you shouldn't live on your own, don't you? You could have been in danger and none of us have known, and nobody near enough to come to help you. It doesn't bear thinking of!"

Poppy knew she was going to cry, and she was cross with herself for doing it. She left the room and could be heard noisily filling the dishwasher. Daisy slipped away to the box room; thinking being grown up was such an awful thing to be. She needed to get out of here. She was soon lost in her music, messaging her friend about what a dreadful family she had, and providing great detail about how much danger they were all in. Of course, if she hadn't come, they would not have found out about it, so she'd helped to save the day.

In the kitchen, Poppy mopped her face with a paper towel and was determined to get herself together. She couldn't bear any thought that anyone would want to harm her mother, and she felt the frustration of just wanting to be able to look after her since Dad died, but not being able to do it. She knew Nancy was fiercely independent and totally capable, while she was still in her sixties. But what would happen later? Poppy always worried about the things that might be and could be in life, something Tim had often tried to get her to let go of. "Take one day at a time," he would say, and infuriate her more.

Just as she was thinking about him, he appeared in the doorway.

"You're supposed to be lying down," she said, not wanting to face him in the middle of everything else.

"I'm fine," he said. "Look, Poppy, we need to talk. I know I've been an idiot. I know I've hurt you. I deserve to be punished. It's over. It was never meant to happen, and I've finally come to my senses, though I know that's no consolation for you. I don't know how I can put this right, but I don't want us to throw away what we've had. Please, please, will you give me the chance to try again?"

"Go away, Tim. I can't cope with you right now. I can't think straight, and I need to deal with today. That's what you're always telling me, isn't it? One day at a time? Well today is not your day. I know exactly what you've been up to; I made sure I found out. You must have thought me very gullible, if you thought I was going to fall for all those urgent business calls and reasons why you had to stay in London. You have lied and cheated, and I'm in no mood to even begin to forgive what you've done. Very convenient that you fainted tonight, wasn't it? What was it, Tim, did you think someone was going to tell everyone what you've been doing? Is that it? Do our children know what you haven't told me?"

Tim felt the panic engulf him again, but he couldn't let it win this time.

"Why did you give Jake the car? Was that it? Was it to keep him from telling me? What does he know?"

"He knows. Look, I'll tell you everything later. Not here. Don't blame Jake. It's my fault. It's all my fault." He leant on the worktop, overwhelmed by guilt and regret that he hadn't allowed himself to feel until now.

"I'm sure it is. Who is she? Anyone I know? One of our friends?"

"No-one you know, Poppy. Just someone I met at a conference. I didn't mean for anything to happen. I don't know why it did."

"Huh! It happened because you let it happen, Tim. Don't give me any lame excuses. They won't wash. You betrayed me, us, our marriage. Just go back in the lounge, will you, and leave me to deal with my mother. I can't deal with you now. Go! Get out of my mother's house as soon as possible!" She turned her back on him.

She hoped he would go back on his own and feel as bad as he deserved to feel. She was not about to show him any understanding or forgiveness, and there were more pressing matters tonight. The damage was already done, as far as she was concerned, and it was no good expecting to confess and be forgiven, as if that was all it needed. She was not even sure she wanted to try. She'd always thought they were honest with each other, that the commitment they made twenty-one years ago had stood the test of time, unlike some of their friends, who had been divorced, remarried, and some of them divorced again in that time. Had she been living a lie, all this time? What else did she not know? She'd heard from the investigator that he'd been on his own in the flat last night. So far, there had been no-one else going in there, so there was no evidence of the woman. She would like a photo, but there didn't seem to be one. She would like to know who to hate, but she didn't know. She was full of so much rage and hurt that all she wanted to do was throw Tim down a very steep set of stairs. How dare he bring this here tonight? She wiped her hands and walked back into the dining room, determined to ignore her husband until she decided she was prepared to listen.

"I'm so sorry, Mum. We should have told you what we knew, I guess, but we just weren't sure what to do until that last message came." Jake looked at his mother with sorrowful eyes, and as she saw before her the child saying, "I don't know what to do", she softened slightly.

"Jake, you, of all people. I didn't think you would shut me out. How could you think anything but that you should tell me, when my own mother might be in danger? How would you have felt if you were me?"

"I didn't think of that."

"No, you didn't, but you should have done. You and Cassie. Thank goodness she talked some sense into you, but now, here you are, the pair of you. You should be knuckling down in Cambridge, and she should be enjoying her first couple of weeks in Leeds, before the workload goes up. And you still haven't told me all the secrets, have you, Jake? I can't help feeling a bit disappointed in you, but then, I can imagine the dilemma you faced, when you found out what your father was up to."

"What?" Jake was floored by the last comment, not knowing what she now knew and didn't know. Oh no! More decisions! What was he to say now? Telling himself to tread super-carefully, he asked, "Does this mean Dad has told you?"

Nancy was looking from one to the other, wondering what else her family had been keeping to themselves. It all seemed very complicated, and she judged it best just to keep out of it for now.

"Dad didn't have to tell me, Jake. I'm not an idiot, and I'm not easily duped, as you well know. If you two learnt anything as teenagers, it was that it was no use trying to lie to me, or hide things from me, because somehow or other, I always worked it out or found it out! I know your father. I've known him for a lot of years. When someone's behaviour changes, it kind of registers, you know? I had my suspicions a few months ago, but I didn't want anything to affect you two, so I kept quiet. But that doesn't mean I didn't do anything about finding out."

"Oh!" was all Jake could manage. He looked at Cassie, who was staring at her mother. Ben was looking embarrassed and holding Sarah's hand, at the same time as rocking Harley back and forth in the buggy, hoping he would stay asleep, despite the raised voices.

"Look, maybe it's time we got going, " he said, much to Sarah's relief. "I'll ring in the morning, Mum, or maybe we could do a video call, so that we can all decide what to do next. Sarah's bushed, and Harley's not going to stay quiet much longer. I do think you should consider what Poppy has been saying about moving, you know. It would be so much better for everyone's peace of mind. We care about you, Mum, and being on your own is not going to be the best option, as you get older, is it?"

Nancy listened, her stomach knotting at the idea that Ben was now siding with Poppy. She felt like shouting at them, "I am not old yet. I'm still quite capable of looking after myself, thank you", but she judged it not to be wise this evening. She bit her tongue and mentally dug her heels in further. She was not about to be written off in her sixties, when she was still doing everything that she did before James died, apart from being with him. The last thing she wanted was to be answerable to someone else for her every move, every decision, every problem that she could sort out herself. However, she had to acknowledge that this time she might have to accept some help ... from a distance.

"Oh, right, of course. He is gorgeous, you know, that baby. It will get easier. Enjoy being in control of him, because one day it might be you sitting here like this, with Harley deciding what you should do!" She tried to laugh, to lighten the awful tension in the room.

Ben smiled back at her, that possibility seeming extremely remote at the moment. He bent to kiss Nancy goodbye, before steering Sarah and the buggy towards the door.

"Bye everyone!" they called. With varying degrees of cheeriness, the others called back. As he passed the lounge door, Ben put his head in, to see Tim standing up, turning off the television and looking far more alive than he had not so long ago.

"Bye, Tim. Glad to see you're feeling better. Look, I know I shouldn't interfere, but whatever it is you've done, mate, you need to sort it out. My sister's an absolute gem, and I can tell there's something far more wrong than being worried about Mum. Don't you dare hurt her anymore. You hear me? Get whatever it is sorted, and wise up. She deserves better." He turned on his heel, before Tim could answer.

As soon as Ben and Sarah were safely gone, Tim gathered up his things and crept out, not wanting to face anyone else. He didn't want his children to witness any quarrelling, and he knew he would not be wanted here by anyone, except, perhaps, Daisy, who would wonder why he hadn't stayed. Perhaps she would understand that he couldn't since she thought he was not well.

Chapter 16: Cassie and Nancy

Cassie hugged Nancy as she said goodbye. Jake had offered to give her a lift to the station, so that she could catch the last train back to Leeds. The house was a bit full, and she could tell her father was going to be occupying the sofa, so Jake agreed it seemed best if she left them all to it. She'd done what she needed to do, and Jake was visibly relieved that he'd had his sister by his side. At least now Poppy knew what had been going on, and Ben being there had been an added bonus. She couldn't stand secrets, and there was no point in interfering in her parents' spat — that was something only they could sort out.

"Goodbye, sweetheart," said Nancy. "I'm so sorry you had to come charging up here, when you're only just settling into your hall. We haven't even had a chance to talk about it, have we? Send me a photo, so I can picture you there, will you? And good luck with the lectures. I hope they're all fascinating. You're at the start of an exciting time, Cassie, so make the most of it, and make lots of new friends. I'm still in touch with some people I went to university with, you know. One of them lives in Italy now. There's a great big world full of knowledge out there, so you grab your slice of it!"

"I will, Nana. I've met some decent people already, and the campus is quite something. Leeds seems to have tons of stuff for students to do, so I don't think I'm going to get bored any time soon!"

"Just don't get too drunk!" interjected Poppy. "And watch what you spend your money on. You know there won't be any more!" Her tone was softened by the smile on her face.

She knew Cassie would make mistakes, but she also knew Cassie would not go so far that she'd end up in trouble she couldn't get herself out of. She had a healthy streak of cowardice that would pull her up, if she saw signs of things going too far. Poppy tried to drum into both her and Jake that they needed to judge wisely, when it came to who they spent their time with, as some would take advantage of their good nature. They were good kids, these two. She wished she could keep them safe, but she had to trust them now. They'd done the right thing tonight, and that was a good sign. She still had to tackle Jake about keeping his father's secret, but she was not so bitter that she didn't understand the position he'd been caught in, not wanting to betray his dad, and not wanting to hurt his mum.

"Is Dad going to be all right, do you think?" Cassie asked, motioning towards the lounge with her head.

"He's perfectly all right, Cassie, just facing up to some unpleasant truths, thanks to you and Jake."

"You know, don't you?" It had dawned on Cassie that Jake had been the keeper of more than one secret, and her mother had not been terribly sympathetic to Tim's fainting fit. It had been Nana who had knelt down to find a pulse.

Poppy looked her daughter straight in the eyes, as she said, "Yes. I know more than you think, Cassie. And Jake, I know what you didn't dare to tell me. Don't ever underestimate your mother's powers of intuition, kids. That would be a big mistake!"

Jake's shoulders dropped, as the tension he hadn't been aware he felt slid away. He'd struggled with keeping one secret, but two had burdened him beyond the level his conscience would let him shrug off. *I've had enough of hiding things and collusion. It was hard work!*

"I'm so sorry, Mum." *I'm saying it again! How many times do I have to say that before I've said it enough times to feel better about what I've done?*

"Look, now is not the time to deal with this. Cassie, stay safe. Jake, make sure she's on the train before you leave her. Drop me a text when you're back in your room, Cass, and make sure you lock the door over night, won't you?"

Cassie laughed. "Stop worrying about me, Mum. I've been well primed, haven't I? I'll be OK."

Mother and daughter had one last hug, and Jake led the way to his car.

When they were left alone, Nancy turned to Poppy and said, "OK, you know what my secret was, so now tell me yours, young lady. What has been going on with you and Tim? Whatever it is, it seems to be affecting Daisy, and the other two seem to have had to bear the burden of knowledge they wish they didn't have. Come on, sit down, and tell me about it. I may be getting older, but I'm still your mother, and just as you worry about Cassie and Jake, I worry about you. It never stops, you know, just because your children get older or just because they start to worry about you. It simply becomes two-way traffic, and the less you tell me, the more I'll worry. So, shoot..." She handed Poppy a glass of wine and picked up her own.

"Oh, where do I start, Mum? I didn't want to tell you about it. You've always been fond of Tim, and it might have sounded as if I were over-dramatising. For a while, I couldn't be sure, anyway. He just started to have sudden business meetings that meant he finished work so late he might as well stay at the flat another night. I thought nothing of it at first. But then it turned into a whole weekend, thanks to some businessman visiting from overseas, and he just had to host him. He must have thought he was doing a good job of fooling me. I couldn't tell anyone, to be honest, because I had to be able to voice my feelings without losing control and wanting to cry. I was hoping the kids hadn't noticed anything, but of course I was wrong.

I don't know when it started. I guess it kind of crept up on me. All I know is that he was away more than he was at home last term, but I was so snowed under at work that I welcomed not having to deal with his comings and goings at first. Daisy started asking questions about where her dad was, and why wasn't he coming to watch her performance in the school play, and I didn't have any answers, apart from telling her he was working. When he was home, he made a fuss of her, and with me he was just his normal self, except that I noticed he offered to do a bit more cooking. I thought he was just trying to make the most of family life.

Then I noticed the phone calls. Sometimes, he would say he had to take the call, but he'd take himself into another room, or out in the garden. Again, it was all plausible at first, but I started to get more suspicious with each little hint. I said nothing to the kids, but last month I decided I needed to find out what was going on. Money had disappeared from our bank account, and he tried to tell me he'd just had an expensive month, and he'd be claiming it on expenses, but no expenses ever went back into the account. A friend of mine knew someone who had set himself up as a private investigator, so I went to see him a couple of weeks ago, and I got him to do some digging. He had someone he knew in London, who could tail Tim. I knew it would cost, but by then I just had to know, one way or the other.

Sure enough, he'd been to the theatre in town, which he told me he'd done, but he didn't go alone. He'd also met the same woman in Hyde Park. Then it all went quiet, and she doesn't seem to be around anymore. He's been on his own in the flat this week. I had decided to confront him with what I knew, when he got home, but tonight has just accelerated things. I wasn't going to tell you, until I'd heard his version and decided what to do."

"Exactly like me, I'm afraid, aren't you, Poppy? Look at us both, not telling. I knew there was something wrong with Jake from the time he arrived, and maybe now I understand. I thought if I gave him time and space, he would eventually feel he could tell me what was bothering him, why he felt he had to escape to someone who would listen and still love him. By the sound of it, Tim put him in an impossible position, though goodness knows how he found out. I'm not surprised he told Cassie, because those two have always bounced off each other and been so close. I should have known he'd tell her about the messages, too!"

The front door banged, as Jake came back into the house.

"All done!" he called. "She's safely on the train, in a carriage with another woman."

"Thanks, Jake," called Poppy. She stopped him in mid-step, as he was about to avoid their conversation and head upstairs, by saying, "Jake, please would you come in here?" He guessed what was coming.

"Look, I'm not going to have a go at you, but I need to know what you know about your father's antics, Jake. I know what's been going on, but what I don't know is how you found out."

"I saw them."

"Where?"

"I went to London to see an old school friend, didn't I, a few weeks ago?"

"Oh Yes! I remember saying what a pity it was you couldn't meet up with your dad, when he would be working, and you said you were staying at your friend's house in Camden."

"I did. We went to Camden market, and we were making our way through the crowd when I spotted him. It's not hard, when he's tall and ginger! I was pretty sure he saw us, too, but instead of heading for us, he steered some woman he was with in the opposite direction and hurried off. I messaged him later, to ask him if he'd spotted us, and he told me to call in at the flat before I came home. That was when he spun me some story about a colleague, and they were there on business, and I wasn't to tell you, because you might get the wrong idea. Then he said I could have his old car, since he was going to get a new one... but if I upset you, there was no way he was going to let me have the car, so I'd better keep the peace."

"I see," said Poppy quietly. Nancy reached across and touched her arm.

"I didn't know what to do then. I took the car, and I had no proof he was lying, but I didn't like having to keep what I'd seen to myself. I came to Nana's because my head was hurting with going round in circles about what to do. Did I tell you and upset you, and maybe cause trouble between my parents, or did I keep quiet and feel like some conspirator? I needed time away from everything to think, but the thoughts just tied themselves up in knots, anyway."

"You should have talked to me, Jake," Nancy said, gently. "Maybe it would have helped."

"But then I'd have been leaving you with the same problem, Nana, wouldn't I? You would know what I know, and you'd have to decide whether to hurt Mum by telling her or leave well alone."

"Ah! The dilemma born of growing up, Jake, eh? You would have had to blurt it out, when you were a little boy, but now you think about others as well. You know, that makes me very proud of who you are busy becoming." Nancy felt herself close to tears, as she walked to the other end of the table and hugged her grandson.

"You know, I saw her, that woman, when we went to the gardens." Emboldened by the hug, Jake decided he might as well tell all now.

"You did? How strange! Maybe she was visiting the area!" Nancy was trying to work out when he may have seen her, replaying their visit in her mind's eye.

"Yes. She was with another woman. They didn't see me, but then I don't think she'd have known who I was, anyway, and Dad was in London, so she wasn't meeting him."

"That's true," said Nancy. "What are we going to do about Tim tonight? He's obviously not your favourite person, as things stand, but I'm not sure he's fit to go anywhere."

"He's gone." Poppy's tone was emphatic.

"Oh! I didn't hear him go!"

"No. I sent him packing, Mum, and he crept away. Just as well. Not something we can sort out tonight."

"Well, I guess we'd better finish clearing up and get an early night. You'll have Daisy to deal with in the morning, and Jake's got to get back to Cambridge. We'll sort out phoning the police before you go, I promise. OK?"

Jake returned Nancy's hug. "Thanks, Nana. What would we all do without you?"

"You'd get along just fine, Jake. You know what's right, and I think you're learning to use that instinct now. Night-night, my love."

"Night, Nana. Night Mum." He pecked his mum on the cheek. "Are we OK, you and me?"

"Yes, Jake, we're OK. Just don't keep anything like that from me again, right?"

"I won't." It was a very relieved Jake who took himself to bed. Everything was going to be all right. Mum would sort Dad out, and they would either get it together or not. He couldn't do anything about that. He couldn't hate his dad — he was his dad — so he hoped they would work it out. And Mum would sort out Nana's problem. He drifted off into the best sleep he'd had for weeks.

Nancy told Poppy to leave her to lock up and turn out the lights. She went to check the front door, after all the traffic through it, and there she found it. A folded piece of paper lay on the tiles, presumably having slipped to one side when the door was opened. It hadn't been there earlier. She picked it up with some trepidation, anticipating yet another prank.

Nana-Nana Boo-Boo.

The words were typed in huge letters and froze her to the core. This was not a nursery rhyme; this was her name, distorted, taunting. Why? She climbed the stairs with leaden feet, feeling now a sense of terror she hadn't felt with the other messages. This was personal. She was so very glad she had Poppy here tonight.

Chapter 17: Nancy

Nancy often had trouble getting to sleep, especially since she'd lost James. Sometimes, she tossed and turned most of the night, even without the provocation of the note she'd pushed to the bottom of her pocket, as though hiding it would make it go away.

She woke with a start, finding she'd been checking upper sixth coursework, for some reason. She hadn't done that for the past year, but somewhere in her brain, it obviously still bothered her that some of her students had struggled. It took a few seconds to register what was happening, as she heard a loud screaming noise from outside the bedroom door. Her half-asleep self could make no sense of it, until she dragged herself out of bed and opened the door.

Coming up the stairs towards her was a coiling mist, like standing at the seaside in a heavy mist. But she was not at the seaside; she was in her own house. Shock woke her up with a jerk that shook her whole body. This was smoke! The noise, it dawned on her, was an orchestra of smoke alarms, from up here on the landing, downstairs in the hall and in the kitchen, all of them shouting at her that something was alight, like some tormented ghost screaming "Nancy Brewer, wake up!". Illogically, what went through her head was yet another of the nursery rhymes she'd looked up:

"Ladybird, ladybird, fly away home. Your house is on fire. Your children shall burn". Her children. Poppy, Jake, Daisy!

It seemed like minutes, although she realised, later, that it had only been seconds, before she shouted, as loudly as she could, "Fire! Get up everyone! Fire! Get out!" She thundered on bedroom doors, all the years of training she'd done telling her that they didn't have long. Two minutes, the fire brigade had taught them, and it felt as if some of that precious time had disappeared faster than she could use it. Her heart thudded so hard; it seemed as loud as her fist pounding on wood. Strangely, she felt no panic, as if she'd floated into a parallel world, where this was the dream and reality had been her sleeping self.

Thankfully, Poppy emerged from her room, and seeing the smoke for herself, her eyes wide with startling truth, she went to rouse Daisy, while Nancy knocked again on Jake's door, until she got an answer. She shouted again, "Jake! Fire! Get up! Get out! Quick, while we can still get down the stairs!"

She ran back into her own bedroom, where last night's clothes lay on the chair, waiting to go to the laundry basket. She scooped them up, knowing there was no time to get dressed. Her handbag lay on the floor, under the dressing table, her phone inside it. She grabbed it. She knew the best chance they had was to call the fire brigade as quickly as possible, so, seeing Jake emerge in a zombied trance, but registering what was happening, she started down the stairs, calling to him at the same time, "Get yourself out in the garden, Jake. OK? Remember what you learnt at school. Keep low! Don't breathe in the smoke. Run!"

He nodded, as she made the turn of the stairs, where the smoke was thickening around her. All he saw was her disappearing body, enveloped as she got herself down to a crouch and headed for the front door.

Poppy screamed at him to get himself safe, while she shook Daisy awake, ear buds still in her ears, to block out the adult world she'd decided she didn't want to be a part of yet. She moaned, as Poppy desperately pulled her upright and pushed her to the door. Still locked in her dream of being discovered by a talent scout, she resented this intrusion into her alternative reality. Poppy could smell the smoke now, and she knew it was getting nearer. If she didn't get Daisy to move fast, they would not move at all.

"Daisy, please! Daisy move! Come on, will you? Take those damn things out of your ears!" She got hold of one of them and tossed it onto the bed. "The house is on fire, Daisy. If you don't move, we're both going to be trapped up here. Do you understand? I need you to understand now. Come on!"

Daisy's face reflected the horror that suddenly hit her, as if she were standing on a precipice, looking over the edge and knowing she had to jump.

"Mum? Am I dreaming, or is this for real?"

"This is for real, Daisy. It's horribly for real! Quick! Move!" Poppy had gathered up a dressing gown and slippers, without even knowing she was doing it. No time to put them on, she pushed Daisy towards the door. As she opened it, she knew they might only just have time to make it to the stairs. The smoke was wrapping itself round the landing like dirty cotton wool, sinister in its serpent-like movement, as if it was coming to get them. She took Daisy's hand and felt it shaking now. There was no time for sympathy, no time for conversation, as she got her to the top stair and gave her brusque instructions.

"We're going down, Daisy. Now listen! Try not to breathe until we are at the bottom, then keep low. If we have to, we crawl to the front door, because that's nearest, OK? I can't see any flames yet, but they might suddenly start. You get yourself to safety, whatever happens. Right? If we can't get to the front door, we try the kitchen. Don't stop."

With that, she started down the stairs, a fast as she could with Daisy attached to her. The grip on her hand told her what words couldn't. Daisy was terrified. She had no time to feel anything herself. Like Nancy, all the years of fire drills had taught her something, and now she was grateful that she'd had that routine practice and could put herself into automatic self-preservation. Watching for flames that wouldn't be a cardboard cut-out blocking a staircase this time, she got them to the bottom of the stairs.

The front door was not going to be an option. At the bottom of the stairs, she could see the curtains smouldering, as if they could burst into flames at any moment, something already burning the door mat, the fire licking its way towards the underside of the stairs. She yanked Daisy towards the back of the house, through the kitchen, where the dials from the cooker at least gave a glimmer of light. Nancy had left the back door open, and a full moon welcomed them outside, as they stumbled through it.

"Thank God!" Nancy hugged her daughter and granddaughter at the same time, tears of relief streaming down her face.

"Where's Jake?" Poppy asked, the urgency in her voice fed by the night around her, as she saw no sign of her son.

"It's OK. He's out, Poppy. He's gone round to the front of the house, to wait for the fire brigade. They're on their way."

Daisy, by now, was shivering uncontrollably, her pale face the colour of the moon and empty of expression.

"I've got a blanket in the car," said Nancy, as she headed for the garage. She'd always cursed having a garage yards away from the house, but tonight she was extremely glad. Opening it, she knew they had at least a little shelter from the elements. She always took her car keys upstairs at night, to avoid the risk that someone could break in and steal them, never thinking for a moment that it could turn into such a boon. She opened the car, and Daisy climbed into the back seat and wrapped herself in the blanket.

"Let's leave her in there for now," said Nancy. "If it gets too dangerous, we'll have to abandon it and go to the end of the garden, but we can keep her warm for now. I'm going to get dressed back there, behind the car."

123

"You've got your clothes, Mum? How did you do that?"

"I don't know, Poppy. Instinct! I just had them on the chair, so I brought them with me! I've given Jake my extra jumper. What about you? Look, I've got my old mac in the boot. Why don't you put that on?"

"Thanks. Good idea. I'll get it."

Nancy disappeared to the dark at the back of the garage, where she pulled on the clothes she'd rescued, emerging just as blue lights were reflected on the white wall that separated her garden from next door. Jake appeared on the drive, to tell them the brigade had arrived, and she went with him to the roadside. It felt as if she were back in a dream, as she watched the two appliances pull up outside the house, while she could see the flames flickering behind the front door.

One of the men approached her, as others prepared the hose. She watched them put on breathing apparatus, and her mind started to race. How much damage was there? All she'd been able to think of immediately was getting everyone out, but the reality of their situation was seeping into her consciousness now.

"Where do you think the seat of the fire is, madam?" asked the fireman.

"It seems to be in the hall," she answered. "Behind the front door. I'm afraid I couldn't see any more than that, because I had to go in the opposite direction to get out."

"That's OK. You did the right thing. Best not to hang around. We'll get in there. Have you got a key for the door? It would save us forcing it, if we can get it to unlock."

Keys. Had she got a key? In her mind's eye, she could see the key on the hall table, but then she realised she did have one she could give them.

"Yes. I've got one in my handbag. I'll get it for you."

She heard the crew discussing how to tackle their task, as she hurried back to the garage, where she'd left her bag. Poppy and Jake had found the garden chairs and were sitting like some leftovers from a late BBQ, facing the drive and well away from the house.

Nancy watched, as the crew soaked the front door, before trying the key. Thank goodness it wasn't a plastic one, she thought, or it would be melting. The old oak door was not giving in so easily. She couldn't bear to watch, as the door opened into the smoke and flames, and the firefighters disappeared from view. Unable to do anything now, she went back to the others.

"Daisy's fallen asleep in the car," Poppy told her. "I think she still thought she was having a bad dream."

"I wish it were a bad dream," answered Nancy. "Usually, if I'm in a bad dream it wakes me up when it gets too uncomfortable, but I'm not waking up. This is only too real. Two of the men have gone in. I dread to think what they'll find."

"We'll worry about that later, Mum. At least we're all out! Thank goodness the others have gone!" She reached out and squeezed her mother's hand. "You could always come home with me, Mum, if it's bad. You know that."

Nancy patted Poppy's hand. "Thanks, Poppy. You're a treasure, you know that don't you? Maybe I don't say it as often as I should, but I do appreciate how much you care. I really do, my love." Her head hung, as she felt her eyes fill.

"I do care, Mum. I only want what's best for you. I worry about you since Dad died, and I don't like what's been going on here."

"I care about you, too, Poppy. I care very much about what's happened between you and Tim, about Jake and Cassie, and about Daisy. It's so tough, being fifteen and people thinking you don't notice things, but you do. Do you remember being her age?"

"Well, I remember my version of it, Mum, but it's probably not quite the same as your version, is it?" Poppy smiled, remembering how they had often clashed, how she'd felt her parents didn't understand, when they said no to something she desperately wanted to do. "I think it takes being a parent to see things from the other side," she offered.

Nancy laughed. "Yes. You were pretty wilful, as I remember. You certainly knew your own mind, and it didn't always match ours! When Daisy's being difficult, hang on to the fact that you turned out all right, Poppy! She's struggling with finding her own identity at the same time as trying not to accept that her parents are going through a difficult time. She must pick up on the tension, mustn't she? And she's old enough to be very aware that Tim has been missing more. She'll have friends whose parents have been there. Everything is so intense when you're fifteen!"

"I was, of course, perfect, wasn't I Mum?" offered Jake, glad of a chance to distract himself from the fire.

"Huh! I don't think so! I seem to remember picking you up from a party and having to bundle you into the back of a car before your dad caught sight of you, when you had very obviously been drinking!"

Jake was quite relieved that she didn't recount any of his other misdemeanours. He would settle for that one. Nancy's agitation overcame her patience at this juncture, and she could anchor herself to a chair no longer. She strolled down the drive, not wanting to get in the way, but needing to see what was happening.

She doesn't know the half of it, Jake thought to himself, remembering some of the things he'd got up to at school, which had not been relayed to his parents. One advantage of being at boarding school had been not being under their watchful eyes all of the time, so his house parents and pastoral staff had dealt with a lot of antics without passing on every detail. Luckily, he'd been well liked; his winning smile, easy-going personality, and being extremely bright had gained him forgiveness. In truth, he'd never done anything drastically wrong, apart from the time some of them had gone a bit too far with putting bubble bath in the fountains.

While Jake mused, the fire-fighters had been busy, and one of them approached Nancy. "It's out, Mrs Brewer. Luckily, it looked far worse than it was, as the flames hadn't spread very far. You did right to call us straight away. It could have flashed over at any time, but if you can find us some window keys, we'll get the smoke clearing."

"Oh! Of course! Thank you so much. Can I go in through the back door?"

"Yes. You're OK to go in that way now."

"Right, I know where the keys are, so I'll get them for you."

One of the fire-fighters was detailed to follow her to the back door, and she handed over the window keys. He stepped inside and she heard his boots on the stairs, as he set about opening all the bedroom windows.

As the hose was rolled up and the men removed their apparatus, the crews readied themselves to leave. Nancy could see that the front door was charred on the inside, but it had withstood the heat. In her scrambled brain, she thought that was good, as at least she would be able to lock it again.

The window keys were returned to her, and she assumed she now had to go and clear up the mess, but before the second vehicle left, there was one last message, as one of the men held her door keys in his hand.

"Mrs Brewer, it looks as if this could have been a deliberate attempt to start a fire. I'm afraid I'll have to ask you not to touch anything around the seat of the fire until our investigator has been in the morning. Just use the back entrance. You may find you hear from the police as well. I'll lock the front door from the outside for you, as it's probably best if you don't touch it again tonight."

"Deliberate? But we were all in bed asleep," protested Nancy. "None of us would have done this deliberately."

"Maybe not, Mrs Brewer, but it does look as if someone did. The fire originated near the front door, and there is nothing there to start a fire, is there?"

"Well no." Nancy was trying to process what he was saying. He was right. There were no electric wires; there was no source of heat. Why would it start by the front door, unless... unless someone had put something

127

through the letter box? She kept her thoughts to herself, thanked him again, and went back to the others.

"Well, if you can bear it, we can go in now," she said. "The bedrooms were obviously full of smoke, so I don't quite know where we spend the rest of the night."

"Let's take a look Mum," said Poppy, as she led the way back into the kitchen, not wanting her mother to discover the damage first. "Jake, would you wake your sister up gently, and bring her in when she's had a chance to come round?"

"Will do," answered Jake, glad to have some kind of purpose.

The smell hit Nancy and Poppy as they came over the threshold. Nancy was reminded of the time, many years ago, that they had a chip pan fire, nothing like tonight, but the smell of burning was even stronger, like standing too near a bonfire. It was as if there'd been a blocked chimney in every room, and every one had been sending smoke back into the house. The actual cloud was gone, but a layer of soot clung to the walls and the ceiling in the hall, and a pool of water drowned the soggy remains of the doormat. The curtains hung in tatters, scorched at the top and burnt at the bottom, and the carpet sported a brown track across the floor towards the stairs. From every corner, and every edge, hung black cobwebs, like something from a Halloween film set, and it felt as if any moment, giant spiders would appear. How had they got there? Surely there were not cobwebs there before the fire? Nancy stood still, expecting "Burning Down the House" to start playing in the background, unable to do anything but stare at what was in front of her. Her instinct was to want to clear it up, remove the signs of what had happened, as far as she could. She wanted, even at three o'clock in the morning, to wash the surfaces, bring back some kind of normality.

"I just want to clean," she plaintively said to Poppy, "but they said we mustn't touch anything."

128

"Why's that, Mum? Can't we just take photos for the insurance company? You have kept up the insurance, I presume?"

"Yes, yes. I'll ring them in the morning, but apparently, it might have been started deliberately, Poppy. Who would want to do that?"

Jake had come up behind them, just as Nancy spoke. "I've got Daisy into the lounge, Nana. She's on the sofa. I hope that's OK?"

"Of course. Thanks, Jake. Is it bad in there?"

"No, it's not, luckily. There's a smell, but it's not as bad as out here, and the smoke doesn't seem to have caused any damage in there. It was good that all the doors were shut; they seem to have kept the worst of it in one place. Look, Nana, I know you don't want to think about it right now, but could this have anything to do with those messages you've been getting?"

Nancy blanched. "Oh dear God! I forgot!" She pulled from her pocket the note she'd found on the doormat as she'd gone to bed. "This was down there, last night." She pointed at the melted centre of the mat. "Just about there!"

She passed the note to Jake, who shared it with his mother. The two of them looked at the note, looked at each other, then looked at Nancy. Poppy wanted to cry. How could anyone do this to her poor mother, who couldn't possibly have done anything to deserve it? Jake's eyes expressed the anger he felt inside that some lowlife had dared to do this. Enough!

"I was waiting till the morning, to ring the police about all of them. They might come anyway, now, apparently, because the fire will have to be investigated. An investigator will probably arrive tomorrow morning."

"They report it if they suspect arson, don't they? I think they automatically notify the police, to get a crime number. You'll need to tell them all of it, Nana."

"Yes, I suppose I will. It all seems a bit unreal, doesn't it? This kind of thing happens to other people, not to me, not here. It just beggars belief! Oh dear! I suppose we shouldn't have handled the note, should we? Right, we're not in any fit state to do any more tonight, and I think we need to try to get some more sleep, don't you? Let's see what the bedrooms are like."

"I'll kip down here with Daisy, if you like," volunteered Jake. "If she wakes up, at least there'll be someone around then. I can use the armchairs."

"That's good of you, Jake. Thanks. I think she'd be terrified, if she woke up alone."

Poppy gave her son the biggest hug she'd given him for some time, and he let her. No-one was saying what everyone was thinking. They felt lucky to have got out before the fire took a hold on the house. Each of them knew they might not have been able to have this conversation, had it not been for the smoke alarms, and that was chilling. Someone could have killed them all if this had been deliberate.

Processing the thoughts was becoming exhausting, and that, together with the shock and tension they'd all been through, made them ready to do as Nancy suggested. Poppy double-checked the back door was locked and would have liked to do the same with the front door, only the threat of investigation stopping her from depositing fingerprints anywhere, now that they had realised their mistake with the note. She made her way up the stairs, avoiding touching the coated banister, and Nancy soon followed. They left their windows ajar, to let the smell out and fresh air in, but they were too tired to feel the cold or to smell the cocktail of smoke and water, as they fell back into bed. Nancy didn't bother to undress a second time, wrapping herself in her dressing gown and a blanket, rather than climbing under the duvet, in case that was just tempting fate.

Chapter 18: Nancy

They woke later that morning to a crisp, blue sky, innocent-looking, as if nothing bad could have happened. Nancy felt it should have been shrouded in fog, like a gothic tale, because it seemed that evil was at large, and she'd found herself in some kind of fiction.

She was up and dressed before anyone else, after a restless few hours of dreams that were no help at all in making her feel rested. As she woke, she'd been trapped in a lift, and no-one was hearing her shouts. This time, at least the nightmare was just that, and she was relieved to see that she was back in her bedroom.

Poppy had been busy making a late Sunday brunch for all of them, not that Daisy wanted any. She looked even more pale this morning, and she sidled up to Nancy, throwing her arms round her neck and landing a childish kiss on Nancy's cheek.

"I do love you, Nana."

Where did that come from, out of the blue? thought Poppy, watching her daughter, as she sat at the table without her phone in her hand.

"I love you too, precious," returned Nancy. "We had a bit of a dramatic night, didn't we? They're sorting it out now, so it'll be OK." She sounded far more confident than she was.

"I can't believe someone actually wanted to burn your house."

The others stopped themselves from reacting, each of them hearing that Daisy had taken in far more than they had given her credit for. Poppy had to acknowledge that her mother had been right. She picked up what was going on around her, even if she seemed not to be interested. There was more going on behind the earplugs and the Instagram than she was letting on. Had she deliberately manipulated her father into coming this weekend, hoping to mend things that seemed so very broken in her world?

"Eat some breakfast, Dais," her brother told her. "I know it's not what you want to eat, but just eat for once, so that Mum doesn't have to worry about you starving yourself. There's enough to cope with, you know."

Daisy didn't argue. She pushed her sausage round her plate, prodded the egg, then stabbed a piece of mushroom and put it in her mouth. Jake tried to look as if he wasn't watching her out of the corner of his eye, as she took a piece of toast and ate it dry, salving her conscience by at least not eating fat.

As if someone had flicked a switch, Daisy suddenly found her voice, her outburst pouring like a tap someone had turned on too hard. "You all think I know nothing, don't you?" she shouted, slamming her fork down on her plate. "Just the kid, so you don't have to tell me anything, confide any of your secrets in me. You expect to know mine, though, don't you? How is that fair? I have to do what you want, but you don't do what I want. It's all one-way traffic in this family, isn't it? Do you honestly think, Mum, that I haven't noticed how up tight you are? I have to live with it, don't I? It's been all Cassie this and Cassie that, because she's been about to leave home, and she's your precious older daughter. You think she never does anything wrong, but you don't know her as well as you think you do. And what about you and Dad? Where is he now? You've sent him away again, haven't you? Never mind that I might have wanted him here! And you're no help, Jake, are you, choosing where you go and who you tell, and cosying up to one sister, but not the other one, because she's only fifteen, isn't she? What does she know? Well, I hear it all, I see it all going on, all of you playing your silly games of hide and seek, and I am not a baby! I'll be sixteen next month, old enough to join the forces, old enough to get married, old enough to make up my own mind about a lot of things, won't I? The only one who really listens in this family is Nana, and you haven't even given me the chance to talk to her, with all your comings and goings. And last night was just the pits. Who the hell is trying to kill us all, I'd like to know? Yes! I'd! Like! To! Know!"

Everyone else sat very still, dumbfounded by Daisy's confrontation. She stabbed her sausage, whole, and suddenly bit into the middle of it, hard, as if taking revenge on it, when she couldn't take revenge on them.

The spell was broken by a tap on the back door. Standing outside, holding a casserole dish full of food, was Janet, from number 14.

"I hope I'm not intruding, Nancy, but Fred saw the blue lights in the night. Are you OK? Is there anything we can do?"

"Oh, how kind, Janet! Thank you so much! Yes, we're all OK, as you can see." She opened the door wider, so that Janet could see everyone gathered at the table. "Luckily, it was only a small fire, and it didn't get the whole house."

Janet stood there, waiting for more detail that was not forthcoming. *Don't give them anymore,* thought Nancy, *or it'll be all round the neighbourhood someone tried to set fire to us.*

"Oh, right. Well look, I'll leave this with you, and we'll keep our eyes open, so if you need help, you just call, OK?"

Nancy was sure they would keep their eyes open — they always did — but at least they had bothered to check whether she was all right, whereas the other neighbours, she noted, had not. No doubt they would all be gossiping about the drama today. Fred's self-appointed guardianship of the close could be useful.

"If you could spread the word, Janet, that we are all safe and not much damage done, that would save me having to tell the story over and over again."

"Of course I will. We noticed a police car in the close earlier, so that must be reassuring."

"Oh, were they around? They haven't been here yet, Janet, but it's good to know they're there, isn't it?"

"Absolutely! We don't want any more damage done by any vandals with nothing better to do with their time!"

"No. Well, if you'll excuse me, Janet, we have a lot of formalities to deal with, but I do appreciate the casserole. It looks delicious."

Janet beamed, handing over the dish and departing with a wave to the family.

"She'll have an excuse to come back for that," Nancy said to herself, at the same time feeling ungracious in view of the fact that Janet had made the effort to cook it for her. "And now she knows exactly who my visitors are!" She wanted to chuckle, which seemed so out of place this morning.

She put the casserole on the worktop, and Poppy claimed her attention.

"Right, Mum, we'd better let the insurance company know what's going on, hadn't we? Have you got their number?"

"I'll get it. It's in the bureau. Daisy, would you like to come with me?"

Daisy didn't answer, but she placed her cutlery on her plate, carefully this time, and scraped her chair back, as she stood. Nancy took her hand, and they left Poppy and Jake to finish their breakfast.

"Whew!" said Poppy. "Where did she find the energy to throw all of that at us? Have I got it wrong, Jake? Should I have told her my suspicions about your dad? I thought she would just round on me, tell me I was being a bitch, blame me for saying anything. It's so damned hard being a parent sometimes. You can never get it all right!"

"You do your best, Mum. I can see that now, but I probably didn't when I was Daisy's age. We're all different, as you well know from school, so what works for one doesn't work for another, does it? I don't think I'd have wanted you to turn me into your closest buddy when I was her age. I wanted to be separate, with my mates, not part of your world other than for you to be my parents, that I could moan about to my friends. You have taken Cassie into your confidence more, though, haven't you, and she seems to thrive on that. There's a Daisy there, somewhere, that we don't know now, isn't there?"

"It was so much simpler when you were all little, Jake! When you turn into young adults, I have to get to know you all over again. Maybe I lost sight of Daisy's blossoming adulthood, when she can still seem so much a little girl at times, the baby of the family!"

"Exactly. It seems your baby, my baby sister, is not such a baby anymore!"

Chapter 19: Nancy with Daisy

I took Daisy with me into the study, to avoid any awkward exchanges after her outburst. My goodness, this child has been bottling things up! Poppy's been so busy trying to protect her from the truth that she's cut off the one way she might have helped, by talking to her child! Poor love, she tries to make everything right in everyone else's world, and she wants to take the burden of caring for us all on her own shoulders. She has to stop trying so hard. Sooner or later, Daisy was going to find out, and then not forgive any of them. She must have felt all on her own with it, somehow.

So, I kept Daisy busy for a while. She was intrigued, when she saw inside the bureau, because the children have never been allowed anywhere near it. We didn't want them rifling through papers or tampering with important things like passports, so it had always been kept locked, and now I was letting her into the secret of where the key was kept. I could have told her not to tell anyone, but today was not the day to tell anyone that. I just reached inside the desk drawer and pulled out the key.

"Here you go, Daisy. Would you be kind enough to unlock the bureau for me? I need to get the insurance renewal document out, so that we can use the number on it."

I passed her the key, and she looked at me, as if to say, "Do you really trust me to do this?"

I nodded at her, and she crossed the room and turned the key in the lock slowly, as if she were afraid it would break something if she did it quickly. She pulled down the hinged door, to reveal the compartments stuffed with years of bits and pieces, some of which could probably be thrown away.

"Right," I said. "Would you go down to the bottom drawer now, Daisy? They'll all open now. You'll see a big white envelope in there, saying 'House insurance'. Would you pass it to me please?"

Daisy sorted through the top layer, as if everything inside the drawer were marked 'fragile'. She found the envelope and passed it to me, without saying a word. I sat down at the desk, and she took my cue and sat on the window seat, looking as if she would like to hide herself behind the curtains.

"Nana Boo," she said, avoiding my eyes. "Nana, do you think my mum and dad are going to split up?"

Well, that put me on the spot, but putting someone on the spot was what Daisy obviously needed to do.

"I don't know, is the honest answer, Daisy. I wish I could tell you of course they won't, but I can't, and I won't lie to you, you know that don't you?" I thought, *Now is the time when she needs to be able to trust what she's being told. No more hiding things from her.* She nodded, looking down at her feet.

"Carolyn's mum and dad split up last year, and she had to choose who to live with. How do you do that, Nana, choose between your parents? Whatever he's done, he's my dad, and I love him, just like I love Mum."

"I know you do, Daisy. He's been a good dad. Why wouldn't you love him? You can't take sides, and no-one would expect you to. You have to remember that he hasn't abandoned you, and he still loves you. You can still be loved by both parents, even if they aren't together, and I don't think your mum, or your dad, would make you choose. They would want what's best for you. Sometimes, things go wrong in relationships, and sometimes people make silly mistakes. If we're lucky, our silly mistakes are ones that we can put right, and there are no casualties but ourselves, but sometimes people mess up in a way that affects those around them. It looks as if your dad messed up, but he's sorry, and all you and I can do is wait to see whether or not it all sorts itself out. It's a big ask of your mum, and you can leave worrying about her to me, just like she worries about you. The best thing you can do is hang on to the fact that you have two parents who care about you, and one way or another they will sort out the mess and find a way forward. You can't sort it out for them — they're two adults — and you can't make them happy together, if they would be happier apart. Just be you and let them in to love you."

I didn't know if I'd managed to find the right words, but she didn't interrupt me once. I watched her face, tilted towards the window but very obviously listening to what I was saying. It wrenched my heart, to see silent tears running down her cheeks, streaking the eye make-up she'd so carefully applied that morning, but I resisted the urge to cross the room and throw my arms around her, as if she were a little child, to give her the chance to process what I'd said and to keep her armour intact.

"One thing I want you to promise me, Daisy," I said, her response being a look of alarm shot in my direction. "If things get you down, you won't bottle it all up and do anything silly. If you need to talk to someone, yell at someone, rant at someone, you phone me, or message me, OK?"

It was a long shot, because I was pretty sure she'd rather tell her friends, but I had to throw a safety net under her, as much for my own peace of mind as for hers. Another nod. Good. We had got somewhere, even if I wasn't quite sure where.

"Right. I've got the piece of paper I need. Would you please put the envelope back and lock up the bureau? Pop the key back in the drawer, and we'll get back to the others. You never know, your mum might let me phone the insurers myself!" She returned my smile, locked the bureau and carefully deposited the key exactly where she'd seen me take it from.

I didn't promise not to tell her mother we'd talked. I didn't ask her not to tell anyone. I wondered how long it would be before Poppy knew what had been exchanged that day, but I knew she would trust me, and I knew I could trust her not to ask. Daisy took the stairs as we left the study, taking the opportunity for some time on her own. *Good*, I thought. *She can mull it over, adjust her thoughts and plan what she does now.*

I took the insurance company number to Poppy, and together we tackled the insurance company's 24/7 help line. It was easier than I expected it to be, thank goodness, so now I have to wait for them to send someone to have a look. That's that hurdle, at least. Now for the police.

Nancy breathed a sigh of relief, once she'd told the police officer about the messages. She wondered why she hadn't done it before. She thought they might just tell her it was something she should ignore, but it seemed that the fire service had alerted them that something was amiss with the way the fire had started, and they were very willing to listen to what she could tell them. She was to keep any evidence safe because an investigator would be coming, and he would need to collect anything she could give him. She was also given a crime number for the insurance company.

"You see!" exclaimed Poppy. "You should have told them in the first place, Mum!"

Nancy chose not to rise to the answer she would have liked to give, accepting the rebuke as partially true.

"They said it was useful that you had witnessed the phone messages, Jake. They might ask you for a statement. Is that OK?"

"Of course it is, Nana. Anything I can do to help. I feel awful about having to leave you today. I've got to get back, so that I'm on campus tomorrow, but what about you?"

"She can come home with me," interrupted Poppy. "She can't stay here on her own."

Nancy could feel her hackles rising. "Yes, I'm afraid she can, Poppy. I have to be here, don't I, for the investigator and the loss adjuster? I can't deal with this from miles away, so you will just have to trust me to look after myself. If anything else happens, believe me, I shall be straight on the phone to the police. I have to let them do their job now, and find out who has been doing these things. I promise the doors will be locked, and I'll seal up the letter box. Simon can bring my mail to the back door. I don't think they'll try the same thing again."

"Mum, we'll be worrying ourselves silly over you!"

"I know, and I'm grateful that you care, but you have to allow me to be a responsible adult, Poppy. You have to go home and deal with your own problems and let me deal with this one. I'm not an old lady yet. I can still read, listen, think, and I won't let anything drive me out of my own home. The police are going to cruise by now and then, they said, so if anyone's watching, I hope they see a very obvious police presence and it puts them off. Now Jake, you get yourself going, and have a wonderful term. I'll look forward to hearing all about it at Christmas!"

"OK, Nana. If you're sure. I'll text you in the week, all right?"

"Oh, that would be lovely, Jake! I'll keep you updated. Now don't you worry about me. Just concentrate on what you've got to do. Go and make me proud!"

Jake collected his belongings and took a last look at the familiar scene outside the window. He picked up his phone and deleted the frantic messages from his father. They were irrelevant now because it was over. Everyone knew, and that was another secret he didn't have to keep. He was ready to be just a twenty-year-old student again, to leave the others to sort themselves, while he picked up at least some of his carefree playing hard, alongside a little working hard. He said his goodbyes, once he'd piled his things into the car, and sped off down the road, waving into the rear mirror with one hand and just about keeping the car in a straight line with the other.

"How can I go home and leave you here with all this?" Poppy asked, as she swept her hand through the air, indicating the blackened walls and ceiling. "Look, Mum, if you won't come home with me, for goodness' sake don't try to clean this up on your own, will you? Leave it to the insurance company. And ring me tomorrow evening. Keep me posted. If you get any more messages, promise me you'll ring the police immediately. I know there isn't much damage, as it has turned out, but if we hadn't woken up, it could be a very different story today, couldn't it? We could all have been killed! The house could have burnt down!"

As the day had worn on, the full potential of what they had experienced in the night had tightened its grip on her stomach and her mind. Last night, it had only been possible to focus on dealing with the emergency, but today the horror she didn't have time for last night had planted itself in her consciousness. She didn't want to leave Nancy like this. She had to go to work and get Daisy to school, but she was sorely tempted to play truant, to make sure her mother was all right. The trouble was that Nancy was right, when she said this could go on for some time, and not going in tomorrow would not be a solution. Tomorrow could be fine, the day after, or the day after that, not fine.

"Mum, if you need my help, you just phone. I'll get compassionate leave. I'll come back, right?"

"Bless you, Poppy, I know I can phone you if I need to. Thank you. Now you concentrate on talking to Daisy and getting somewhere with Tim, because we're going to be busy worrying about each other, aren't we? I'm not going to tell you what to do, other than to find time to get your head together, so that you can work out what you want. Whatever decision you make, you know I'll support it."

Nancy reached out and took her daughter in her arms, and Poppy rested her head on her mother's shoulder.

"Love you, Mum."

"Love you more, daughter." They shared a smile.

Chapter 20: Felicity

I don't have a clue what I'm going to do now. I've never seen Chas that bad before — pure rage! I suppose I should have seen it coming. He was bound to find out at some stage, but I was hoping against hope that he wouldn't. It's over. I'd finished it. I wanted it dead and buried, a folly of middle age that should never have happened. It was never going to come to anything, with him married and me with Chas, and it was so stupid! I can't believe it was me, behaving like a silly school kid.

Chas has always been a bit controlling, if I'm honest with myself, but I let it go. Nothing serious, but sometimes I admit I felt a bit crowded in and never good enough, compared with his late wife, who was obviously a saint. They say you don't know someone till you live with them, and that was certainly true, but I did love him at first. I think I was putting off facing the truth, once I saw what he could be like, and then I was suddenly swept off my feet with flattery and kindness, caught in a moment of weakness. I could come up with all sorts of excuses, but that's what they'd be, wouldn't they? I just looked across the table, and there was Tim, smiling at me, and something flipped. I felt sixteen again, catching his eye, knowing he was looking, and him knowing I knew. It was a harmless game, to start with.

I shouldn't have left my phone on charge in the kitchen. Stupid move. He shouldn't have looked at it, of course, but when it rang, he just picked it up, and there it was. Missed call. Tim.

"So, who's Tim?" It seemed such an innocent question, if I'd had an innocent answer. I could feel myself panicking, going red. I must have looked guilty, whatever I said.

"Who is he, then?" His voice sounded harder than I'd never heard it before, hard as a piece of flint, waiting for me to sharpen my wits on it. They felt anything but sharp. I needed to think quickly.

"Just someone I met at work," I said, feebly.

"Why would someone you met at work be phoning your personal mobile, Fi? Your work one's over there." He pointed at the shelf, where I'd put it down when I came in. He reached out, flung it at me, and it crashed to the floor. The muscles in his face clenched, distorting his mouth and heightening his cheekbones, as if he were blowing up some outsized balloon. His arm was rigid, but shaking, as he glared at me. The pupils in his eyes seemed to have shrunk to pinpoints, as he waited for me to explain the inexplicable.

"I don't know. Maybe I gave him the wrong number," I tried, knowing it would not fool anyone, let alone him. He'd been investigating fraud for far too long, sifting the genuine from the tall tales people would spin to make a profit. He could see through fabrication as clearly as if someone pressed a button on "Would I Lie To You?", and the light behind her head illuminated the word "Lie"!

"Where were you, at work, to give someone your mobile number? Don't they see you every day? Don't insult my intelligence, Fi! Who is he?"

"It was when I was in London," I started, not knowing where I was going with this. Did I confess, throw myself on his mercy, or pile the lies on top of each other, until I no longer knew what was true, or what I'd said. I couldn't do that. I wasn't prepared for this. I could feel the tears starting to scald my eyes. "He was at that conference I went to down there, you know,

143

back in the Spring. He was friendly to me when I was in a strange place. He said he knew me."

Six months ago, I realised. I'd let this go on for six months, each time I said "no more" caving in to his persuasion and wanting to believe that he didn't mean to hurt me. I could feel something crumbling inside, as I looked into my partner's eyes, that could be so soft and warm, and were now looking at someone he saw as his enemy. How could one person be two such different personalities? No-one who knew us socially would imagine he could be like this. The stronger his rage made him, the weaker I became.

"When did you see him last, then?" his voice threw at me. "Yesterday? Last week? When? Has he been there when you've been away on business? Just how friendly is he, Fi?"

I couldn't hold back the tears any longer, however much I tried. It was no use. My guilt and fear engulfed me like a dam bursting, flooding my brain, and making my legs feel like melting ice. Suddenly, he reached forward, grabbing me by my arm.

"You're hurting me!" I cried. His hand landed across my face.

"I'm hurting you? What do you think you're doing to me? How could you do this to us? Doesn't our relationship mean anything to you, you selfish bitch? Tell me what's been going on. You owe me at least that!"

"I'm so sorry, so very sorry," was all I could manage, my throat catching as I tried to speak. I knew it was no good trying to tell him he'd already damaged our relationship. He would only ever accept that it was all my fault. Everything was always my fault.

"Sorry for what? Tell me!" He yanked my arm and raised his fist, as if he wanted to punch me in the stomach. He wouldn't do that, would he? I wasn't sure. I had seen this person in front of me before, but never with so much reason to lash out. He'd been a bit rough, and cross, but this was more. I'd unleashed something in him he'd kept well and truly hidden before we lived together. I twisted round, freeing my arm, backing towards the lounge door, but he was quick. He pinned me to the door jamb, leaning over me like a volcano about to erupt. It was almost a growl that came out of his throat, as he used his body weight to trap me. For the first time since I'd known him, I was genuinely afraid, not just that he would hurt me, but afraid for my life.

"I met up with him a couple of times," I said. "As friends."

"Well, if he was such a good friend, how come you never mentioned him to me? Don't treat me like an imbecile. You're lying. I know you're lying."

He pushed me, and I fell against the kitchen island. I can still feel the bruise on my side. Again, he leant over me, and I felt he could do anything now. His fist landed like a hammer on the worktop. Was it going to land on me next?

I ducked under his arm and headed for the bedroom, though Lord knows why, trying to keep the door shut as he pushed against it. I was no match for his strength. He was in the room with me before I could get anywhere. I could feel myself staring, as he stood there, fists clenched. My eyes fixed on the back of his head in the mirror. There was no escape now. He grabbed my hair and threw me down onto the bed.

"Tell me!" he shouted. "Tell me who he is!"

"He works for another accountancy firm. That's all I know. I've seen him a couple of times. I won't see him again, I promise you. I've told him I don't want to see him again."

He grabbed my bag, looked at the phone again. It was pointless, trying to stop him. He held it up in the air and looked at my contacts. There he found him. Tim Castleford. The triumph he should have had all over his face suddenly disappeared, as his shoulders sagged. I thought he was going to cry, but instead he reached up on top of the wardrobe, flung a case down next to me and roared:

"Get out. Just get out! Of all the people in the world, I thought I could trust you. I thought you loved me. You're no better than Sadie was, are you? The same miserable excuse for a woman! Michelle's the only one who was

145

worth having, and she died and abandoned me. Well, this time, I'm not playing the game. This time, I make the decision. You take what clothes you can pack into that case, and leave. And don't ever come back. You came with nothing; you go with nothing. I never want to see your sorry face again. If I do, I won't be answerable for my actions."

He stomped out of the bedroom, and I heard him shut the bathroom door. He bawled "No!" at the air, and I pictured him standing over the basin, his chest heaving with angry sobs he would not let me see. Part of me wanted to comfort him. I heard the smash, as he must have thrown the mirror across the room. I heard the thud, as he kicked the wall and the door, like a wild animal about to destroy its cage. I knew I was next. My gut tightened, and I could hardly think. I just knew I had to move fast before he came back into the room.

I didn't know what I packed. I pulled things out of the wardrobe and drawers, caring little what I took, apart from my passport and a few sentimental things. I willed my hands to stop shaking, but my whole body felt as if it were being tossed back and forth. The faster I tried to be, the slower I seemed to be able to fold. I crammed as much as I could into the case, before I shut the lid and heaved it to the stairs. I couldn't carry it — he would normally have done that for me — so somehow, I slid it down the stairs and on to the front door. I picked up my car keys. Thank heavens he couldn't take that because it was mine.

He must have heard me shut the door behind me, and before I could make it to the car, like some medieval soldier on the battlements, he rained things down on me. I should have grabbed my laptop, but I was in no fit state to think. I heard it land among the old CDs and other things I'd left behind. All I knew, in that moment, was that I had to get as far away from him as possible, while I still could.

Where was I to go? I headed for Lisa's. She would, I knew, take me in for a night or two. What happened after that, I neither knew not cared, as long as I was safely away from him. I put my foot on the accelerator and drove.

Chapter 21: Nancy

With everyone gone, the house seemed very quiet, and Nancy ventured into the hall, where she could see beyond the blackened walls to the detail of what had been damaged by the smoke. She knew she didn't dare touch anything yet, but her eyes rested on the shelves under the stairs, where the overflow from a lifetime's collection of books had rested. She and James, between them, had so many relics of their studies and their teaching that their personal keepsakes had been squeezed out of the space they had for day-to-day use. The study had been a workplace, not to be cluttered with memorabilia. She was not even sure she could remember what was there, in the shadow of the staircase. Bending down had become less easy as the years passed, and doing so, to peer at anything, inevitably meant the pain of banging your head as you straightened. She sighed and took herself into the garden, despite the wind whipping across the fields at the back, to fill her lungs with fresh air and freedom. She missed them all, with their noise and their clutter and their company, and she found it unnerving to think about going to bed, alone in the house, but at the same time she felt relieved that she could just please herself again.

"Count your blessings," she scolded herself, as she dead headed her last surviving rose. "You're lucky to have them care about you."

Her tightened muscles told her that, however much she loved them, she was not yet ready to be old and cosseted, or worse still — controlled. This was her home, the home she'd shared with James, and this was where she wanted to be. Not given to praying very often, she found herself muttering, "Please God, let them find this idiot who tried to burn it down!"

The phone rang in the middle of the morning, and Nancy hesitated to answer it, but told herself not every call could be a prank. It was just as well, because this time it was the Investigating Officer who introduced himself and said he was on his way. He understood that he couldn't use the front door, and he didn't want to startle her, when he came to the back. He would need to look inside the house, but he would have his ID with him.

He arrived, a young woman with him, dressed in a white disposable boiler suit and clutching a case. She didn't look old enough to be out of school, in Nancy's eyes. Oh, how she now understood how her own mother had felt, when she said all the doctors and policemen seemed to be getting younger, the older she got herself! Politicians looked as if they were far too young for running the country, and part of her life was history to television presenters. It was somehow quite alarming that younger people were in charge of everything now, when not so long ago it had been her contemporaries.

She led through to the hall and showed them where the damage had been done.

"Mrs Brewer, do you have any reason to believe that someone would do this deliberately?" asked David Henson, an earnest expression on his face, as he handed her his ID.

"Well, no," Nancy started. "But you see, I did have some strange messages on the answerphone and a note through the door. I don't know why, or whether they are even connected."

David exchanged glances with the young woman to his left. Nancy knew what they were thinking, even if they were saying nothing. For them to be here at all meant the fire-fighters suspected arson, and they were looking for clues.

"That's where I found the note, the night before." She pointed to the hole in the doormat.

"Do you have the note, please, Mrs Brewer?"

"Yes, I'll get it for you. There's still one message on the answerphone, if you'd like to hear it," she offered. "I'm afraid I deleted the first one, because I thought it was just a silly prank, and someone had got the wrong number."

"Anything you've got, please. If there's been criminal activity here, Mrs Brewer, the police will be involved, and we need anything that could help them to find the culprit."

He explained the procedure to her, and the woman took out her phone, to record the message, as she played it. Nancy felt herself shudder, as she heard it again.

"Would you mind writing it all down for us, Mrs Brewer? If you can give us dates and times, and the exact content of every message, that will be really helpful."

He was talking to her gently, as if she might be too frail to deal with the demand, she realised, but never mind, his intentions were good.

"I can do that for you now," she said, standing as upright as she could and sounding as capable as she could. He'd just better not call her "dear", or she would not be able to cope! She wondered what he would make of her writing down nursery rhymes! She found she was glad of the evidence on the phone and on paper, to prove that it was not a figment of her imagination or a sign that she was going senile. She'd make sure she included the fact that she was not on her own when the fire happened, too, or they might think she'd done something daft.

"My daughter and grandchildren were here the night of the fire," she volunteered.

"Ah! Well, if you list their names and contact details, we'll follow that up, Mrs Brewer. We'll need statements, but we can deal with that after we've examined the scene."

She left the investigators to their job, saying she'd be in the kitchen, when they needed her. They seemed to know what they were doing, as they picked up the doormat and put it in a plastic bag and started examining the door.

Sometime later, a knock on the kitchen door interrupted her as she attempted to keep her hands and her head busy by tidying her cupboards.

"We've finished for now, Mrs Brewer. We've taken photographs and gathered up what we need. I suggest that you take your own photographs, for the insurance company, before you move anything. It's okay to do that now, if you want to."

"Thank you. Would you like to come through, to go out of the house the same way you came in?" asked Nancy, knowing how strange it sounded to be upholding the Yorkshire custom, in the middle of everything so surreal.

The young man smiled at her, and he and the woman with him walked past the pile of tins on the table, nodding "Goodbye" as they passed.

Chapter 22: Nancy

The loss adjuster sat at the kitchen table, his folder open in front of him.

"Mrs Brewer, let me explain the procedure from here on."

"Please do. I've never been in this situation before. Where do we start?"

"I'll alert a recovery company when I get back to the office, and they'll come to sort out what needs to be disposed of and what can be salvaged. They'll make a list of everything they condemn, so that we'll know what needs to be replaced. We then appoint people to validate the claim for any items you have lost. We'll be in touch with the police and fire service, and they'll make sure we're kept informed of the outcome of their investigation. The recovery company will also clean things up for you, so there's no need for you to try to do that."

"I see. Is there anything else I need to do?"

"No. Leave it to us now, Mrs Brewer. We'll be in touch. Just check the list the recovery company makes, so that we know they've got it right. They'll probably discuss it with you, anyway." He folded his notepad carefully, and slowly placed it back in his briefcase.

"You were very lucky, as it happens, Mrs Brewer. It's as well you had good batteries in your smoke alarms. We'll have to get the house back to normal, but rest assured we'll get the builders to repaint the hall and stairs, to get rid of the smoke damage. I'm afraid you should be prepared to lose everything in the hall, because some of it will not be economically viable for cleaning. The police or fire investigators may have removed some things themselves, of course, so let us know what they've taken."

"I see. Thank you."

"Now I have to go to someone else who's had a fire. She has very little left." He shook his head, seeming genuinely concerned. Nancy wondered how he could do his job, when it meant facing the misery of other people's lives every day. He looked a thoughtful young man, not the sort of person she was expecting at all. She thought the loss adjuster would come to see what he could avoid paying for, but this one seemed to be trying to sort everything out, without any tussle at all. Maybe that would come later.

She shook his hand and showed him out, feeling lucky in comparison to the poor person he was going on to see. When she'd shut the door behind him, she stood in the hall, looking around at the blackened walls. Hanging over the stairs was the tapestry they'd bought on their honeymoon. It had faded over time, despite being behind glass, but they had treasured it, along with the memories. She took it down, revealing one clean rectangle, almost like a window of light. She took it into the kitchen and wiped it down, hoping to see that she could save it. Her heart sank, as she saw the smoke had seeped its way behind the glass, and the fabric was smeared with black, its beautiful colours hidden, as if behind a cloak of coal dust. She took it to the garage and placed it against the back wall. She knew she should probably leave it for the recovery team to deal with, but they wouldn't know its value to her, and there was no material value she could put on it. If she left it here, she could still come to look at it now and then, even if it were no longer perfect.

She was now determined to look under the stairs before anyone could dispose of anything else she held dear. She ducked under the return, reached past the bookcase, and pulled out the wicker hamper that had been living in the shadows of the lowest part of the under-stairs cupboard for so long. She couldn't remember what was in it now, only that it had once been in the loft, before they'd attempted, and abandoned, a clear-out of detritus that had accumulated from the time when the children were small.

The hamper was heavy. Not daring to lift it, she slid it across the floor towards the kitchen, where she grabbed a chair and sat herself in the doorway. She lifted the lid and recognised, immediately, the packets of old photographs from years ago. There were also some old cables and some floppy discs, that must have been a good few years old. She didn't think she even had a way of reading them anymore. In a little box, however, she discovered a couple of memory sticks, and she was intrigued. Why would James have put memory sticks in here? Surely, they would have been stored in the study? Maybe he didn't want to write over whatever was on them.

Feeling like Miss Marple, Nancy booted up her laptop, wondering what she would discover, and imagining James to have hidden something she was not supposed to find.

Unlike Miss Marple, as soon as she told the laptop to open the files on the memory stick, she was filled with delight, not suspicion. Well, well! The equivalent of holiday snaps was here! He must have backed them up, to make sure they didn't lose them, if the computer broke down. She opened the folder labelled "Madeira 2017". That was the first Christmas after James had retired, and they'd decided to try a week in the sun in the middle of winter. As she opened the photos, one by one, she was lost in the memories, and she so wished she could turn around and share them with him.

"Oh look!" she would have said. "There's that cable car you got me to climb into. I've never been so scared in my life as I was on that!" Never as scared, until last night, when so many of her precious ones were under her roof, in danger. She would rather be back on that cable car than have anything harm one hair on their heads. It dawned on her that part of her relief at them going was that they would be safer elsewhere.

She turned back to the photographs, and there he was. James was smiling at her, the sunshine making the peak of his cap shadow his face, with only his mouth clearly visible. There was James by the giant Santa Claus in the centre of Funchal, with locals in national costume dancing nearby. There was James tucking into his meal in the restaurant they'd visited twice, because it was so good. And there they were together, standing on a glass platform that jutted out across the sea, when a fellow passenger on the trip had offered to take a snap of both of them. She hated having her photograph taken, and she avoided it whenever she could, but she was glad she'd let that happen. Maybe she could get it printed out. Unlike some of her friends, she had few photographs on show, because James hadn't been keen, and they did cause more dusting. She'd kept some on display in the dining room, where he didn't have to see them all the time, but she had to be very selective. Now, she realised, she could have as many as she liked on show, and no-one would complain. It shocked her that she felt pleased about that. Any relationship, however good, involved compromise, and now she didn't need to compromise any more. How strange that felt!

By the time she'd trawled her way through the rest of the photographs on the stick, the dark was descending around her, and she realised she needed some light. She knew there was no rational explanation, but she wanted lights on all over the house. There had been no more messages, no more pieces of paper through the door, since everyone had gone, and she would have liked to believe that whoever it was had done their worst and made their point, whatever that point was meant to be.

She dragged the hamper into the study, where it would be safe. She wanted to be sure that she could go through everything later, when she had the energy. There were memories in these things, and if she couldn't share any more of her life with him, she wanted to preserve the images they'd made together. It was strange. She'd lived with the man for so many years yet ask her to draw his face and she would not know where to start. How much had she really noticed it, rather than just recognised its familiarity in their everyday lives? When she looked at the photographs, she noticed the mole in the centre of his right cheek, but she'd never studied it, when it was there before her. She noticed how he stood, in every photo, with one foot rested on the other, as he leant on something or someone. Did he always do that? Had he needed to do that, and she'd never noticed? She'd often complained that he paid her no compliments, when she dressed up to go out, and he certainly wouldn't have registered her wearing the same jeans day after day. She now thought maybe she'd been just as selective about what she saw in him. His lopsided grin had been one of the things she'd loved about him when they first met, and her eyes responded to its presence without her brain analysing where his wrinkles were or how his sunhat always tilted in the same direction.

She'd better report in, she realised, or Poppy would think she'd been hit over the head or fallen down the stairs. Better make the call before her supper was ready, or she might sit down and fall asleep.

"Hi Mum! You OK today? Did the loss adjuster come?"

"I'm fine, Poppy. Yes, he came. There'll be someone coming soon, to sort out the mess. What about your end?" *Keep it vague*, she thought. *Don't pry.*

"I've had a heart-to-heart with Daisy, Mum. I don't know what you said to her, but she tells me she's going to deal with things differently now. Tim's back home, at least temporarily, and when Daisy goes to her friend's for a sleepover, we're going to sit down and talk. I don't know how I feel right now, other than wanting to throw him out and punish him, and he knows he's treading on thin ice. We'll see. Have you heard anything from Jake?"

"Well actually, he sent me a text while the loss adjuster was here, but I've only just read it. It's brief, as you'd expect from Jake. He's saying nothing about anything much, other than the fact that he got back safely, and lectures have started. He has said he's somewhere up here for a friend's birthday party at the week-end, so he's going to come back to check on me. Goodness knows why!"

"Because you're his Nana Boo, and he loves you?" Poppy laughed. "He's turning into a good man, my son. If he's coming this week-end, I'll leave it till the following week, then, so that we don't all descend at once. I'll get him to give me a report!"

Nancy laughed, but she felt herself forcing it. She didn't want a fuss. She was quite capable of carrying on as she had been, before all this silly nonsense had started, and she hadn't suddenly aged ten years in as many days. She knew they meant well, but she also knew they would wear themselves out, travelling back and forth, and they couldn't keep it up without starting to resent it. The last thing she wanted was to be a burden.

They started to say their goodbyes, with Poppy extracting a promise that Nancy would lock the doors and saying it was her turn to phone tomorrow.

"Look, why don't you leave it a day, Poppy? Then I might have something to tell you about when the recovery team is coming. I'll phone you, if there's a problem, and you can assume that no news is good news for a day or two."

"If you're sure, Mum."

"I am. Now go and have some evening. I'm sure you've got a pile of marking to do."

The call ended, Nancy went back to the photos and spent the rest of the evening lost in memories of good times and sunshine. There was Venice, in all its glory, filmed on the video camera as they rode up the Grand Canal. She'd fallen in love with Venice, and they'd become experts at riding the vaporetti, to get from place to place. There was a photo of the glass on Murano; she still had the little vase they had bought as a souvenir. There was St Mark's Square, with all the hawkers driving them mad with their pestering. She'd been very glad she'd done her research before they went, because they might have sat down at one of the white-cloth-covered tables and ended up with a bill, had she not known to avoid it. And there was Rome, on a whistle-stop tour, with the Pope appearing outside the Vatican. She'd never forgotten the magic of the Sistine Chapel, where the tourists were expected to file through in respectful silence. She could feel her heart beating with the remembered excitement. She could re-live, in her imagination, touring Scotland with the old tent, in the rain, or basking in sunshine in Cornwall. She could feel the smile on her face, as if she were back in the past.

She suddenly realised how late it was, and thought she'd better get to bed, in case someone turned up to clear the mess early in the morning. She closed the folders on the memory stick, extracted it, and turned off the laptop. For a while, she'd been able to forget the fire, forget the messages, forget that James had gone. She carefully stowed the memory stick back in the hamper.

She knew she'd locked the back door earlier, and the front door had been kept shut and locked, but she had to go round again, checking every door and every window, to make sure all was secure. She checked the tape that had been put over the letter box, so that nothing else could come through it. She told herself everything was shut. It was all right. No-one was going to come. She knew it was true, but she struggled to convince herself that she was safe, as she turned out lights downstairs and went to bed. She left the landing light on, just because.

Chapter 23: Fred and Janet; Jake

"Fred, come here! Take a look at this!" Janet pulled at the curtains, giving Fred a better view.

"What? What are you on about, Jan?" He was irritated at being made to move when he'd just made himself comfortable.

"Quick! Look! That awful man across the road. He's packing his car, going somewhere."

"Not before time, if you ask me. Good job he cleared up that mess out there! As if he didn't make enough noise creating it, he made another racket piling it into bin bags, and I bet the dustmen don't take it all. He needs to get it to the tip, not leave it all in the front garden, so that we all have to look at it. It's like a slum over there! Disgraceful behaviour!" Fred tutted and went back to his newspaper, sitting in his favourite armchair, facing the window obscured by Janet's ample frame.

"Never a dull moment lately, is there? I've never known it to be so traumatic, living here!"

Janet clutched her duster, as she wiped it round the window frame. The car outside number 10 screeched its way off the drive, spun itself round and sped off. She was almost disappointed to see an end to the action.

To her amazement, she didn't have to be disappointed for long. An hour later, just as she brought the tray of tea and biscuits into the lounge, where Fred was now engrossed in the grand prix, lo and behold, another car drew up. She placed the tray on the coffee table, which reflected her surprise back at her.

"Well! Will you look at that, Fred!"

"What now? Can't a man have a bit of peace on a Sunday morning? I want to see the end of the race!"

"She's back!"

"Who's back?"

"She is. That woman. So, he's gone and she's back." She mused, as she watched the woman take what looked like a very light case to the front door and let herself in.

"That could be fireworks, then, if he comes back and finds her there. We'll have to keep a watch, make sure nothing terrible happens." Fred's self-satisfied chin descended onto his chest. "Good job the police have been round, if you ask me."

"I might have to pop over to Nancy later, to collect my casserole dish. I hope she enjoyed the meal, but I could do with the dish for tomorrow's dinner." Janet convinced herself, easily enough, that it was vital.

"Righto." Fred put an end to conversation, as he turned up the volume and the cars roared round the track. "Come on!" he shouted at the driver he knew should win.

As he'd promised, Jake had returned to see Nancy, to make sure she was all right. He'd arrived early that morning, much to her surprise, though he looked as if he'd hardly slept. Student parties, she remembered, were not ones that offered much opportunity to do anything but crash out on someone's floor. Somehow, when you were young, you could sleep almost anywhere, and James had begun to perfect the art again in his sixties, but Nancy needed a comfortable bed. She'd ushered Jake in and plied him with coffee, strong, as he liked it. She was relieved that he'd walked the half mile from the station, instead of driving when he was so obviously tired.

He looked round the hall, taking in, for the first time, just what a mess it was. It had only been a small fire, but the smoke seemed to have got everywhere. As he sat at the kitchen table, eating a roast dinner Nancy had insisted on cooking for him, but which he   didn't have much stomach for enjoying, he thought again how lucky they had all been. It didn't look as if someone had meant to torch the whole house, just to frighten someone, but it seemed twisted and cruel, especially when it was a pensioner living alone. He was glad the police were now involved in trying to track down who had done it, but he knew the statistics. He'd read that only ten percent of all arson cases result in an arrest, and only one percent of all arsonists are convicted of the crime. He didn't want to dampen Nancy's hopes, but he didn't think it very likely that the culprit would be brought to justice, and while he, or she, was still out there, Nana Boo might still be in danger. Cassie had done some more research, and she'd made the link, now between Nana Boo's name and the last message.

"Do you know," she'd informed him during the week, "that in Canada and part of the States, there's a taunt that children use. If they're chasing someone they might shout 'Nana-Nana Boo-Boo, stick your head in doodoo', so it's in the urban dictionary, and there's even a song on YouTube with the words in it? Amazing! You didn't know what you were doing, when you gave her that nickname, did you?"

"OMG! I've never heard of that before!" he'd exclaimed, feeling yet another burst of guilt for his actions. But maybe, he consoled himself, this meant it was not personal. Maybe it was just a taunt, and not a deliberate use of her name.

Nancy assured Jake that she was all right, and there had been no more messages. She showed him what she'd been rescuing and told him what the investigator had taken away. He'd already been contacted and asked for a statement, so he told her he would get that done in the next couple of days. They had also contacted Poppy, apparently, so they were piecing things together. He wanted to make sure he hadn't forgotten anything important, so they ran through what he'd seen and heard. He knew he didn't register much, when Nancy had woken him up, because it was such a shock, but at least he knew exactly what he'd heard on the answerphone, and what she'd shown him, when she found the note.

"It's like something out of an Agatha Christie novel, or like 'Death in Paradise' on the television, isn't it, Nana? We need some clever spark to work it all out, gather everyone together, and tell us who did it and why!"

"That would be wonderful, Jake!" Nancy loved how this boy could bring a smile to her face, even in the midst of all this stress.

"Is there anything I can do for you while I'm here, Nana? I know we can't clear up, but if you need help with shifting anything you want to save, I'll do it."

"No, it's OK, thanks, Jake. It's been lovely to have your company for a few hours. There is one thing you could do for me, though. You see that package over there, on the telephone table? It's a bit smoky, but it's not mine, so I can't let them throw it away. Would you mind popping it across the road for me? I took it in before all of this lot started, and with everything that's happened I forgot about it, but it needs to go to the right house."

"Of course I will." Jake picked up the parcel. Nana gave him a paper towel, to get rid of the worst of the smoke deposits and told him not to hold it next to his clothes.

He set off across the road, wondering who had cleared up the pile of things that had been in the garden. He was a bit apprehensive about approaching the house, wondering if there was someone in there with a screw loose, but he didn't want Nancy to do it, either.

He rang the doorbell, softly at first, almost hoping no-one was in. He rang it again, and footsteps pattered down the stairs. As the door opened, he felt his mouth open with astonishment.

"You!" was all he could manage, as he stared at her face.

"Well yes, it's me. Who... " she stopped in mid-sentence, the figure in front of her suddenly disarmingly familiar. She paled. "What do you want?"

Jake shoved the package into her hands, wanting to run away as fast as he could, but his feet were rooted to the spot. "This was at my nan's house. She asked me to get it to you. Apparently, she took it in for you a few days ago."

She clutched the package, a black smudge appearing on the sleeve of her jumper.

"Your nan. But you're...."

"Yes. I'm Jake Castleford, and you're the woman I saw my father with in London, aren't you? You're the one who's been causing havoc in my family." The bitterness was something he couldn't conceal. He didn't want to be standing here, but somehow, he couldn't leave.

She felt the heat rising from her neck, and she knew she was turning scarlet. She wanted to cry. "So, you're his son? You know we only saw each other a few times, then, don't you? It's over, Jake. It's over. I know it should never have happened, but I was so unhappy, and he was kind. He's a good man, your dad. He loves all of you."

"What are you doing here? Why did I see you at Harlow Carr?"

"I live here. We've been renting this house, my partner and me. When you saw me, I was staying with a friend. It's a long story." She looked down at the package, wiping a finger across the surface and staring at the black deposit. She looked inquisitively at him.

"There was a fire. Someone tried to burn my nan's house down. You're lucky that survived. Some nasty piece of work has been leaving her messages, death threats in nursery rhymes, and then decided to torch the house in the middle of the night."

"We haven't lived here long, so I don't know her very well. Is she OK?"

"No thanks to whoever did it, but yes. She's OK." His brain was whizzing, and he stilled it with determination. "Does my father know you live here?"

"No. He only knows I live in Yorkshire. We... we didn't exchange addresses, only telephone numbers. I've just come to collect some of my things, then I'll be gone."

"Good, because I never want to see you again."

Jake spun round and marched across the road. He could feel his heart pounding in his chest, the anger moving to his hands, that had formed clenched fists. How could SHE be living across the road from Nana, and none of them know?

By the time he got through the door, he'd managed to control himself. He took a deep breath, put on his smile, and called out, "All done, Nana. I gave it to the woman who was there."

"Oh! She's back, is she?"

"She says she's collecting some of her things. Apparently, she's leaving for good, so we got the parcel to her just in time."

"Right. They seemed a nice young couple until the other day, but I don't know them to talk to, other than an occasional "hello", and they seem to have had their own crisis. The whole close will know about that! Anyway, I'm glad that's out of the way. Thanks, Jake."

"I'd better get going, then. Got to catch the train. Are you sure you'll be OK, Nana?"

"Yes, yes. I'll be fine, Jake. You take care now and get down to work. You can't afford to waste this last year!"

"No, I know. I'll get there! See you soon, then." He planted a kiss on Nancy's cheek, as she hugged him, and strode down the road towards the station. "*I've done it again,*" he thought to himself. "*I didn't tell her who was living in her street, did I? I don't know whether I should have done or not, but maybe it's best if she doesn't know.*"

He pulled out his phone and sent a text to Poppy.

Jake Castleford to Poppy Castleford
Been to Nana's. She's OK. Talk later. On my way to catch the train.

Job done, he set about answering messages from his friends that had pinged their way to his phone while he'd been at Nancy's house. It had taken quite a bit of control not to look at them, as his teenage self would have done, but for a few brief hours he'd tried to be the adult his mother needed him to be. He'd be falling into the Union Bar when he got back, ready for a drink and some company of his own age.

Chapter 24: Nancy

Nancy watched as the recovery company piled things in the front garden, to be taken away. She was glad there hadn't been more damage, but she wasn't looking forward to having to replace what they decided was to go. It was astonishing, their willingness to throw things away. She heard them ripping up the carpet, taking down the curtains, clearing the shelves of books that couldn't possibly be cleaned. She was very glad she'd rescued the hamper because it would have been tossed unceremoniously onto the pile. And then there was the hall table. Oh, she'd desperately hoped they would just clean it! It had seen better days, but it was one of the few things she'd that had belonged to her mother, and she knew she could never replace it. Its old, barley-twist legs and inlaid top had been so familiar for so many years, but the flames had obviously licked the feet and stained the legs, and now, after standing there so proudly for so many years, it was condemned. Out it went, smashed onto the gravel as if worthless, added to the lists on pink sheets that were to be the only record of it ever having existed.

The young woman in charge of clearing things out was pleasant enough, with a jolly smile and a willingness to literally get her hands dirty. She did bring to Nancy the brass letter rack that had sat on the table in case it had sentimental value. It looked old, and it was, but Nancy didn't have the heart to tell her it had come from a junk shop down by the river.

Agitated by the noise, Tommy Tucker screeched and called over and over again, "Gissakiss", until Nancy wanted to throttle him. He hadn't been the same since the fire when they had completely forgotten about him in their rush to get out of the house. Luckily, the smoke had done no damage in the lounge, so he'd survived, but it had occurred to Nancy, eventually, that he might have died of night fright, which seemed to kill some budgies. They could feel fear, but she didn't think their sense of smell was very good, so maybe he hadn't picked up the smell of the burning. What seemed to spook him was strange noises, and he'd certainly had plenty of those. Maybe he would have screeched a different word, if he'd ever learnt more from her, but that was a lost cause now, and "Gissakiss" or "Watcha Tommy" was all they were going to get, whether he meant that or not. At least he seemed to have dropped "Rockabye" and "Georgie Porgie", much to Nancy's relief.

As she made herself a pot of tea, needing something to comfort her, the phone made her jump. She still couldn't shake off the feeling that every call was going to be another ridiculous rhyme, part of an unsolved riddle. On the contrary, this time it was the fire investigator.

"Mrs Brewer, I just thought I'd update you on where we are with your fire," he said, as if she owned it, somehow. She wanted to say, "It wasn't mine; it was someone else's, to be accurate," but she stopped herself. It was no time to be churlish when he was just doing his job.

"Thank you. That's kind of you. I have people here right now, clearing out anything that was damaged."

"Right. Well look, we know that this fire was started deliberately, and your insurance company will be told that, and we need to try to find out who did it. Could I come to have another chat with you this afternoon? Would that be convenient?"

"Yes, of course. Would about two be all right?"

"Two it is, then, Mrs Brewer. It shouldn't take long. I just need to check a few facts with you."

Nancy's first reaction was to be pleased that someone was doing something, but as she ended the call, she began to think about the words "check a few facts". Did they think she did it herself, for the insurance money? People did that, it seemed. As she drank her tea, she found she wasn't feeling as welcoming as she might.

The investigator found his way to the front door, through the debris, and rang the doorbell. Nancy approached from the kitchen and told him to come round to the back, where it would be easier to get in. As they shook hands, she realised she hadn't fully registered his appearance at their first meeting, when she was still raw from the shock of the fire. He had the bearing of someone used to authority, and she'd thought him younger than he was. He held his file under his arm, and his immaculately groomed hair topped a generous smile and clear grey eyes that were obviously taking in every detail of where he was. Without the protective clothing, she saw the pressed trousers and tailored blazer, with shoes that shone as if he'd been in the army. As fast as he was noticing her, and judging her to be astute, she was judging him to be worthy of a discussion.

He had, of course, seen her before, but he was struck by the fact that he was not dealing with a fragile old lady here. She was probably just about old enough to be his mother, and his mother was not to be messed with. He would choose his words carefully.

"Hello again, Mrs Brewer. I wondered if I could just have a chat about your statement, to see whether there's anything else you could add that might be helpful. Is that OK?" He turned on his most friendly smile, hoping to put her at her ease.

"Yes, of course. Please sit down. The kitchen table is probably the easiest place to be. You can put your file on it." She spoke briskly, making him feel as if he were back in school. He took a seat and opened the file.

"Would you like a cup of tea or coffee before we start?" she asked.

"No, I'm fine thanks."

"Right. What do you want to know then, Mr Henson?"

So, she'd remembered his name, he told himself. Nothing wrong with her memory, then.

"When I was last here, my colleague and I listened to the answerphone recording, and my colleague recorded it on a department phone, so that we could listen to it again, when we got back to the office. It does seem strange that it was talking about Georgie Porgie, Mrs Brewer, not a woman, but a man. Had that occurred to you?"

He could see the impact of his question.

"Well, I have to be honest." She shook her head. "I haven't really thought beyond the impact of the call itself. Is that important, do you think, Mr Henson? The whole thing was so strange that I couldn't get my head round what was being targeted." Her fixed eyes told him more than her words. However much she tried to brush it aside, it had unnerved her, and this point had just struck her.

"Can we go back to the first message, the one you deleted?"

"Yes. That one took us by surprise when we got in."

"We? That's you and your grandson, I presume?"

"Yes. Jake had only been here since the previous day, and we'd had a lovely outing to Harlow Carr garden, and that spoilt it, as soon as we came through the door. I wished I hadn't bothered to check the message, but it was unusual, you see, and I thought it might be my daughter, and urgent."

"Yes, I see. And that was 'Rockabye Baby'? Was it just the first line, first verse, or more, Mrs Brewer?" He didn't want to be accused of leading questions, but he knew he had to press this point. He tried to keep his face expressionless, his head slightly tilted on one side, as if he were very open to answers of any kind.

"It went as far as the bough breaking and the cradle and baby falling," recalled Nancy. "I wondered why someone was singing a lullaby down the

169

phone. I thought maybe someone had got the wrong number, and I didn't think it that malevolent. After all, it's something we sing to, and with, small children, isn't it?"

"Exactly. I gather that you've researched the origin yourself now, Mrs Brewer, as one of our officers has done. If we look at it from that perspective, it's not quite so pleasant, is it?" He allowed himself to look puzzled, hoping she had got there before him, drawn the conclusion he wanted her to draw. "It seems it didn't go on to the last verse, which tells the baby not to fear, because mother is near. It stopped at the unpleasant idea of the cradle falling, the baby being harmed, didn't it?"

"Yes, it did. I wonder why we still put it in nursery rhyme books, when it's aimed at killing a Catholic baby! It doesn't exactly fit with equality and the twenty-first century, does it?"

He nodded in agreement. "The note that said 'Three Blind Mice' said nothing else, so perhaps by then you were meant to work out the rest of the rhyme. As I'm sure you know, this was yet another allusion to the battle between Catholicism and Protestants, and again about killing off the enemy. When we put these messages together, Mrs Brewer, it begins to sound as if someone was not playing games, at least not pleasant games." He knew he was in danger of heightening her sense of continued threat, but he had to dig deeper.

"Could we just clarify, did you have any messages at all before your grandson arrived?"

Nancy's shocked face indicated that she'd never considered this relevant. "Well, no. I didn't, but surely that was just a coincidence?"

"We have to consider all possibilities, don't we? We know it was a man's voice, but not one you recognise. We know it was threatening someone in this house. When it began, there were just the two of you here, weren't there?"

"Yes."

"So, we can eliminate the possibility that anyone else in the family was a target. Unless someone had got the wrong house and the wrong phone number, it had to be aimed at you... or your grandson. Wouldn't you agree?"

"I suppose you're right, but I can't see why Jake would be a target, any more than I can see why I would be one!"

"Had he upset someone over a woman, maybe, Mrs Brewer?"

"No. Jake doesn't have a girlfriend, as far as I know. He did have a sweetheart from his school days, but that relationship fell apart last year, as they were at different universities, and they drifted apart, if what my daughter told me is right. He has a circle of close friends, I understand. The only thing worrying him, when he drove up here, was that his father had been having an affair, and he'd found out."

"He drove up here, Mrs Brewer? He's twenty, isn't he? Could he have antagonised anyone with his car, been involved in an accident and not owned up, anything like that?"

"Well, no, I don't think so. He's only just got the car. His dad gave it to him, so he's looking after it. He parked very carefully, when we went out."

"What kind of car does he have, Mrs Brewer? Not a typical student car, then?"

"No, but it's a few years old, so my son-in-law is going to replace it. You can't tell how old it is, because it's in very good condition, and it's still got his personal number plates on it, so it's probably still technically owned by him. It's an Audi something."

"Do you happen to remember the number plate, Mrs Brewer?"

"That's easy. I can't remember the first bit, but I know it has 40 TJC in it. He bought it when he was forty, and it had his initials on it."

"I see. Easily recognised, then. He wasn't here when the fire broke out, was he?

"No. He'd left."

171

"But Jake was, and the car was. You said your son-in-law had been having an affair, Mrs Brewer. Do you have any idea with whom?"

"No, I'm afraid I don't. I try not to poke my nose into my daughter's business further than would be welcome, Mr Henson. When Tim was here, I gathered that the affair was over, but he was not likely to be forgiven any time soon, however sorry he was. When he has betrayed my daughter's trust, it is best if I leave her to decide what to do, because I could be wrong for supporting reconciliation, if that's not what she wants, and just as wrong for condemning him, if she decides to take him back."

Nancy was beginning to see where this was going, but he knew he wasn't going to get any more out of her.

"If you need any more detail, I think you'd better ask Poppy. You've got her statement and contact details, I presume?"

"Yes. I'll do that. I think that's all for now, Mrs Brewer. I'll leave you in peace. Oh - one last question. Have there been any more messages since the fire?"

"No. They seem to have stopped, thank goodness. Maybe someone realised they had gone too far!"

"I see. So, none while you have been on your own at all, Mrs Brewer. Well take care now and thank you for your time."

He rose to leave, shaking her hand and closing his file with a very deliberate action, as if he was thinking as carefully as he moved.

As he left, Nancy felt herself suddenly overwhelmed with tiredness. She must have tensed up far more than she realised. *He knew his stuff*, she decided, as she poured herself a glass of wine. He'd got her thinking, that was for sure, with his questions. He was right - she'd had no messages before Jake came, and none since he and the others had left. She didn't want to think about the implications of that.

Chapter 25: Felicity

Well, I think I've got everything I came for now. It was lucky that Lisa tipped me off that he's had to go to Scotland for a couple of days. At least I've been able to clear out my wardrobe and collect my jewellery. I'll never be able to take everything that's mine, but I don't care now. I'm past that. Most of the furniture was his, anyway. I should never have given up my flat and agreed to move in with him. Big mistake. He seemed so charming when we first met, though Lisa did try to warn me about people you meet on these dating sites. You think you know how to suss them out, don't you? Slipped up there, didn't I? Fine, when we were just going out on dates, and very persuasive. I believed him, when he said he and his wife had been blissfully happy, but I'm not so sure now. I'm not so sure she's even dead. If she discovered the other side of his character, like I have, when he doesn't get his own way, she probably ran for the hills! I thought he was the answer to my prayers. He seemed to have plenty of money, and he said he wanted to look after me. I thought all my money struggles were well and truly over.

I suppose I can't entirely blame him for losing it when he found out about Tim. But maybe I wouldn't have found Tim's kindness quite so special if he'd been kinder himself. Maybe I should have seen the signs, early on, but I just thought he was a bit fussy in restaurants, because he was paying for the meals. I never dreamt he would start to be fussy about what

I did, what I wore, who I went out with. If he'd had his way, I'd have dropped Lisa, and she's been my best friend for years! No way! You could tell he was jealous of our friendship, the way he behaved when she came round. She said he gave her the creeps, the way he seemed to keep appearing, as if he wanted to hear every word we said. I didn't really notice, because he lived here, after all, but after she commented, I began to notice how he did pop up every time I was on the phone, or whenever someone came to the door. He hated it if I phoned my sister, even though she's across the other side of the world and wasn't about to drop in. I told him she was looking forward to meeting him some time, when she came over, or if we went over there. I thought he'd be excited at the thought of a trip to New Zealand, but he seemed exactly the opposite.

And then he started on the meals, what he did and didn't want to eat. I thought I'd please him, and cook his favourites, but after a while there was always something wrong with them. I never seemed to be able to quite get it right, never quite as good a cook as his wife had been. He went off in a strop one night, just because his steak was a little bit the wrong side of rare! He had another strop when I wore a top he thought was revealing - made me go back upstairs and change before we went out. We were only going to the coast for the day, so I wanted something cool, but I got the impression he'd like me dressed up like a nun, in case there were any men around. Funny that, because he seemed to like the way I dressed before I lived with him. He grabbed my wrist that day, hard, and left a red mark.

It was a few days later that he slapped me when I'd been out with Lisa and got home late. Called me a slut for being out on the streets in the evening, when we'd only been in the pub on a girls' night out! When I saw that look in his eyes, I knew he frightened me. The anger in his face completely distorted it, like something out of a horror film. He said he was sorry, it wouldn't happen again, and I wanted to believe him. But then there was the wedding reception… That night, I knew he would do it again, and again, and somehow it was always my fault. I'd heard about the pattern.

Didn't expect it to be me that was caught up in it. I thought I could judge people; I did it all the time at work. I could have started to believe it was all my fault, if I'd stayed much longer, if it hadn't been for meeting Tim. Tim made me realise things could be different, made me stronger. I was planning to leave, anyway, when he found out. I was lucky. He could've just hit me, but he went to the bathroom first. He would've done, when he came back. He would've got beyond the pure rage and been calculating how to make me believe I had provoked him. That's how it started, with words first, so that I knew it was coming. I think he could have killed me. Lisa was right.

He took control of the money when we moved in here. Said I didn't need to worry about it. Luckily, I was a bit more protective of my money than I was of myself! That was one thing I was wary of, after all those stories of people being conned. I didn't think he would con me, but I didn't tell him how much I had in my savings account, and he didn't get his hands on that. He persuaded me to have a joint account, and I can see that he's cleared that out, but haha, Mister Clever! You didn't get as much as you might have done! I've still got my own bank account, and my salary goes in that, so all he got in the joint account is what I transfer into it each month. And then there's the money Tim gave me when I told him I needed to escape. I knew he would want to help. I'm a survivor, and I'll do what it takes to survive. I knew we were going nowhere, when he was married, but he served his purpose. The decent men all seem to be taken, so I have to take what I can, when I can.

I'm never coming back here. I'll just have a last look around, to make sure there's nothing else I need to cram into the car. I can't stay at Lisa's, because he'll find me, but at least I've got a hotel room till I can find a decent flat. Let's check the wardrobe. Done. What about these drawers? He keeps his stuff in these, but I wouldn't put it past him to have something of mine in there, too.

What the heck? He's got a whole wad of papers here, in his sock drawer. What's this lot? I'll sit on the edge of the bed, I think, and have a look. Well, that's a photo he's printed out. What? It's a car. Wait a minute — it's Tim's car outside his London flat. How did he get that? And what's this? A whole load of print-outs of stuff he's found on the web, by the looks of it. But why would he put it in his sock drawer? It seems to be something about nursery rhymes. I think he's completely lost it now! That's weird! I'd better shove it back, in case he realises I've seen it.

Oh! I'm taking that photo frame as well. That was a present from my sister. I don't want the photo of us that's in it, but he's not having the frame. He'd probably smash it, anyway.

Right. I think that's it. I could've done without Tim's son turning up on the doorstep, and I had no idea his mother-in-law was the woman across the road. I don't want to hang about to hear what she thinks of me! At least the package is useful, though. Much to Chas's disgust, I'd ordered a new iPad, because my other one is old now. If it had come any earlier, it would probably have ended up smashed, like so much else! The credit card's in his name, so he can pay for it. Serves him right!

Goodbye, house! Good riddance!

"Well, let's hope that's the end of that, Fred!"

"What?"

"Well, it feels as if this close has been turned into a rubbish dump lately, doesn't it? First young fella-me-lad over the road throwing stuff out of windows, then all that stuff piled in Nancy's front garden, to be got rid of after the fire! It looks like a run-down council estate!"

"Hmm." Fred folded his paper carefully and placed it on the coffee table.

"What do you mean, 'hmmm'?"

"Of course, you're right, dear, and it does seem such a waste of good stuff, when it all goes in a tip."

"Yes, it does, and such a pity, when all your personal possessions are on display to the world! Did you see all those books Nancy had to part with? I suppose it will mean a bit less dusting, though? Such a pity about that lovely hall table! It's a shame they couldn't have saved that."

"Yes. I did go and have a look at it, Janet, to see if it could be saved. I don't like waste, and I can't see why so much has to go to landfill, just because a bit of smoke has got into it. I did manage to save one thing, though." Fred kept his eyes sheepishly on his lap.

"Oh really? What?" Janet could think of nothing they would want to bring into the house. She didn't want any of the muck brought in, making her more work. She'd seen the state of the carpet – nice, expensive carpet, but black all over it.

Fred levered himself up and went to the back door. "Come and see," he called.

Intrigued, Janet followed him, and there, sitting in the back porch, was his reclaimed treasure.

"The bell!" exclaimed Janet. "Oh Fred! That'll be so useful, when you're down in the shed and your dinner's ready, won't it?"

"Yes. A bit of Brasso, and it'll come up a treat. Hopefully, Nancy will get a new one, so she doesn't need the one they've thrown away."

The laptop would take a little longer. He couldn't just leave it there, on the street, to be piled in the skip with everything else that flew out of the window of number ten, when it might be repaired. The screen was cracked, but it seemed to have some life left in it yet. Fred had never had his own laptop before, just his tablet, and he was avidly looking forward to learning how to use it. He'd be able to record his seeds on it and keep a diary for the residents' committee he was going to set up. He would, of course, chair it himself. Maybe the new people would want to get involved in keeping the close neat and tidy, keeping an eye on things. There'd been so many strangers in the close in recent weeks, it was beginning to feel less safe than it used to be. At least the workmen had all gone, and all that to-ing and froing had stopped, but you never knew who might have been sizing them all up, to see who to take advantage of. You had to be on your guard, always.

Chapter 26: Poppy

"Hi, Mum. How are you doing?"

"Hello, my love. I'm fine. I had a surprise visit from the investigator yesterday, and he's got me thinking. Bright spark, that man."

"Is he? What did he have to say?"

"Well, he was asking questions more than telling me anything, but in a roundabout way, he did tell me something."

"That's a bit of a riddle, Mum!" Poppy laughed, making no sense at all of her mother's account.

"Yes, well it does seem as if the messages were a bit of a riddle, Poppy. You know, he got me to realise that I didn't have any messages before Jake came, and I haven't had any since you all went. He also asked about the car registration. It's beginning to sound as if he's linking the messages to someone wanting to frighten someone in the family, but not necessarily me. Jake hasn't got any enemies, has he?"

"No, of course he hasn't! He's a typical student, but he'd never do anything really bad, certainly not deliberately, and he wouldn't hurt a fly!"

"That's what I thought, but you know him better than I do. I see my grandson, who is always on his best behaviour with me. You see him when he's just being himself."

"Hmm. What was the importance of the car, Mum? Do you know?"

"No. He didn't say, but he wanted the registration number, and he seemed very interested in the fact that the car had belonged to Tim."

"Tim," Poppy muttered, almost to herself. "It was Tim's car. Mum, maybe it's something to do with Tim, not Jake!"

"That's what I was thinking, but I didn't like to suggest it myself. Is he back home, or is he still in London?"

"He's back here for now, Mum, but we'll see how things go. He is very sorry for what happened, and he promises it will never happen again — the classic lines, unfortunately. I don't know. I still love him, and he's the father of my children, but whether I can ever forgive him is another matter. Right now, he can stay in the spare room, so that he's here for Daisy, but all I can manage is to be civil. I'm too hurt, and it's too raw, to forgive, and even if I decide to give our marriage another go, I don't think I'll ever trust completely again. I hired a private investigator. Did I tell you that?"

"No. You didn't." *More secrets*, thought Nancy. How many more were there going to be?

"He seems to confirm that the affair had finished, but I've got him watching for a bit longer."

"Good. Don't be a pushover, Poppy. Tim has always seemed a lovely man, and I'm sure he loves you and the children, but once bitten, twice shy, eh?"

"Too true, Mum. Right, I'll talk to you tomorrow. Don't forget to lock up, will you?"

"Of course I won't! Give Daisy a hug from me. 'Bye."

Nancy shook her head, as she put down the phone. There it was again, that hint that she was getting old and might forget what she needed to do. She knew it was kindly meant, and all Poppy was guilty of was caring, but somehow, she had to hang on to her independent life. She was an intelligent woman, and she was only a few months older than she'd been when she and James had been a couple, when no-one assumed she was past it. Yes, she was a bit less agile than she'd been, and yes, she sometimes forgot things, but widowhood didn't equal dotage, and she had to cling to the knowledge that she was perfectly capable of living on her own, even if she felt lonely sometimes.

"Hello, Tommy Tucker," she said, as she prodded the cage in passing. "At least you don't think I'm any different, do you?"

"Gissakiss Tommy Tucker. Gissakiss!" the budgie squawked, its head on one side, as it moved back and forth on its perch. For the first time, she wondered whether the budgie was lonely, stuck in that cage all on his own.

"Oh, I do wish James hadn't said that in front of you," laughed Nancy. "You haven't got any answers for me, have you?"

Jason Mercury straightened his tie. It had been a tough week, and he knew he was going to have to give evidence in court the following day. He'd done it before, on many occasions, but he knew the defence lawyer, and he was in for a grilling. He swigged his coffee, hoping being up half the night preparing his notes was not going to show, as his secretary showed Poppy into his office.

"Good morning, Mrs Castleford!" he said as cheerily as he could muster, peering at her over the top of his glasses.

"He sounds like Mum's budgie chirping," thought Poppy, noticing the dark lines under his eyes.

"Good morning, Mr Mercury. I thought we should have a chat, as things have moved on, and I don't think I'm going to need your services anymore."

"Oh! Is that good news, Mrs Castleford, or have you decided to part amicably?"

"I'm not sure what the outcome will be yet, Mr Mercury, but I don't think it will be necessary for you to continue to track my husband's whereabouts. He is back home, though that may be temporary, and we are going to see where we go from here. He says the affair's over, and I'm inclined to believe him."

"I see. Well let me just fill you in on what we now have. You know most of it, but there has been an interesting twist in our investigations."

"Has there? What's that then? Don't tell me he's been up to something else I don't know about!"

"Not exactly, but you asked us to try to find out who the woman was, and we think we have."

"I'm not sure I want to know, to be honest, but fire away."

"As you know, she didn't appear at the flat again, but one of our investigators was detailed to track her down, and she has come up with something rather interesting. It seems the woman in the photograph here," he indicated, as he passed the photograph across the desk, "has recently taken up residence in London again."

"To be near Tim?"

"It would seem not, as they don't appear to have met any more. She took a trip to Yorkshire last week-end, and our investigator has unearthed her previous address, to which she seemed to go. Mrs Castleford, it is very strange, but she was living in the same street as your mother, with a partner who also seems to have left the house."

"What's the relevance of all of this, then?"

"Coincidences are often not coincidences, when they lead to unusual circumstances. Our investigator met some neighbours, walking a dog, and she posed as someone looking to buy a house in the area. They were very forthcoming, it seems, and full of pride in their environment. They went to great pains to say that the fire that had happened was not the kind of thing that usually took place there, because it was a very quiet, respectable area."

"Right. It is, actually. Where's all this leading?"

"Mrs Castleford, I may have a suspicious mind because I've been doing this job a long time, but have you considered the fact that the fire could have some connection to your husband's affair?"

Poppy felt her heart suddenly beating faster. "Ye Gods!" she exclaimed, part of her brain telling her that was not the thing to say in the presence of

Mercury and Mars. "I had not made the connection myself, but my mother was beginning to wonder whether his car was a link in a chain."

"I think you should pass the information I've given you to the police, Mrs Castleford, so that they have it as part of their investigation into the fire. It may be irrelevant, but you never know."

"Yes. Thank you, Mr Mercury. Can I point them in your direction if they need to talk to you?"

"Indeed. They may well want to do that, anyway."

Poppy's head was spinning, as she got up to go. She knew Jake couldn't be responsible for the fire, but Tim? "Thank you so much for your help," she managed, as she shook his thin hand. "Email me your bill, and I'll sort it out as quickly as possible. I hope I don't have to see you again, Mr Mercury, for the best of reasons."

He smiled at her with kindly understanding.

Chapter 27: Felicity and Tim

Felicity unpacked her car, piling her belongings into her new home and thinking she must sort out some of her clothes for the charity shop. They weren't all going to fit into this tiny space, where she had one double wardrobe, instead of two. Her shoes ended up in a pile, with no rack to put them on. She looked round at the sorry state of the room, which was in desperate need of decorating, despite the exorbitant cost of the flat. Right now, the faded wallpaper and curtains with the lining showing beneath them seemed a perfect reflection of how she felt. She'd been on a rollercoaster of a year, but all the joy had been bleached out of it by recent events, and she was going to find it hard to disguise her emotions, so raw and in need of healing time and space.

Tim had gone back to his wife. *No surprise there, then. Wasn't that what they usually did?* Hadn't she been told that? She wanted to see neither of the men that had caused her such misery, ever again. She was not sure she wanted to see any man ever again. She felt washed up, in her thirties, always the bridesmaid and never the bride.

As she put her things away in drawers, she thought about what she'd found in the house. The papers stuffed in the sock drawer bothered her, but she couldn't quite work out why they should, when they just seemed to be innocent children's nursery rhymes. But it was weird. She began to wonder whether she should have looked for any evidence of child abuse. *That couldn't be it, could it? Surely, even though he's a maniac when his temper was up, he's not a paedophile as well!* She told herself she would have spotted something. *No. He couldn't be. Did wives and partners always know? Maybe not.*

She started to wonder what Tim's life was like with his wife. She'd only seen her once, and that was before the affair had started. She seemed a bit up tight, but very nice. *A teacher, he said. Three children, he said. Three.* Was she ever going to have the chance to have even one? You needed a relationship to have children, and she wasn't going into another one for a long time. Tim seemed very proud of his children, and one of them was not that much younger than her. It was that one that had landed on her doorstep, out of the blue. The one that had seen them together in London, when he'd been there with his friend. He'd had real hatred in his eyes, when he'd delivered that parcel, and she thought he would probably have thrown it in a bin instead, if he hadn't been under orders from his grandmother. She couldn't blame him, when Tim had told him to keep quiet, and not to tell his mother.

As she pictured, in her mind, Jake delivering the parcel, she stopped folding her jumper in mid action. *What was it he said to her about the fire over the road? Someone had started it deliberately? Someone had been sending her messages? He said they were death threats, but he said something about them being in nursery rhymes. Nursery rhymes! He wouldn't, would he? Surely, he wouldn't go that far?*

She sat on the edge of the bed, not wanting to think what she was thinking. She rubbed her wrist, remembering the bruises, the shouting, the wanting his own way. She picked up her phone, and her fingers hovered indecisively over it. Then she dialled.

Tim didn't want to take the call. He could see who it was from, and he'd, so far, kept his resolve to show Poppy that he was genuinely sorry, that she was the one he loved, and he desperately wanted to make their marriage work. He didn't know how he was ever going to convince her that he would never be so stupid again, but he knew he had to. He wished he could turn back time, change the way that day had gone, but he knew that was just fantasy, and this was real life. He'd never meant to hurt anyone, and now he'd hurt all the people he cared most about, and he'd messed up Felicity's life, too. He'd been drawn to her sunny smile and her sadness that wiped it out, as she talked about her life. She seemed to have had such a tough deal, marrying young and her husband being killed in Afghanistan. He'd felt himself warming to her, but he was not prepared for the sudden, overwhelming need for her, after a meal that was intended just to keep her company on a night away on business. They hadn't been alone, that first evening; they'd been with three others, all men. Somehow, he'd ended up sitting next to this beautiful woman, whose eyes had captivated him across the meeting table, whose hair looked so soft he just wanted to touch it, and who quietly talked to him, while the others cracked jokes only men would enjoy. It seemed harmless enough, to offer to escort her back to the hotel. It was harmless, until he was faced with the impulse to kiss her, as he wished her good night. Oh, that kiss! It ran through his body, gripping his stomach muscles as if he were lifting a heavy weight.

They parted, both embarrassed by the passion they had just felt for someone they had only just met. He felt obliged to apologise, though she'd been as eager as he had. She'd looked down at her feet and told him not to apologise for making her happy.

At the next day's meeting, they'd avoided looking at each other, both unsure what had happened to them. But as they brushed past each other at the coffee break, he felt the tingling in his fingertips, like being out in the cold, and before long they were standing next to each other, as if pulled there by strong magnets. They'd talked again, and before he knew what he was doing, he was suggesting another meal, just the two of them, that evening, before they set off home. It was as if he was living in another time and space, the unreal world becoming the one he'd inhabited for so many years. He thought he could keep them separate, be two different people, but he realised he'd been kidding himself, especially when he saw her at the wedding, and Poppy was there, too. He'd hoped his loss of control had just been put down to the alcohol, but he knew it had dangerously loosened his tongue. He was no good at this double life. She'd pretended not to know him, and her partner had, fortunately, been at the bar, so he didn't see or hear anything. But Poppy did. He had to hope he'd been convincing in his excuses.

When she'd said it had to end, he knew she was right. Reality crept up on them, as they walked across town on a fresh and sunny day. They were lost in their cocoon, heading towards Camden Lock, when he saw, ahead of them, as if he'd come through a gate from another world, his son, strolling along with that friend of his with the mop of black hair and beard. He'd stopped, grabbing Felicity's arm, and hissed at her, "My son. That's Jake. We have to go."

Too late, he'd realised. Jake had seen them, and it was going to take some explaining. Back in the real world, he'd panicked and pleaded with Jake not to tell Poppy, not to hurt her.

"Hurt her? Don't you think you're doing that, Dad? What are you doing?"

Like stepping out of a fancy-dress costume, Tim had suddenly become his other self, wondering, indeed, what had he been doing. He loved his wife. He loved his children. He was not living in a fairy-tale, and he was in danger of losing everything that meant so much to him.

"Jake, I'm so sorry. It was a stupid mistake, and it's finished. It should never have happened. If you tell your mum, it will only cause upset she needn't have. I've learnt my lesson, I promise you."

Jake had looked daggers at him, and he felt he deserved every single blade.

The phone had switched to answerphone. He heard her voice, speaking to the machine.

"Tim. This is just to let you know the police may want to speak to you. I'm sorry. I won't contact you again, but I thought it only fair to warn you. They know about us. They know about my past. They may want to ask you a few questions. There is nothing to hide, and you have nothing to be afraid of. Just tell them the truth, all of it."

The police. What's all that about then? Tim could feel the stress making his breathing shallow, and he could hear his heart thumping through his ears. He had no idea why they would want to talk to him. Was Felicity all right? Had that brute of a partner of hers hurt her? He knew he mustn't let himself be drawn back in, and she didn't intend it, but he would prefer to stay out of temptation's way. It was all too much, this caring, like being caught in quicksand.

Chapter 28: Nancy

Nancy had steeled herself for what she had to do. It was time to go through the garage, to decide what she should try to get rid of. She'd given Ben the option of taking whatever he wanted, but he was not like his father; he was more interested in using his brains than his hands, and if he was going to create anything it would be on a screen. James had been a brilliant teacher, in her opinion, and he'd taken science to a new level at the school where he taught. He had a knack of grabbing the imagination of the children and taking it with him. They'd built rockets and let them fly across the grass pitches. He'd somehow got them interested in building their own robots, imitating Robot Wars in the playground. She wasn't going to have any use for his tools, and it was time to gather them up and let her friend Sally take them to a car boot sale, to sell in aid of the hospice. At least that way they would do some good.

She moved the car out, to make more room, and she'd just started to fill the wheelbarrow with a heavy drill, a sander, and other bits of electrical paraphernalia that she couldn't see herself ever using. Just the weight of some things was enough to make that impossible. She had her own toolbox in the utility room, full of things she could use, if she needed to.

Someone came up the side of the house and called out. "Mrs Brewer, are you there?"

She caught sight of a young woman, who looked vaguely familiar, craning her neck to see who was crashing about in the garage.

"Hello. Yes, I'm here. Can I help you?"

"Mrs Brewer, I work with Mr Henson. You may remember that I came with him, when we did the initial investigation of the site of the fire."

"Oh yes. I'm afraid you were rather heavily disguised in protective clothing at the time! I thought there was something familiar about you."

"Could we have a chat, please? I have some news for you."

"Of course. Let's go into the kitchen, shall we?" Nancy led the way, wondering what was coming now. She'd tried to put the threats out of her mind, focusing on letting the builders sort out the mess and get the house back to normal. She would prefer not to think about it again.

As they sat down, the young woman pulled a file out of her briefcase. She placed it carefully on the table in front of her, keeping it closed. Her hands were folded over it, as though she were reluctant to open it.

"Could I ask what your name is, please?" asked Nancy.

"Oh, of course! I'm so sorry. Look, here's my ID badge." She held out the badge, so Nancy could see her name, Lydia Kowalski.

"Thank you. We weren't introduced last time, were we?"

"No." Lydia didn't want this job. She'd tried to say she wasn't experienced enough, that her superior should do it, because it was going to need careful handling. But there was no luck there. He was on another case that required his presence, so she had to step up. She found it difficult to raise her eyes from the table, to look straight at Nancy's enquiring face.

"We've had a new development, Mrs Brewer, and we thought we should talk to you about it." There. She'd done it. At least she'd opened the dialogue.

"I see. So, what's come up then?"

Lydia slowly opened the file, making the contents clearly visible to Nancy. The first thing Nancy saw was the photograph of a woman she didn't recognise. She was quite striking, with her long, flowing hair peeking out under a stylish hat. She wore the kind of coat Nancy might have worn a few years back, with a tie belt, that can make some people look like what her mother would have called "a sack of potatoes". This woman wore it elegantly, and she walked on heels the like of which Nancy had never worn.

Having let the photograph do its job for her, Lydia gained a little more confidence. "We have an identity for a woman who apparently lived in this close, Mrs Brewer."

She turned the photo round. "Oh yes, of course! I thought she looked a bit familiar. I think she's part of the couple that were renting the house over the road, but I think they've gone now." How much did she tell now? Should she describe the mayhem of the row and things being thrown out of the window? She didn't know what this girl was after, so she'd better be cautious, and not sound like a gossip.

"Did you meet her partner, when they were here, Mrs Brewer?"

"Well, I didn't exactly meet him. I saw him a few times, if we happened to be outside at the same time, but it was only to wave at and say 'hello'. He didn't seem all that eager to make friends, to be honest, but it might have been because he was in a hurry."

"I see." Lydia produced another photograph, this time of a very smart man, getting into his car. She placed it in front of Nancy. "Would this be the man?"

"Probably. Of course, only seeing him from a distance, I wouldn't say I could definitely pick him out at an ID parade or anything, but he certainly looks like the man I saw."

"Thank you. That corroborates the statement made by some other people, who have been extremely helpful."

Fred and Janet, Nancy thought to herself. Aloud, she asked, "How's that, Miss Kowalski?"

"We understand that there was something of an altercation between these two. Can you tell us anything about it, Mrs Brewer? We have one account, but we'd like to understand exactly what happened, if you can help."

Wondering what on earth this had to do with messages and a fire, Nancy was instinctively beginning to feel that there was something she was not being told, in order to get information from her. She'd seen these games played in television drama, even if she'd never been on the wrong side of the law in real life. *Cassie would have loved this!*

"I can't tell you what was said," she began, "because whatever it was, it must have happened before the noise grabbed my attention. I just suddenly heard things smashing, and that's something that's hard to ignore, so I looked out of my lounge window. I'm afraid what I did see was various items being thrown out of a window, though I couldn't honestly say who was doing the throwing. I assumed it was the man, because the woman was getting into her car, in a hurry. She drove off, and I stopped watching. I know the front garden was cleared up the next day, but again, I can't tell you who did it, or even any detail about what was there."

"Have you seen either of them again?"

"No. No, I haven't. I don't think there's anyone there now, but someone must have been in last weekend, because my grandson was able to give someone a parcel I had taken in before the fire. I had to get it to the right house before the recovery team threw it away with my things!"

"I understand. You see, your grandson says he gave the parcel to a woman, and that woman was someone he'd seen before, but he didn't feel able to break that to you."

"More secrets," muttered Nancy under her breath. "Why on earth would that be?"

"It seems the woman is someone he saw when he was in London with his friend. She was with your son-in-law, Mrs Brewer. Would you happen to know anything about that?"

"Oh dear! It seems that dots are starting to join themselves, doesn't it? She was the woman my son-in-law had an affair with! I had no idea it was with someone from round here! How can that be? They can't have met here, because she's only been in this close for a few weeks, and Tim hadn't been here in that time." Nancy was wishing she had a brain like Mrs Marple. There were bits of this jigsaw missing, but she had a feeling Lydia had more of the puzzle than she'd let on so far.

"May I ask how you came to make that link?"

"I can't reveal my sources, Mrs Brewer, but we have it on good authority that the woman who lived across the road was one and the same as the woman who was in London and was seen with your son-in-law. Your grandson's identification confirmed what we had been told. We have also been told that her ex-partner left in rather a hurry."

"Well, you must also know, then, that Tim has stopped seeing her, that the affair was very short-lived, and he is back with my daughter."

"Yes, we do know that. We have spoken to your daughter, and her husband. It seems the woman — let's call her Miss A — had an abusive relationship with her partner. Did you ever see any signs of his having hurt her?"

"No, but then I wouldn't, would I? These things happen behind closed doors. Has he done her some harm now?"

"Thankfully not, but it seems that neighbours had heard a great deal of shouting, the day Miss A left, and it is quite possible that he'd found out about the affair. We'll track him down, Mrs Brewer, and have a chat with him, but we just want to establish as much as we can before we do that. Could you now please look at this photograph?" She pulled out a photograph of Tim getting into his car.

"Can you confirm that this car belongs to your son-in-law?"

"Yes, of course. That's him getting into it, outside his London flat." As she finished saying it, she spotted that there was someone in the passenger seat. She couldn't make out any features, but there was definitely someone there. Like fairy dust landing on her eyelids, she suddenly realised what she was looking at. "Is that... is that her, in the passenger seat?"

"Yes, it would appear so. This was taken by someone in the street at the time. We have reason to believe that Miss A is the passenger."

"I see. But you realise that's the car he let my grandson use, don't you? That's the car Jake drove up here, just before the messages began." As she said it, very slowly, she began to realise what she was saying. "You think he was mistaken for his father, don't you? Is that what you're telling me?"

"We have been able to visit the house across the road, Mrs Brewer, after a tip-off. This is a photo we found in the house." Nancy stared at her own front door; the car parked on the drive.

"... kissed the girls and made them cry," she said, almost under her breath. "Did Tim run away, when her partner found out? But "rockabye baby"! Were his children the targets? Oh, my goodness! Three blind mice, and he has three children. What kind of sick mind wants to kill the children for what the father has done?"

Nancy's eyes filled with tears, and she could hear her voice crack, the horror of what had just dawned on her feeling too much to take in. She'd coped with being a target herself, with it probably being some kind of sick prank, but this! This was talking intent to kill. This could have been murder.

Lydia didn't know what to do. She hadn't dealt with anything like this before. She'd practised how to tell someone a relative has died, and she'd shadowed investigators delivering bad news. This hadn't harmed anyone, and yet it was like something from a horror film, surreal. She'd done her best to reveal the information a little at a time, let the other person work it out, if she could, so that it didn't have to be spelled out or seen as any kind of bias. But what did she do now? Here was a woman looking distraught, and she had no idea what the procedure should be. She could hardly give her a hug when she didn't even know her. Nor could she just leave.

"It seems it may well be as you suspect, Mrs Brewer. You were not the target at all. Jake arriving started a chain of events because that made him accessible. Maybe the messages were just meant to frighten, and maybe it was assumed that Jake would tell his father, rather than keep it to himself.

The perpetrator cannot have known what Jake knew, so he may have assumed that, in a normal family, the son would tell the father, if he was unnerved. I gather he didn't even tell his mother, did he?"

"No. He didn't want to worry her, and nor did I. That's hardly the point though, is it? Where is this maniac now?"

"We believe we know where he is, Mrs Brewer. He will be picked up and taken in for questioning. Now that we've searched the house, we have evidence to link him to the use of the nursery rhymes, and it seems he'd been tailing his partner, after her first trip to London, taking photographs of where she went and who with."

Chapter 29: Chas (Charles)

The mist was rolling around the motorway, like smoke curling in the wind. It was as if it were trying to wrap its arms around the cars, to catch them as they passed, as they escaped. It was getting dark now, and the headlights coming towards him were blinding him on the bends. He'd cleared Leeds with no problem, cutting through the town. He still hated driving on the loop, trying to get himself in the right lane, even though he'd done it, now, many times. As he headed upwards, the traffic thinned, the rush hour now over. *I just hope I've remembered everything.* His passport was in his briefcase, and he wore his suit, looking as if he were going on a business trip. He'd done it before. He knew the drill. He'd bought himself a business class ticket, so that he could sleep on the plane and avoid sitting next to other people. *There's always someone who wants to chat, when you're on your own, and right now I don't want to talk to anyone.*

The money was safe in his bank account, and he had plenty in his wallet. He couldn't carry too much on him, but he'd made sure he had his cards and the funds had all been transferred into his own name. He would be able to survive for a while, until he could make the necessary arrangements.

The mist thickened with the descending darkness. It was becoming more and more difficult to see very far ahead. He was tired. It had been a

196

long week, and he'd needed his wits about him. He wasn't sure whether or not the letting agent had accepted his story that his wife had left him, and he needed to terminate the contract with immediate effect, but when he'd tried to go back into the house, the locks had been changed.

Bitch! She must have gone back there. He'd hoped to be able to get in and clear out his papers, although he'd already got his clothes out to the caravan he'd rented by the A1. Anonymous was what he wanted to be, and no-one questioned why the pleasant man with plenty of money had turned up and asked to rent an empty caravan in an emergency. His mother was dying, and he needed to stay in the area for a while. They took pity on him, couldn't do enough for him.

He'd seen that old couple watching every move in the close. *Nosy old biddies!* He hadn't dared to park outside the house, because they would have noticed, so he'd parked round the corner, pulled on an old coat over his hoodie, and waited until nightfall to try the door. They would have had him arrested as a burglar, if they had seen him, and he didn't want to draw attention to himself. He didn't want to meet the police right now.

She's gone for good, that's for sure, and any chance that she was carrying our baby. She didn't deserve him, anyway. *The cheating slut. She said she wasn't going to her lover, but I'm gonna make things as difficult as I can now.*

He'd teach that pariah a lesson he wouldn't forget. *He even had the nerve to have his car on show, outside the house over the road, like flaunting it. The old woman was obviously connected to him, or it would not have been there, and I wanted to make damn sure he didn't get the chance to leave. Pity, the fire didn't seem to catch very well — not something I'm an expert in, after all. I'll have to think of something else next time.*

He'd never done that before, and it was tricky, lighting the rags, as he pushed them through the letter box. The petrol would keep them burning, he hoped. It was satisfying, when he saw the blue lights appear, and heard the commotion outside. Now, though, he had to put some distance between him and that house before anyone started poking about and asking questions. It was a close thing when the police drove round. He thought they were heading for him, but they just cruised round, taking a look at the empty street, and went away again. *Huh! Thick as two planks! Can't see what's under their noses!* He laughed.

He pulled in at the service station, glad of a break from peering through the windscreen and needing black coffee, to keep him awake. Not that far to the airport, once he got off the M60, so this would be the only stop he would need.

He sat down on his own and picked up a newspaper someone had abandoned. He didn't buy one himself — seemed a waste of money, when he could get the news online. It was a bit more interesting, as it was the York Press, rather than a national rag, and he flicked absent-mindedly through the pages. His hands froze, and he flicked the page back, having just turned it over.

What was that? Down at the bottom of the page, there was a piece on a case of arson that could turn out to be attempted murder. The police were looking for someone, a man. The description fitted him pretty well, although, as always, the height was guesswork, and they'd overestimated it by a couple of inches. He was, luckily, average height, now with indistinct greying hair and ordinary brown eyes. There was nothing to make him stand out from the crowd. He kept his parka wrapped round him, trying to look like anybody travelling, saving the business image for the airport. He closed the newspaper and headed out of the door, casually stopping to look in the window of the newsagents, so that he didn't appear to be rushing.

He clambered back into his car, taking a deep, calming breath. He had contacts. He would be OK. He would stay out of the country for a while, and then he would come back as someone else, or not. *Maybe I'll just stay in the sunshine!* He smiled at the thought.

It was on the M56 that he first noticed someone's headlights had been in his interior mirror for an irritating amount of time. Whoever this idiot was, he was tailgating, and the light was becoming a nuisance. There was no-one else on the road by now, so he sped up a little, to try to lose the menace. It didn't work. The other car stuck to him, as if it needed him to show the way in the dark. *Must be someone who doesn't like driving at night, but I wish they wouldn't follow my tail lights quite so closely.*

He turned off toward the airport, where he'd booked himself into a hotel, so he could park the car there and grab something to eat. It would be a while before the staff realised he wasn't coming back to collect it. Too bad that he had to abandon it, but it would hardly go in the hold with his case, so there was no option. He'd check into the hotel, but he would only be there an hour or so before he had to check in for his flight. He had it all planned. He would head for his parents' holiday home in Spain for now. *Good luck with trying to find me, Felicity! Two can play at keeping secrets!* Felicity had no idea that he'd inherited the villa just before she moved in. He'd been letting it out, but at this time of the year it was empty. A bolt hole.

He was surprised when the car followed him right into the car park and parked a couple of rows away from him. He didn't want to be greeted by the driver, so he pulled out his cases as quickly as he could, wheeling one in each hand, his briefcase on its long strap across his shoulder. It didn't seem much to be able to take with him, but he could buy what he needed when he got there.

He headed for the check-in desk, and the foyer was, thankfully, empty.

"Good evening, Sir. Ah yes! I see your reservation. I won't keep you long, Sir. I'll just go to get your key."

The young man on the desk disappeared, and he paced up and down while he waited what seemed like ten minutes but was probably only two or three. His eyes shifted quickly back and forth, reassuring him that there was no-one to recognise him. He tapped on the counter, impatient to get out of the public area. He'd never had to wait like this before; usually keys were there, at the desk.

As the key was put into his hand and he said a grudging "thank you", he turned towards the lift, down the corridor, where it was still very quiet, completely deserted. As he approached the lift, a man and a woman came up behind him surprisingly quickly, presumably needing the same lift, but as he pressed the button to summon it, the man spoke.

"Mr Campbell, would you please leave your cases there and come with us?"

He spun round, the shock showing in his rigid body. His brain whizzed. What to do? Run or talk? He shoved the cases into the legs of the woman, forcing her to bend in half, and ran past her toward the door. He still had his car keys. He could do this.

He got as far as the door, but outside were more police in uniform, and he was not going to make it past the wall they made against the door opening. He turned back, only to find himself confronted by the man who had spoken and the woman he'd hit with the cases. Behind them were hotel staff. He knew he was trapped.

"Mr Campbell, you are under arrest for the crime of arson. You do not have to say anything, but it may harm your defence if you do not mention when questioned something which you later rely on in court. Anything you do say may be given in evidence."

He felt the handcuffs being slipped round his wrists, as one of the officers guided him to the police car, waiting outside.

"What about my cases!" he shouted.

"Don't worry, Mr Campbell. We'll take care of those."

Chapter 30: Sergeant O'Malley

Sergeant Daniel O'Malley had no patience left with people like this Tim Castleford. *Plenty of money, nice house, wife and kids, and he gets to middle age and turns into a stupid teenager again, ending up with police having to waste their time sorting out the havoc he's caused.* Dan was due to retire soon, and he just wanted a quiet time for the next couple of months. He and Erin had been childhood sweethearts, and they were planning to celebrate with a long-awaited cruise. *I couldn't imagine either of us playing around like this idiot's done.*

Dan walked into the interview room, where both Mr and Mrs Castleford sat, having been invited to come in for a chat. They'd been assured that they were not in need of legal representation, as they were obviously just helping with enquiries, and they may have some information that would help.

When she'd phoned on leaving Mr Mercury, Poppy had asked if she could talk to the investigating officer. Tim had been warned that he might be spoken to, so they sat very quietly, nervous but not anxious. Each of them felt unsure about what the other would say, and neither of them had told the other about the contribution they could make to the enquiries.

Dan sat himself down, and a young woman constable, looking remarkably fresh and eager, sat down next to him.

"Thank you for coming in, Mr and Mrs Castleford." He tried to sound pleasant, kept the smile fixed on his face, banishing his irritation to the side. "We need to have a little chat about what each of you can do to help us to convict the person responsible for Mrs Brewer's fire. Are you happy to talk?"

"Of course!" Poppy jumped in, before Tim had a chance to say anything. "My poor mother has been terrorised by whoever this is, and we'll do anything we can to make sure it stops now, won't we Tim?" She looked straight at him, and their eyes locked for the first time for weeks.

"Absolutely," he said. "How can we help?"

"Right. Now then, we gather that you, Mr Castleford, had been having a liaison with a woman called Felicity Dawson." Hit him with it now, was Dan's thinking. Get that elephant out of the room. She knows anyway.

Tim reluctantly said, "Yes. For a few weeks, but it was over before the fire."

"So, I gather. Now, Mr Castleford, it seems that this Mrs Dawson was still with a partner at the time, a Mr Charles Campbell. Did you ever meet Mr Campbell?"

"Well no. I've never met him, as far as I know." Well, he hadn't, as far as he knew. It had been a shock, when he saw Felicity as a bridesmaid, but he hadn't been introduced to whoever she was with, so he felt he was justified in telling the truth.

"You are not able to identify him, then?"

"No, I'm afraid not. All I know is that he was not a pleasant character, as far as Felicity goes. He gave her bruises on more than one occasion, and he tried to control her. She was afraid of him, I think. You'll have my statement, I presume? Have you spoken to Felicity?"

"Let's stick to what you can tell me, shall we, Mr Castleford? Did you see any evidence of the domestic violence, Mr Castleford, or is that just what she told you?"

"I did see bruises on her wrists."

"Well, as you know, we have been given information that suggests the couple lived opposite your mother, Mrs Castleford. Did you ever observe them having an altercation when you visited?"

"No. I think you know I didn't, but you have the account my mother could give of the show-down they had just before the messages started. They hadn't been there long, so I never had any reason to notice them particularly. If I visited, I just went into Mum's house."

"We do indeed know about the messages, though that does not prove that he was an arsonist." Let that hang in the air. Dan was getting them ready to answer the questions he ultimately wanted answers to.

"OK. Here we have a couple living opposite your mother-in-law, Mr Castleford, but you had never met them in that location, and you first met Mrs Dawson in London. Doesn't that seem a little strange?"

"I can see that now," said Tim, wondering where this was going. "As my wife said, they hadn't been there long, and I've been away from home a lot, so it was just my wife who visited my mother-in-law. I don't know whether they had seen me before, but I hadn't seen them."

"And Mrs Castleford, I gather that you had your suspicions about your husband's conduct, before your son saw him with Mrs Dawson in London."

It was a statement of fact, but it sounded like a question. "Yes. The reason I asked to speak to someone was that I had asked a private investigator to find out what was going on, because he was away more than usual, and I knew he wasn't telling me the truth."

"What?" Tim's amazement was evident in his voice. This was beginning to sound like something from a counselling session, or a television programme that made people confront each other with untold truths. He'd never imagined that Poppy would go that far, in trying to catch him out. He should have known that she would see through his excuses when they'd known each other so long. She'd heard a million excuses from teenage boys, and he'd proved himself no better than any one of them. But a private investigator? That seemed to be taking things a bit too far. She was usually so pragmatic, and this seemed more like a drama from Daisy's diary, which he'd come across once, when he was changing her bedclothes.

The silence hung in the air for what seemed like minutes but was probably only seconds.

"Yes. He was recommended by a friend of a colleague, and he'd been a police officer himself, so I trusted him."

Dan nodded. He'd seen the statement she'd handed in. He remembered Jason Mercury as Jason Manners, but he didn't blame him for adopting a pseudonym for his business purposes. Mercury was fast and clever, and Jason had certainly been that; it seemed an appropriate choice that he was, among other things, responsible for guiding souls to the underworld. He smiled to himself. Trust Jason to choose something like that. Good man, was Jason. He would've done a thorough job, and Dan had quite enjoyed catching up with him over the phone.

"I understand he told you to pass on the information you've put in your statement, Mrs Castleford, and we have now spoken to him personally. It proved to be fortuitous that one of his operatives was keeping an eye on the whereabouts of your husband and Mrs Dawson, which is how we discovered that Mr Campbell was also watching. He's been identified as the man seen in the street, outside the London flat, on more than one occasion, as the operative thought his behaviour rather strange and took a photograph of him. What we couldn't do was link him to the Yorkshire address, until Mrs Dawson told us about her partner and gave us the information about what she'd found."

"She thought it was him?" asked Poppy, unaware that Felicity had phoned the police as soon as she'd found the nursery rhymes.

"You know that don't you, Mr Castleford?" Dan was going to make these two be honest with each other, even if it was like pulling teeth.

It was Poppy's turn to look astonished. "How?"

"I couldn't tell you, because I promised you I would have no more contact with her. I swear, I didn't answer the phone, but she left me a message. She didn't tell me what she'd found, but she did tell me the police would want to talk to me. I wasn't sure why."

"It seems that Mr Campbell saw your car outside your mother-in-law's house, Mr Castleford. The same car as he'd seen his wife get into in London. He recognised the number plate, so he assumed you were in the house. He had no idea how you were related, but that didn't matter. For all he knew, you were Mrs Brewer's son. But he set about warning you off, because he blamed you for the affair with Mrs Dawson. She'd left, so he couldn't take it out on her, but it seemed you were available. So, he started leaving the nursery rhymes, riddles that threatened harm and accused you of being a coward, when you were found out. But then it seemed too good an opportunity, when there were more people in the house. He wanted you to get the blame, you see, for everything. It was only when he was asked whether he'd seen anything the night of the fire that he began to panic, we think, because he could see that it was being investigated, and the police were involved. He is an intelligent man. He knew it would only be a matter of time before the connections were made, and he would be found out."

"It's unusual for people to know the origins of the nursery rhymes though, isn't it?" Poppy asked.

"It is indeed, Mrs Castleford. I didn't know them myself until this happened, but it seems that Mr Campbell's ex-wife was a history teacher, which might explain it."

"Ex-wife? I thought his wife was dead?" Tim exclaimed.

"It seems that's what he told Mrs Dawson, Mr Castleford, but it seems that is not the whole truth. We have identified Mr Campbell as one Charles Carson, whose wife is very much alive and very glad to be shot of him. It seems your Mrs Dawson has had a fortunate escape, as Mrs Carson was not so lucky, and she and her baby only escaped to a refuge after he hurt her so badly that she ended up in hospital. We have no proof, so I can only tell you that she believes he was the one who set fire to their house, when he thought they were asleep upstairs, because she was seeing a counsellor, and he certainly didn't want her telling anyone about what went on in their relationship. If she is right, he was very careful to leave no clues, and we couldn't convict on probability. We would need enough evidence to ensure that he is held responsible."

"So does the information from Mr Mercury help, then?"

"It does indeed, Mrs Castleford, together with the testimony of Mrs Dawson and the items she discovered in the house, which we can definitely attribute to Mr Campbell. The trouble with fire is that it tends to wipe out the truth, other than confirming the materials used to start it. We often can't prove who actually lit the fire, because whatever might have had prints on it has been destroyed. This time, we have his fingerprints on the documents that match the notes put through the door, and we have experts on analysing the recording on the answerphone, to match his voice. Although you didn't intend your private investigator to investigate a crime, he has helped us to solve one. There is just one more thing. Mr Castleford, did Mrs Dawson ask you for any money?"

Tim blushed. "I didn't pay her, if that's what you mean."

"No. I don't. Did she ask you for any money, to help her to escape the relationship?"

"Well, not exactly, no. But she did ask me to lend her some, because he held the purse strings. It wasn't much, but she told me she had nothing, and she needed to pay her credit card. She couldn't let him see the bill, or he would have hit her."

"Quite. Unfortunately, Mrs Dawson is not entirely as honourable as she might seem, Mr Castleford. In this instance, she certainly did pick the wrong person, but it seems she thought she'd found someone who would keep her in the manner to which she would like to be accustomed, without having to use her own money at all. She'd carefully stowed away quite a bit of money, even before planning her escape, as Mr Campbell paid the household bills, and she'd taken advantage of his credit card from the time she moved in with him, rather than using her own. She'd been accruing considerable savings. I'm afraid she duped you somewhat on that score. It seems she has ensured that she is comfortably off, and she has just bought herself a flat in the suburbs. I don't think that is the action of a woman with nothing, do you? Did it ever occur to you that she may have chosen you for a reason, that your relationship was not quite the happy accident you thought it was?"

"She said she would pay me back, but then she said we had to call it off, and I knew she was right, and once we split, I could hardly turn round and ask her for money, could I?"

"No, indeed, Mr Castleford, because that would not be honourable, would it?" Dan hoped he picked up the irony.

Tim looked at Poppy. Poppy looked at Tim. Dan thought it would have been interesting to be telepathic at that moment in time. Was she feeling sorry for him, or calling him all the idiots she could summon from her vocabulary? Was he asking for pity, excusing himself, or what?

"Do either of you have any more information you can give me, or are we all done here?" Dan was thinking they might be all done here, but they would not be all done when they left here! He didn't reckon Tim's chances, judging by the steely look in Poppy's eyes. If she let him stay, it was very obviously going to be on her terms, and there would be no more chances. Justice would be served.

Chapter 31: Nancy

"Nancy? How are you?"

"Oh, hello, Rosie! I'm fine, thanks. How are you?"

"Hmmm. 'Fine' is what we all say, isn't it? I've seen the piece in the paper about a fire in your neighbourhood. It sounds as if it might have been your house. How fine is that, then?"

Nancy might have taken umbrage at the tone of the inquiry, had it not been one of her oldest, dearest friends. She and Rosie had been friends before they were married, had supported each other when the children were small, and they'd seen each other through so many ups and downs, sharing laughter when laughter was the only way to cope with the mayhem of life. You didn't make many friends like Rosie in your life. Rosie had empathised when her parents died, when the children left home, and more recently, when James died, her own husband having died a couple of years before. Of course, Nancy had been there for her, too, and their shared joys and griefs made them able to discern emotion in a change of tone, understand the implications of a sentence spoken, when so many remained unsaid. They were separated by about two hundred miles these days, but when they were together, it was always as if they had seen each other the day before. Rosie was like a sister to Nancy, who had only had an older brother, and when he'd only survived her parents by a couple of years,

208

she'd felt the blow of becoming an only child. In a world full of missing people these days, Rosie was a comforting voice and presence.

"All right, Rosie, I know! No-one was hurt, luckily, and there was not a lot of damage to the house. Poppy was here that night, with Daisy and Jake, so it could have been a lot worse, and I wasn't on my own. The mess is being cleared up and the fire is being investigated. Is that fine enough for now?" She laughed at their mock crossness with each other.

"Whew! How did it happen?"

Nancy gave her the story, making light of the possibility of arson, to avoid alarming her. She didn't mention the threats. She had, of course, no idea that Poppy had already written to Rosie, to gather in her support and influence, largely for her own peace of mind, but also because she thought it would be good for her mother to have some company right now.

"Look, Nancy, I was wondering how you would feel about me coming up to stay for a couple of days. Could you cope, or would I be a nuisance while you're sorting things out? Be honest!"

"That would be wonderful, Rosie! When were you thinking of coming?"

"How about tomorrow? I've got no reason to put it off. I haven't got my grandson to look after for the next couple of weeks, because Gavin and Teresa are going to the Canaries for a break. So how about I have a break, too? Would that be all right?"

"Would it be all right? Oh, wouldn't it just?" Nancy was absolutely delighted, and not just because she always looked forward to seeing her friend. Maybe Poppy would be reassured, while she had company, and that would give her a bit of head space to deal with her own problems.

"That'll be fantastic, Rosie! Are you driving up?"

"Yes. I'll aim to be there some time in the afternoon, so I'll stop for lunch on the way. Looking forward to a good old catching up session!"

"Absolutely. See you tomorrow then. Take care, and good luck with the road works!"

Rosie laughed. When were there not any road works? They said their goodbyes, and Nancy set about getting a bedroom ready. She hadn't yet had the energy or motivation to sort out everything Poppy and her children had used the night of the fire, and Jake had been again, so she spent the rest of the day cleaning and tidying. She'd kept the windows open, just in case she was now nose-blind to the residual smell of the burning, and by the evening the big spare bedroom was full of fresh air. The bed sported a flowery duvet cover to go with the vase of late-flowering bits and pieces Nancy had managed to arrange rather well on the window ledge. She plumped the pillows one last time and was eventually satisfied that her old friend would be comfortable. She found herself humming as she dusted, something she knew she used to do as she worked, because James had often found it irritating, but it took her by surprise that she felt in such a good mood that she wanted to sing. She hadn't felt that for a while, and certainly not in these last couple of weeks. She caught herself saying aloud, "Bless you, Rosie!".

Rosie was one of those people who came through the door laden with bags. She gave no opportunity for Nancy to give her the enormous hug that would come her way eventually, and the bustle of her arrival avoided any emotional outpouring of relief that might have been triggered. Nancy's smile seemed to be trying to stretch her mouth from one side of her face to the other, and her eyes twinkled, like they had the day that James had first noticed her. She held the door open, as enormous bags for life dangled from Rosie's arms and made their way to the nearest floor space. Nancy marvelled at how she could need so much for a couple of days but knew there were probably goodies stashed in one of them, in preparation for an evening of sharing, talking and laughter, to which she was looking forward with all of her being.

"There!" Rosie straightened up, smoothed down her jacket and took a deep breath. "Now, my friend, let me look at you!"

Nancy met Rosie's open arms with her own, and they hugged as if they hadn't seen each other for years. It felt like years, Nancy realised, since the funeral, and she'd done a lot of adjusting to becoming one of two since then. Rosie had known her when she'd been one before James, and she knew her perceptive friend would spot any changes, without being told.

"I'm not going to bother to ask you how you are, because I don't want the 'fine' answer, Nancy. Let's just skip that bit and start from now. We do what we're good at, you and I. We carry on carrying on, and I'm sure that's what you've been doing since I last saw you. Now, let's get that coffee made and get started on a conversation I fully expect to last for two whole days!" She chuckled, waving her scarf in the air as she removed it with a dramatic flourish. "This blasted fire of yours. I want to know all about it, but not until you have told me about the family."

"Well, that could be tricky, because unfortunately the two are very much inter-twined."

"Oooh! Fascinating stuff then! Now, where would you like me to dump my stuff, while you sort the coffee?"

"It's what was Poppy's room, where you slept last time," Nancy offered.

"Good! That's the one next to the bathroom, isn't it? Handy, when you're my age!"

Rosie had a way of making even the basic trials of an ageing bladder sound amusing, and Nancy felt the kind of comfort that comes from being able to talk about anything, because nothing is taboo when there is such closeness.

"Don't you want a hand with your bags?"

"Nah! I'll leave that one down here." Rosie pointed to one of the heavier carrier bags, scooping up her other bags and heading for the stairs. "When you've been on your own a bit longer, you find you become very independent, my friend. I do a lot of things I might have expected a man to do, now that there isn't one around. You discover your strengths, and your weaknesses, believe me!"

By the time Rosie appeared in the lounge, the coffee was waiting, and Nancy had sat herself where they could face each other to talk. Rosie breezed in and plonked herself gratefully on the sofa, arranging cushions around herself. "Your sofa doesn't get any smaller, and my legs don't get any longer!" she joked. "Now, start from the beginning. How is my godson, Jake, doing? Last I heard, he was in Spain with a friend. I presume he's back in Cambridge for his last year? And Cassie will just have started in Leeds. And I want to see a photo of Ben's baby."

"Yes, well both of those things are true, and I will show you a picture of Harley," began Nancy, "but it's complicated. If you want me to start at the beginning, I think I'd better start with Poppy and Tim."

She wasn't sure quite how to weave the tale together, but it began to tumble itself out, and the link between the affair, the fire, and the visits somehow achieved a kind of straight line, so that Rosie grasped the overall picture of events.

"And have they caught whoever lit the fire?" was Rosie's last of many questions.

"It would seem so, Rosie. Once you see all the pieces of the jigsaw puzzle put together, it all makes sense, but the coincidences are incredible. If she hadn't lived across the road, and Jake hadn't seen them in town, and if Tim had never met that woman in the first place, but then life is full of 'ifs', isn't it? I'm not sure how safe I'll be here, if he gets a short sentence, but for now, he's safely behind bars, and the house is being re-let, so I can put it all down to experience. I just hope we don't get some diabolical character in that house next time. We don't want to get a serial killer, or a gangster, or a drug baron, but you just never know, do you? Mind you, it must have given a few people a lot to talk about."

"It sounds as if you're determined to stay here, then, Nancy. What about Poppy's suggestion of moving near her?"

"Oh, I don't know, Rosie. I can see where she's coming from, but I'm not ready for a retirement complex yet, and I just get this feeling that she'll be watching my every move in case I do something she doesn't approve of. I don't feel old yet, and I need some time to adjust to being a widow, let alone facing moving somewhere I don't know as well. If James and I had moved together, we'd have got out and about and got to know the place, but on my own?" She shrugged her shoulders. "My head's been going round and round, and it's a bit like that game of pulling the petals off a daisy, where you say 'Do I? Don't I?' and there is no real answer."

"That's perhaps because you're looking for the wrong answer," said Rosie.

"Well, I might know that, if I knew what the right answer was!"

"Just for a minute, take the 'Poppy wants' factor out of it, Nancy. We know Poppy wants to worry less, and we know how she sees that happening, but what you need is the 'Nancy wants' factor. What do you want?"

"I want to be independent."

"Exactly. Just as I do. We are not the sort of people to want to lean on someone else, are we, Nancy? Maybe, if we are unwell, or we make it to being very old and frail, we'll be forced to adjust our thinking. Some people find it best for them to live in a complex where there is always someone to talk to, always company, and that has its benefits, doesn't it? Decide what's more important for you — no-one scrutinising your behaviour, or company?"

"I think, right now, it's being completely free to please myself, and not having to accommodate anyone else. It isn't something I've done since before I was married, and it sounds selfish, but I need time and space to find a different me."

"I get it, Nancy. I know exactly what you mean. The trouble is that's lonely. What about the loneliness? That's what gets to a lot of people in our situation."

Nancy went quiet. When life had been very busy, with husband, children, and job to sort out, a bit of time on her own had been such a luxury, something to be savoured, but she knew that when it was forced on her day after day, week after week, talking to a budgie and only hearing his limited conversation could be enough to drive her mad. Isolation was not what she craved.

"There is another way," Rosie broke into her thoughts. "Let's look at other possibilities, shall we?"

"Such as?" Nancy felt the stark reality of what Rosie was making her face up to.

"Well, you don't have to live with other people, do you? You could get yourself out there, joining things, volunteering, visiting places. You could make sure that you build a new social circle that doesn't feel as if it is missing James. You could focus on what you could offer that would help others. You could pick up the phone more often, too, Nancy Brewer!"

Rosie's scold was captured in a laugh that made Nancy acknowledge that she'd never had time to get into the habit of phoning more often, and she didn't want to be a nuisance by suddenly doing it, just because she didn't have James around anymore. She didn't want people's sympathy, because it just made coping harder, and it took away any genuine pleasure in talking to other people. Rosie nodded, as she spoke, having been there herself.

"The last thing we want is to be a burden on our children, isn't it? The thing is, we have to find out how not to be a burden on ourselves! If we're not careful, we'll waste the good years we've got left, denying ourselves the chance to find a different way through them, so let's come back to the central point. What does Nancy want?"

"I want to travel," Nancy blurted out. "I want to do some of the things James, and I said we would do, but he never got the chance. I want to do them for both of us." She felt the emotion welling up inside herself, as she gave voice to what was stirring deep inside her. Her eyes moistened, and Rosie bent forward and grabbed her hand.

"Then travel," she said. "It's quite simple, isn't it? If that's what you want to do, do it. Do it while you can. Make the memories we know we're going to have to live on, if we get really old. Take the photos. Meet the people. If you're very lucky, I might be tempted to come with you!"

Nancy lifted her head, seeing her own tears mirrored in her friend's face. "Really? Would you be prepared to come with me?"

"If that's the only way to get you to do it, yes. I don't believe, for one moment, that you are incapable of doing it on your own. Who did all the organising of holidays, anyway? Who sorted the paperwork, had the passports and tickets ready, arranged holiday insurance, packed the cases? You did, Nancy. Who asked locals the way, studied timetables, sussed out buses, places to visit? You did. There is nothing you cannot do. You could join one of these group holidays, or an escorted trip, so that you don't have to worry about being alone or unsafe. Think about it. Life doesn't have to be black and white. Start to see the shades of grey. It isn't 'do it with James or don't do it at all', it's 'do it another way'. And then, when Nancy has done what Nancy wants to do, you can come back and re-think where you want to be, as the independent woman you are."

"But Poppy has so much stress to deal with, how can I add to that?"

"Did Ben think about your stress, when he took off to work abroad? Did Poppy ask your permission to have three children, while you worried yourself sick about her giving birth? Did Tim think about you when he had an affair? Did they ask you, before they moved away from here? No. They have lived their own lives, ever since you had to let them go. You have never dictated what they had to do, where they had to be. As parents, we're expected to bring up our children and then accept that they are their own people. It seems to me that they have to accept that we're our own people, too, just as we were before we spent most of our lives putting them first, even if we might need a little help now and then, just as they did. Poppy has to let you do this, or you will end up resenting her for putting the brakes on your life and plunging you headfirst into old age too soon. I'll talk to Poppy. Leave her to me."

"You are the dearest friend a girl could have. You know that, Rosie?" Nancy squeezed Rosie's hand, letting go only to find a tissue to wipe her clouded eyes. "I knew I could rely on you to do some straight talking and sort me out!" She smiled, despite the tears, and they laughed at each other.

"Stroppy, me," said Rosie. "But you would have done the same for me. Now, in that bag in the kitchen is some delicious cake I bought from the baker's first thing this morning. I think we need a huge, sinful slice each, and more coffee, or I'll be dozing off in front of the television this evening!"

Chapter 32: Poppy

"Anita, hi! Poppy here!"

"Oh, hello stranger. How are you?"

"I'm fine. So sorry I haven't been in touch. Things have been a bit full-on. How are you?"

"Oh, I'm OK. Plodding on. We've just booked a fantastic holiday for our silver wedding anniversary next spring, but I'm not allowing myself to get too excited too soon!"

"Wow! Where are you going?"

"Caribbean cruise, Poppy. It's something I've always wanted to do, and, well, we need to do it while we can still enjoy it, don't we?"

"That sounds wonderful." Poppy still wondered whether she and Tim would make it to their silver wedding, but things were improving, slowly. They'd decided to go to Italy in the summer half-term, as she'd always wanted to see where her grandmother had come from, and Ben had said it was beautiful. Why should he be the only one to get there? She noticed Anita hadn't mentioned Tim.

"How's your mum doing now? Is she back at home?"

"Yes thanks. She seems to be doing pretty well, actually. Her friend, Rosie, was as good as her word, and they had a couple of holidays together, including a cruise down the Rhine. By all accounts, they thoroughly enjoyed themselves, though it sounds as if they had as much wine as wayward students!"

They both laughed at the thought of Rosie and Nancy being in disgrace. "She's off again in the spring, this time to Venice, apparently, and on her own. I'm not too happy about her going alone, but she says there will be a rep around, and she won't come to any harm, so what can I do? I can hardly tell her she can't go, as if she's Daisy's age, can I?"

"No, and nor should you, Poppy. If that's what she wants to do, let her do it. Look how fast time flies. Let her use the time she's got, to make memories to keep her company when she can't travel any more. I know how you feel, because I know how I felt with my mum, but I wish, now, she'd thrown caution to the wind and lived her dreams, like Nancy's doing. She waited, and then she had the stroke. You never know what's round the corner."

"I suppose you're right. She's adamant that she's not moving yet. The house was partly re-decorated after the fire, and she's turned Dad's study into her writing and sewing room, so she says she wants to stay put, near the neighbours and friends she's known for a long time. I have to let her decide when she wants that to change. She did, actually, sort everything out herself, after the fire, and she's got a handyman/gardener signed up, doing things she might have needed Dad to do. Apart from missing him, she seems content, and she says she's travelling for both of them."

"Oh, Poppy, that's so sweet! Maybe it actually helps her to feel she's doing what he wanted to do, you know."

"Maybe you're right. Anyway, I've been put in my place for now!"

"What about everyone else, then?"

Here we go, thought Poppy. "Well now, Cassie is still with Miles, which I must say surprises me, but he's growing on me. There's more to him than I saw originally, as he relaxes a bit with us. He is also a good influence, because he's in his last year, so he's facing finals, and I think Cassie is beginning to grasp just what she has to do to get there comfortably. Jake is

Jake, and he is a semi-reformed character. He has been very good about keeping in touch, and I think he's shaken off that Ed that was such a pest last year. He seems to have found himself a girlfriend, so I'm hoping she'll keep him away from online gambling and keep him focused on his work, at least most of the time. And Daisy, ah Daisy! Well, she is a little easier now that Tim has been home more. As far as she sees, things are pretty much back to normal, so she's busy being a teenager. Enough about my brood, what about yours?" She was aware that she, too, had avoided talking about her relationship with Tim.

"Where do I start? How long have you got?"

They chatted on, comparing children and jobs, neither of them daring to comment on whether or not Tim was home to stay. Poppy had no idea how much Anita knew from Tim, and she decided she preferred not to know. It was all too raw to want to discuss it with anyone else. They could never be in love like they once were, and she was still unsure what she wanted. She couldn't imagine her life without him, but she couldn't imagine life with him ever being the life she'd thought they had. For now, she was getting through the days, one at a time, doing her best to allow them at least to be friends again. He'd bought her a beautiful bouquet for her birthday, but rather than delight she found herself feeling resentment that he might think she could be won over with a bunch of flowers. Their anniversary had been a quiet affair, and all she could muster was to sign her card with her name, while he signed his with all his love, for ever. Ever was a long time.

There seemed to be an uneasy truce between him and Jake, but at least it was a truce, and on the surface, they were perfectly at ease with each other again. Cassie had managed to stay just Cassie, somehow ignoring what had happened, or putting it aside. She may not have realised it herself, but she'd become the glue that held them all together. Poppy envied Daisy her focus on life being good or bad according to how much it satisfied her wants and needs on that particular day. Big dramas, full of tantrums or

219

tears, could easily be followed by days of laughter and smiles, just like the daisy closing in stormy weather and opening itself to the sunshine again.

Chapter 33: Nancy

Nancy clicked her case shut and did a last look round the hotel room, to make sure she'd left nothing behind. As she lifted it onto the floor, she was glad she'd gone for clothes that would roll up to almost nothing and cut back on all the additional bits and pieces she might normally take on holiday, so the case was definitely lighter than it might have been. She would only be allowed one piece of luggage on the train, and the overnight bag did the job. She positioned it on top of the case, feeling exceedingly grateful to whoever had invented cases with four wheels, instead of two. It was so much easier to get from one place to another.

"That's it," she said to herself. "Here we go then."

As she wheeled her luggage along the corridor to the lift, she allowed herself just a little bit of excitement, to counter the trepidation. On the ground floor, she was able to check out and wheel her case straight through, from the hotel to the station. The travel agent had been most helpful in getting her a special deal for the journey down to London and the night in the hotel, and it had, thankfully, all gone smoothly. So here she was. She looked around her, marvelling at all the people rushing here and there, taking no notice of their surroundings at all, while she tried to take in the myriad of notices and signs and arrows pointing this way and that. She checked her ticket again, although she knew by heart what it said. The spring sunshine shone through the glass in the roof, as she manoeuvred her way to platform two. She had plenty of time, but she found her footsteps quickening as she approached the clock she'd been told would be a marker. And there it was. Above the door, under one of the magnificent arches, was the sign she needed to aim for: "Venice Simplon Orient-Express". She joined the queue, glad she'd arrived early, as there were obviously others eager to be starting on this journey, and very soon there were many more behind her, seeming to come out of nowhere. Most people were in couples, but she noticed she was not the only solo traveller, and the welcoming, smiling staff soon put her at her ease, as she handed over her luggage and waited for the train to arrive. Emerging from the waiting room, she saw the train's old brown and cream livery, looking as if it had been polished. It stood proudly, ready to launch itself towards Folkestone.

At long last, passengers were invited to find their carriages. Nothing was rushed. Nothing was missed. Her hand luggage had been taken from her and would magically appear in her own sleeping car when she got to France. All she had to do now was to indulge herself in being waited on in the finest possible way. She settled herself into an enormous armchair at her allocated table and waited to meet whoever had been given the chair on the opposite side, looking forward to making a new acquaintance.

By the time the train pulled into Folkestone, she'd exchanged life stories with a complete stranger. Like her, Georgie Butcher was finding his feet in a world without the love of his life, but he'd been here before, and he knew the ropes.

"We came to celebrate our fortieth anniversary," he told her. "This year would have been our fiftieth, so I thought I'd go back to where we went last time, see what's changed. I'm just hoping we don't get a high tide that floods St Mark's Square again. I'd like to be able to roam around it this time, instead of walking the plank!"

He was good-natured and had some interesting times working abroad as an engineer. It struck her that he probably had a tale to tell wherever he went, and she was contributing to another.

"Whatever you do, be careful when you buy a drink in the piano bar, on the other train," he warned her. "The prices are sky high. Last time, I found some people I'd met on the coach doing exactly as I was doing - making one drink last as long as I possibly could!" His white beard and moustache almost hid his smile, but his kindly eyes crinkled at the corners. Nancy found she liked him, and they passed the time pleasantly over lunch.

"Oh, I can take this," she thought to herself, as waiters in white uniform placed food on immaculate china crockery, and she was expected to use the silver cutlery as if it were an every-day occurrence. Somehow, the food tasted even more exquisite in this setting!

At Folkestone, with great aplomb, a brass band played them to the leather-seated coaches, which were to take them across the channel, to join the wagon-lits, and eventually, there they were. She could hardly believe her eyes, when the staff lined up to greet them as if they were film stars or royalty. She'd felt so extravagant, spending so much on herself for this trip, and Ben had questioned the wisdom of parting with the money, but Rosie's words rang in her ears. "Do it! Do what Nancy wants!" and as she looked along the carriages and saw the steward standing to attention at the door to hers, her heart sang. This journey, she was going to do on her own. She'd shared a dorm with Rosie at school, and they had thought nothing of seeing each other dressed or undressed, sleeping in the same room as others, sharing the washing facilities, but they agreed that perhaps cooped up in a tiny compartment would be a little too intimate for them as ladies of a certain age. They'd had a wonderful winter holiday together, relaxing in the sunshine while others froze, and when Nancy had told her about her plan to go on the VSOE, Rosie had said it was a bit expensive for her, so Nancy should just go for it, send her the pictures so that she could imagine her friend by the Rialto Bridge or climbing the Campanile. Poppy had coped with them going away together, and Nancy had promised her that, maybe next year, she would look for a bungalow not too far from her. She had another promise to keep first, a promise to herself and James.

Nancy looked at the iron step up into the carriage and stopped to consider how anyone was supposed to climb these with any dignity. They were very steep. She decided to put her handbag down on the floor of the corridor, leaving both hands free to haul herself up, hopefully without falling flat on her face. The steward tactfully looked the other way, as she felt as if she'd stepped into a comedy programme for a few minutes.

Safe in her compartment, she saw that her case had already been put in the luggage rack. She explored the wash basin, tucked away inside an impressive mahogany cabinet, and found the souvenirs she knew she would take home, rather than use. She had her own toothbrush in her bag, so one in a special box would stay pristine. She would be glad of the dressing gown hanging on the wall, as this was no en-suite, just a basin. The trip down the corridor to use the toilet was not something she was looking forward to, but she was soon distracted by enquiries about which sitting she would like to attend for dinner.

Before long, the train was under way, and they were speeding through the countryside, as dark fell. During dinner, in such comfort that no restaurant would ever live up to it, she felt as if she'd stepped back in time. The Lalique glass in the windows graced the polished mahogany decorated with inlay, shouting "luxury" at all who dared to look. Her mind filled with images of Agatha Christie novels, and she half expected Poirot to appear with a tray. After a sumptuous meal, with more new acquaintances, she returned to her compartment to find her bed made up with crisp, white cotton sheets, and it wasn't long before she fell asleep, the gentle rocking of the train on the track not unlike nights she'd spent being rocked by the wind in a caravan, in her younger days. She didn't want, or need, a lullaby... For the first time since the fire, she slept without hearing the nursery rhymes playing in her mind.

She woke in the early morning and jumped out of bed, so quickly she almost lost her balance. She could hardly believe her eyes. The mountains rose around them, their snowy magnificence shining through the window. She'd never been this close to such giants before — you could hardly count Snowdon alongside these. She washed and dressed as fast as she possibly could, throwing open the door to the corridor, so that she could almost run from one side of the train to the other, drinking in the sense of awe and beauty. They were just like the pictures of the mountains she remembered on her bedroom wall, as a child. She felt exhilarated, moments of pure joy, her spirits lifted somewhere she couldn't define. She gave up clicking the camera, because she didn't want to watch them through the lens; she wanted to watch them with her eyes, fix them in her memory.

"Look at that, James," she whispered. "I'm seeing them for both of us. Wouldn't you just love this?" She peered out at the front of the train gliding round a bend, wistfully seeing his smile in her mind.

When they arrived at the wonderful chaos that was Santa Lucia Station, her water taxi was waiting to take her to her hotel, thanks to her travel company's representative being there to meet her. She stepped into the taxi, looking around at the buildings and the water, feeling the thrill of another adventure about to begin. She'd try to find the places she and James had visited together, to rekindle those memories, so that she could hold onto them for a little longer. She was ready, now, to not be afraid to live this dream … for both of them.

Poppy scrolled through the photos Nancy had posted on Facebook. There she was, doing a selfie in St Mark's Square, which had, fortunately, stayed dry for her visit. There was the Grand Canal, taken from a vaporetto, as she passed the Venice equivalent of a fire engine, speeding down the canal. She'd obviously visited the Basilica and the Doge's Palace, resplendent with its golden staircase and its paintings. Sometimes, she was on her own, but sometimes, she was with another woman, who must have taken the photo of her on the Bridge of Sighs. Her sheer joy was all over her face, and Poppy realised she'd rarely seen her mother this happy since her father died. Thanks to modern communications, there was not to be a new postcard, but there would, no doubt, be tales to be told, and she imagined Nancy's voice, animated as it used to be when she was enthusiastic about some new experience or new idea.

Daisy came strolling in, trailing her bag, and looking bored. The contrast was stark. Poppy offered to show her the photos.

"Oh, she's just so lucky, isn't she, Mum? Look how she's shining like the sunshine, surrounded by those buildings, and the gondolas! It's got to be so much better than being stuck here, expected to study. Go Nana! Freedom!" She held her fist in the air.

She sauntered back out of the room, grabbing a packet of crisps from the cupboard on the way. Poppy had to admit Daisy was right. Her mother was shining with happiness, as she waved at the camera. She'd been so full of the Orient Express, when she'd video called the previous evening, making Poppy imagine the grandeur of the mountains, the chalets on the hillsides, the splendour of the vineyards, as she'd drunk in every last detail. She'd almost succeeded in making Poppy envy her, with her personal steward looking after her and her magnificent meals, where she'd met new people and had such an interesting time. Whatever the future brought, she had wonderful new memories to lay over the old ones, and Poppy was glad her mother had stood up to her. Under her breath, she whispered, "I just hope I'm as strong as you, Mum. You are teaching me well."

The phone rang, and Tim got there before her. He came into the room, holding the mouthpiece at arm's length, having put the caller on speakerphone.

"Say it again, Cassie. Go on! Your mum can hear you now."

"OK. Mum, are you sitting down?"

Poppy's heart went to her boots, as she imagined, in that instant, what kind of bad news was coming.

"When does Nana come back?"

"At the end of next week. Why?"

"Well could you start investigating venues, please? I think we may need a party."

"What for?"

"Miles proposed to me last night, and I accepted. He passed the Nana test, it seems, when I took him to meet her. We have her blessing. I hope we have yours, too."

Poppy's first instinct was to be afraid that Cassie was too young, that she should stay free for longer, but she pulled herself up. This was Cassie's life, and Cassie's happiness. She had a right to make her own decisions, and maybe Miles actually was the decent young man her mother had judged him to be. Sometimes, Nana Boo could see things differently, when she was not, like Poppy, caught up in the net of fear, born of trying so hard to protect those she loved. There was something to be said for the encouragement of the young to take a leap of faith. Jake had given Nancy that. She must learn to trust Cassie's judgement now.

"Oh, that's wonderful, Cassie!" she heard herself say. "When Nana gets back, we get planning. Something to look forward to."

She watched Tim leave the room, his shoulders drooping once he'd ended the conversation with his daughter. She felt the tugging of the shredded fabric of love she'd felt for him. It was going to take time to build the trust again, but maybe there was a future to look forward to. Daisy was growing up fast, her sixteenth birthday party having been a rip-roaring success, thanks to Nancy's support. They just had to find a different way forward, with their different selves, as Nancy had done.

Acknowledgements

I would like to acknowledge all those who have made it possible for *Nana Boo* to come to life in these pages. There are several women who have inspired Nancy's character, and I won't name them here, but I hope they feel proud of themselves. There are also those women who, like Poppy and my own siblings and peers, have balanced caring for parents and caring for children — the generation in the middle. I salute them.

My gratitude goes to Willow River Press for finding a place for this, my second novel, following the 2022 publication of *Shadows of Time*. I'm delighted to have had the opportunity to work with the team again.

Special thanks go to my editor, Penny Dowden, for her considerate and thorough work on the manuscript, including researching British English idiosyncrasies that are not part of American life. I appreciate all her hard work and her patience.

I would like to thank all those people who have encouraged me and supported me in my writing, including my husband, who has put up with me taking over the study and being engrossed in my writing! Family and friends are too many to mention, but there is an inspirational group of writers in the north of England, including my sister, Bonnie Meekums, without whose generosity in allowing me to join them over Zoom during the pandemic, "Nana Boo" might not have existed.

I would like to thank those people who often remain anonymous, but whose willingness to read advance copies and give feedback is so important. Some have been prepared to read a second manuscript for me, which is heartwarming.

Last, but not least, I am grateful to Yorkshire, my northern home for thirty-four years. As they say: "You can take the [woman] out of Yorkshire, but you can't take Yorkshire out of the [woman]". It gave me beautiful settings to inspire me, as I walked and planned.

Having retired to Somerset after many years teaching in Yorkshire, Jackie Hales is a member of the Society of Authors, whose début novel, "Shadows of Time", was published by Willow River Press in 2022. She has been writing as a hobby since childhood, contributing to poetry anthologies since her undergraduate days. She also enjoys writing short stories for friends, family and students, including children's stories and even a story about her son's wayward cat for the rescue centre's blog! She has read her work on YouTube for "Poetry Archive Now" and has had various submissions published online, including micro-fiction and flash fiction on "Paragraph Planet", "Roi Faineant" and "Flash Fiction North". Publication of a piece of creative memoir by "Dear Damsels" in 2019 was a precursor to a unique collaboration with her sister, Bonnie Meekums, on a creative non-fiction memoir of their 1950s childhood, "Remnants of War", published in 2021. Jackie has a Facebook page and writes a blog (as Jotting Jax) about her walks and inspiration in the Yorkshire and Somerset countryside, interspersed with the challenges of life as a seventy-something woman.

Milton Keynes UK
Ingram Content Group UK Ltd.
UKHW021311220924
1783UKWH00021B/81